CONTENTS

LUKE HARROWER

Cover design by: S. Crow

1

The Highs & Lows Of

FLATROCK

Luke Harrower

LUKE HARROWER

Note From The Author:

Hello. I made this novel because no one had written the book I wanted to read: A cosy, low stakes, funny story that follows likeable characters in comical situations. I wanted every chapter to read like episodes to a sitcom (with some continuity), and I hope I have achieved that, and that you enjoy it. I don't particularly care about fame or profit, but I do like the thought of myself finding this book 20 years into my future, reading it again, and still laughing at my own jokes (I am, after all, my own target audience.)

From this point on, I can only wish you happy reading, and to anyone who isn't happy, your local library could always use another donation.

CHAPTER ONE

The Start Of Something Else

"Oops," said God.

These words were uttered just after the creation of the planet that would be called Flatrock. Maybe it was his old age getting to him, but God wasn't so good at making new worlds anymore. Flatrock is, as its name suggests, a flat planet. To make up for his mistake, God made Flatrock face the sun, and instead of rotating that planet on an axis to create a day and night cycle, a flat moon was created to block out the sun at regular intervals; it wasn't perfect, but it was, at the very least, functional. Having a flat planet did create some other complications, however; for one, the climate. Heat rises up in the atmoflat (not atmosphere; the world isn't round), meaning desert climates are found exclusively in the north, while tundra is only found in the south. Feeling this planet was destined to turn out a bit weird anyway, God experimented with adding what we would call "magic" into the world. Magic works by speaking in the language of God, like a prayer or a wish, and the desired effect becomes reality, although it's not that easy. The difficulty with performing magic stems from the fact that God's language is incredibly complex, and even the greatest minds spend years researching and remembering each word to perform magic effectively. That being said, there's a second method of learning magic which involves stubbing your toe repeatedly, and accidentally discovering new spells through saying pain induced gobbldygook phrases. Either method is equally effective; it just depends on how much walking you intend to do that day. Magic items were also an exciting concept to God; by attuning a mundane item with the language of God, it could carry a magic effect indefinitely. These became incredibly powerful and desirable items, which unfortunately, started an undesirable number of wars (which is to say, more than zero). People cried insults at God, who had accidentally let slip that he existed, and people started their own clubs with the rules they wanted to have. God eventually stepped away from management duties as he didn't enjoy the attention, and let Flatrock be independent from divine intervention.

It was probably for the best.

Some centuries passed, and things got about as good as they were ever going to get; the times of rampant war were diminishing, many countries were on the cusp of technological breakthroughs, alcohol existed; life was becoming pretty comfortable. Comfortable for everyone except a man named Milo; his entire life was about to be shaken up.

It started in a pub, a pub very familiar to Milo known as The Devil's Neckhole; maybe not the best bar in town (in fact, *definitely* not the best bar in town); it was the kind of place where if something interesting happened, it needed to be cleaned up. Across a long bar top, which was lopsided thanks to repairs made by a frequent visitor called "Cack-Handed Cameron," barstools had been set up for customers, while other stools had been left on the floor by visitors who didn't make it to the toilets on time. A snooker/poker/bedside table lay in the back end of the pub which, after most busy nights, was dangerous to go near with a naked flame. The walls were painted a dark red colour, although once cleaned, were actually cream; the colour depended on if the local football team had won that afternoon. On this day in particular, Milo was almost alone, nose deep in a pint glass with only a barmaid for company, who had just arrived for her shift.

"Evening, Hazel," said Milo.

"It's midday," replied Hazel.

"Two minutes past is close enough."

With a red pencil tucked into his pocket at all times, Milo was a middle-aged man with dark brown skin, short black hair, and a face most would describe as "probably trustworthy." Despite the way he was currently spending his time, Milo always kept himself presentable; a navy shirt and black trousers were what he always wore, but today was special, as he'd gone to the effort of adding a tie.

"You're looking a bit posh today," inquired Hazel. "Did you finally give in and pay for a fancy woman?"

"It's just business," replied Milo.

"None of my business, you mean."

"It's for the newspaper. They've asked me to bring along a portrait artist to sketch the people I interview."

"Oo, someone's job is going upmarket."

"Hardly. They'd replace the printing ink with dog dirt if you told The Big Cheese it was trendy."

Hazel had already started polishing glasses, holding the conversation as if she had memorised a script. "Well, good luck to them. It's going to be a hard job."

"This person's a professional; I doubt they'll have problems making a few sketches."

"I meant having to work with you."

"Oh, ha ha," ended Milo sarcastically.

If you couldn't tell, Hazel and Milo have been friends for some time; if you believe in the law of opposites attracting, this pair would confirm your suspicions. Hazel was a pale faced woman with hair colour to match her name; long braids, a pink blouse, and plenty of ear piercing are what you might expect to see her wearing.

"When are you meeting this artist?" asked Hazel.

"Should have been half an hour ago," answered Milo.

There was a lapse in sound around the bar as Milo took another sip of whatever concoction he chose to drink that day, when an unfamiliar woman's voice perked up.

"Excuse me," it said.

Milo looked around to see a short young woman standing in front of him; she was smiling, which unsettled Milo.

"Mr. Point?" she asked.

"That's me," replied Milo.

"Heidi. Heidi Watson. Your portrait artist."

The announcement was made with all the fire of an ill-fated forest. Hazel started to snigger; she could read Milo like a book and knew he had already decided to hate this woman. Heidi wore a white shirt with brown trousers and walking boots; her hair was blonde and hung down to her waist, though had she been a normal sized person, her hair length would not at all be out of place. By her side was a brown canvas shoulder bag with so many zips, buttons and decorations, you'd be forgiven for thinking there was a horrible accident in a tailor's shop.

"It's nice to meet you," said Heidi, extending her arm for a handshake.

"It's a pleasure to meet you too," said Milo, lying.

"Can I get you anything?" asked Hazel, giving Milo a small break to adjust himself.

"Just water please," answered Heidi, still waiting for a handshake.

"Double whisky," added Milo.

Hazel poured the drinks, all the time locking eyes with Milo. Not a single word was spoken, but the phrases "help" and "ha ha" were easily communicated. As Heidi realised the handshake wasn't going to come, she sat down, and Milo noticed the litter of bangles, rings, and bracelets adorning her arms with no sense of pattern or style as they collapsed onto the bar like a skeleton in an earthquake.

"What got you into being a journalist?" asked Heidi.

"I have a friend who got me the job," said Milo bluntly.

"Oh, same as me. My artwork was featured in a gallery north of here. One thing led to another and here I am."

Heidi waited a moment for Milo to say something in return,

but he kept on drinking, barely making eye contact with his new assistant; regardless of this, Heidi continued the conversation anyway.

"I travel a lot," rambled Heidi. "I want to visit every major city and learn about every culture that I can. I just need the money to get there first. Have you travelled at all?"

"No. I like the peace and quiet," replied Milo.

"I guess that comes with age," continued Heidi, not picking up on the hint, "but forgive me if this is rude: You don't look like a local."

"I moved here from the west."

"Oh, I've never been that way. Is it nice?"

"Better than here," said Milo in a sarcastic tone that was lost on his present company. Their small talk continued for a while, Heidi asking more and more questions, while Milo gave answers as brief as possible to avoid conversing. When the time came, the two left The Devil's Neckhole and returned to their respective homes. As Milo walked down the cobbled street back to his small house, thinking about Heidi with the knowledge that they would be working together for the foreseeable future, one thing kept running through his head to give him comfort.

"At least I've got brandy at home."

The next morning came as a wake up call, as is generally the point of mornings; granted, certain nocturnal creatures like owls, fruit bats, and teenagers didn't have the same methodology but as stated before, Flatrock is not perfect. Milo's morning routine consisted heavily of very little. As previously mentioned, Milo worked for a newspaper, and was predominantly an interviewer; it was a line of work that didn't so much interest the man as much as it used to, but it was nonetheless easy; there was very little Milo needed to do in preparation besides have a large glass of water to ease the night before. As Milo was about to pick up his work bag, there was a knock at the door. Milo was surprised, as he didn't often have guests (on account of his personality). Turning the handle, Milo was presented with a familiar young woman.

"Sorry I'm late," apologised Heidi.

"Hello," answered Milo with uncertainty. "How did you know where I live?"

"You asked me to meet you here yesterday."

There was a small pause. "When did I do that?"

"I think it was after your seventh whisky."

"Ah. That makes sense."

"Do you feel like you should maybe cut down on the drinking?"

"No, I can't. I drink to forget."

"Forget what?"

"I can't remember."

"Well, I'm here now, so do you mind if I come in?" said Heidi, already halfway into the living room, much to the annoyance of Milo (although he wouldn't say anything). It was clear to Heidi that Milo made decent money from his job; landscape paintings hung proud on the walls, with pots of flowers sitting underneath (and all the flowers were still alive, which is no small feat for most men.) Despite the impression the owner may give, the house was far better maintained than the man was. Every table was clean, each window was spotless, and the furniture was laid out in such a way that you'd expect a protractor was involved at some stage.

"You'll have to give me a moment," called Milo, as he walked into a room opposite from Heidi. Curiosity took hold of the woman for a moment, and she peered through the door as it was closing. Heidi saw a few things, but didn't have a chance to fully grasp the picture. It wasn't long before curiosity won the fight against common decency, and Heidi walked through the door, where she was presented with all manner of items. Graphs, shelves of books, and illustrations covered the walls like patio furniture on a freshly murdered body; not a single bit of wall space wasn't being used for something. Examining the shelves revealed texts from people Heidi had never heard of writing about subjects she didn't realise existed. Some books were as thin as the paper it was printed on, others as thick as a wanker's forearm. It was a lot to take in, and she would have had the time to if it wasn't for Milo being there.

"Hey! Don't touch anything," he shouted.

"What is all this?" asked Heidi.

"Research material."

"For what exactly?"

"Magic items."

Heidi was taken aback. "Wow. I haven't heard about those things since school."

Heidi knew a little about what she was looking at; she knew most magic items were lost in the mess of wars that happened because of them, and that they're incredibly rare in this era of Flatrock, making their relevance to modern society tiny compared to the past. Heidi picked random books off the shelves, Milo keeping a studious eye on her like she was holding his new child. Inside them, Heidi found notes on a lantern that produced a light that would allow people to see through solid objects. Another book was written about a ring that let the user blast freezing cold air from their fingertips. Another was about a mixing bowl that made bread dough rise at twice its normal speed.

One of these books interested Heidi a tad less than the others.

The books were written in multiple different handwritings, and they didn't have any marks to give the impression they were officially published which Heidi questioned.

"That's because I made them myself," answered Milo. "I take all the research material I can and compile it, or copy it down when I need to."

"You made all these books?" said Heidi in some shock. "That's amazing."

Milo couldn't help but smile as a little spring of pride burst forth. "Most of them, certainly."

There was a pause for a moment as Heidi continued to take it all in. "What got you into all this stuff?"

"History. The entire world was changed by these items."

"Even the bowl that makes bread rise?"

"Not all of them, just the powerful ones. Oh, this is my favourite," gushed Milo, picking a book from the shelf with sudden vigour. "You see this?" said Milo with a level of excitement he usually reserved for vodka.

"Yes," said Heidi with a level of confusion she usually reserved for idiots.

Heidi was looking at a page that documented a piece of rope that could extend to any length without breaking, and was struggling to find the interesting part.

"It's a magic rope that was used to tie up a whole castle," explained Milo. "Two horsemen circled the battlements and made an indestructible wall with the item. That castle still stands today because of that rope."

Heidi was somewhat surprised by the sudden burst of excitement from Milo, admiring his dedication more so than the story of the indestructible castle. Milo looked at Heidi, hoping she shared his enthusiasm, but realised she wasn't showing much investment.

"You don't care, do you?" asked Milo.

"No, I do," answered Heidi. "You just caught me by surprise. And besides, it's nice you have something you're passionate about."

Milo's smile returned to him, although the positive energy was quickly drained when he noticed the time, and realised he'd be late for work.

"Oh cack!" barked Milo. "We've got to be going."

Milo grabbed the book from Heidi and returned it to the labelled spot on the shelf, before retrieving his bag and bolting out the front door. Heidi took a look back into the study, not sharing the same level of urgency as her new work colleague, and left the building as well.

It might be worth mentioning now that this story takes place in a town called Pending, located in the country of Belland.

If you want to know what the town of Pending is like, it could be described with a short story. "Pending" is actually short for "Name: Pending." It wasn't originally called Pending, nor was it ever intended to be named as such, but circumstances were stacked against it. Originally, the town was named "Great-Town" as a shallow marketing ploy to make the place sound grander than it really was. Of course, the word "great" implies a level of significance, when in reality, the only significant thing that could be said about Great-Town was its take-aways, the only food service in the world where the one thing greasier than the chips was the person serving them. It wasn't long before several nicknames started circulating, including Hate-Town, Second-Rate-Town and Migrate-Away- From-This-Town (along with some less imaginative names rhyming with spit, cat, and duck) which forced the local authorities to consider changing the name. A vote took place among the population, but the town's people, feeling just, if not more displeased about the place they lived in as the rest of the world, voted the town be dubbed "Tosspot." Ignoring the small matter of what the town's people would be named (regardless of whether it was true), the authorities did not desire to take that title. As such, a transition period was declared where the name "Pending" would become the town's official handle for the time being. That time lasted several centuries, and continues to this day. While it cannot be denied that living in Pending is no one's greatest aspiration, it does have the benefit of not being either of the towns just north and south of the location, which the people of Pending affectionately refer to as "Rock" and "Hard Place."

The newspaper Milo and Heidi worked for was known as The Bystander, and it was a reputable newspaper, at least in comparison to rival publications like The Daily Echo, who had a nasty tendency to repeat their stories. The Bystander was not a newspaper of opinions, presenting only the facts, which unfortunately did not make it popular. As I said before, yes, The Bystander was reputable, but not popular, as most people don't care to think for themselves (or so I've been told). The office building for said newspaper, coincidentally, also refrained from outsider influence, giving off the impression it had been built by a man who thought a saw was an inflammation on the body. The roof was crumbling, the windows were clouded, and to use the phrase "brickwork" is generous; "Brick Had-A-Go-At" is a more reasonable assumption. The building itself was a one-story affair away from the town centre, not a long distance from where Milo lived. Upon entering the office for the first time, Heidi declared, "So this is where the magic happens."

"Yes. This is where the tragic happens," muttered Milo.

Heidi glanced around the walls and met eyes with a handful of staff who had the courtesy of arriving on time. The office desks themselves were small oak tables with piles of documents, reports, and future hamster bedding resting in organised letter trays. Every table had three draws, a desk tidy full of pencils, and a smattering of decorations arranged by the person working there. Twelve occupied desks arranged in an open plan stood in this main office room, apart from a single desk that had walls screwed onto three sides.

Milo sat there.

"I assume The Big Cheese will want to talk to you. His office is just down the hall," said Milo, half-heartedly pointing to a corridor filled with certificates of achievement, including two for swimming.

"Actually, I was wondering if you could show me around a little bit," asked Heidi politely.

Milo would have rather got on with his work, but he wrestled up the energy to say, "Your desk is the empty one. The break room is out the back. The stationary cupboard moves sometimes. I'm sure you'll learn in time."

Milo tried to get along with his work, but Heidi planted her hands on the top of Milo's wall and had plenty more questions to ask.

"Anything else I should know about working here?" asked Heidi. "Any unwritten rules of the room?"

"Three rules," commanded Milo. "Stay home if you're sick, no work during breaks, and don't talk to Rob."

"Who's Rob?"

"I am he," interrupted the man in question.

Heidi looked around to see who was speaking, while Milo looked at the inside of his hands, resting his head in them in the hopes it would give him strength. Rob was a peculiar fellow, according to people who didn't want to use bad language in front of their kids. Rob had a tablecloth sense of fashion (by which I mean his clothes were always stained); he wore a brown corduroy jacket, grey jumper, and thick glasses, hanging around his neck on a chain, despite the fact he never took them off. His hair and moustache, both as thin as a new mother's patience, were the features Heidi was most drawn to upon first glance, on account that they danced like corpses in a tornado.

"Yes, I am the head of the research team. Robert Bobington," said the man, extending his arm for a handshake.

"Heidi. Heidi Watson," she replied, returning the handshake far quicker than Milo would.

Milo interrupted less than a split second after Heidi said her name. "She's the new portrait artist. Rob, this is Heidi. Heidi, this is a mistake."

"Research team," said Heidi enthusiastically, ignoring the warning. "How many people do you work with?"

"Oh, it's just me," answered Rob without a hint of irony.

Heidi paused for a second; she was unsure how to continue the conversation.

"So, you must know some interesting facts," asserted Heidi eventually.

"Oh, that I do," stated Rob. "For example, did you know that wolves will often tear the limbs off new members of their pack if they don't offer food to the leader."

Heidi became concerned.

"Would you like an apple?" she asked nervously.

"Oh, yes. Love one," answered Rob, snatching an apple from Heidi's hand not a moment before it had left her shoulder bag.

Rob held the apple in his hand and continued to stand in front of Heidi; even she was feeling out of her depth.

"Don't you need to see the boss?" asked Milo.

"Yes," remarked Heidi quickly, avoiding eye contact with Rob as she walked past him. Rob kept eyes on her at all times as he watched her leave.

"Lovely girl," babbled Rob.

Rob stayed in front of Milo's desk for a while, much to the annoyance of the occupant.

"Don't you have work to do?" urged Milo.

"Oh yes. I'm going over this fascinating book on snail ethics," claimed Rob.

"Careful you don't die of excitement," whispered Milo, as Rob turned around.

The rest of the day went by rather uneventfully. Heidi had not been assigned any great deal of work, so set to personalising her desk and talking to Milo; as uncooperative as he may be, he would at least entertain her anecdotes. Heidi made sketches of family members on clean paper, folding them so they could stand on their own, and the boss had been generous enough to give her an aloe vera plant, which now sat in the corner. Heidi noticed during the day that she was, by some margin, the smallest in the office; during lunch, she had taken a stiff cushion from the break room seats and used it to prop herself higher on her chair. Heidi watched Milo from her desk; he was clearly focused on something, but the fitted walls brought mystery to the proceedings. Heidi gave a quick glance over the desk walls to see what Milo had been doing; unsurprisingly, he'd been working, but on top of that, she did also notice the total absence of decoration on his desk. Even Rob, who possessed the charisma of a dead fish, had taken the liberty of purchasing a stylish letter opener (which looked very underused). Heidi leaned forward into her desk and made a note in her book, before standing up and saying, "Milo!" in an upbeat tone.

"Heidi!" parroted Milo, faking a smile for half a second.

"I was hoping, would you mind visiting me after work?"

Milo, of course, did mind, but on this occasion, he had an honest excuse. "I can't tonight. I'm playing chess with Hazel."

"Just the two of you?"

"It's difficult to play chess with three people."

"Ah well, never mind. Have fun, and pop over to mine whenever. Any time of the day is fine for me."

"I'll remember it," groaned Milo.

In the evening, Milo sat across from Hazel on her dining room table, a chess board between them. Milo and Hazel frequently played board games together, as they enjoyed the feeling of outwitting each other. Hazel's home was small, although the estate agent described it as "cosy." She lived in the central area of Pending, just within earshot of the wild pub nights but not quite within range of the fires that sometimes followed. Hazel's home had been furnished with all manner of animal paraphernalia: Statues of badgers and shrews crawling through broken logs, glass and ceramic songbirds mid-flight, and hand carved wooden cats standing high, with wide, beady eyes, staring like witnesses to a murder. Milo, in a rare case of fashion, was relaxed, bending forward intently over the chess board in front of him. The game looked to be in Milo's favour at the moment.

"How are you getting along with your new best friend?" inquired Hazel, with a cheeky grin.

"I'm not her best friend anymore," answered Milo. "She's pals with Rob."

"Rob the knob?"

"That's the one. Knows some very interesting things about mutilation, that man."

"Speaking of mutilation, you didn't answer my question about the girl."

"What's that got to do with mutilation?"

"If you don't answer, that's what I'll do to you."

Hazel moved her knight forward to threaten Milo's bishop.

"I'm a bit peeved with her," said Milo. "She showed up at my house today."

"Didn't you invite her?" asked Hazel.

"While drunk."

"That's your natural state."

"It is not," shouted Milo, before taking a sip from his dark ale. "Besides, you don't just show up to someone's house if you don't know them very well."

"You were telling her a lot of things even I didn't know about you," argued Hazel.

"Beside the point," countered Milo. Acting defensive, Milo retreated his bishop. "I'd prefer working without her."

"That's cruel of you," cried Hazel. "She seems like such a lovely girl."

"You only love her because you know I hate her."

"If I loved everyone you hated, I'd be the world's most successful prostitute."

Hazel moved her queen forward.

"She invited me to her house," ranted Milo.

"Aw, I feel so bad for you," said Hazel sarcastically.

"Enough with the tone. I don't want to go."

Milo moved his rook to take an unguarded pawn.

"What have you got against her?" asked Hazel wholeheartedly.

"It's the over enthusiasm," protested Milo. "It's tiring. She *always* has to be doing something, and half the time, it involves talking to me."

"You're the only person she knows right now. This is a new place for her and she's probably feeling really lonely. You remember what that's like, don't you?" Milo paused for a second as he remembered when he first migrated to Pending from the west of Flatrock. It was true that the world seemed to flip upside down when he arrived, and Milo was somewhat frightened of the change. "Back when you arrived here, I was the only one who wanted to be friends with you. Twenty years later and nothing's changed," said Hazel. "I'll do you a deal. If I can win this game, you have to visit the girl."

"Deal," agreed Milo.

Hazel moved her queen and took an unguarded knight.

"Checkmate," she declared.

Milo looked at the board astounded. He had just been played like a violin.

"Come on. What's the worst that could happen?" asked Hazel. "You visit that girl tomorrow."

Milo wanted to groan, but Hazel, reading the man like a book, gave him a stare that could turn an army against their king.

Milo kept quiet.

The next day was a day off work, so Milo didn't need to go to the office. Normally, Milo would spend days like this either reading, writing, or regretting, and today was the turn of the third. Heidi had told Milo her address on the way to the office yesterday, which Milo had remembered well, on account of the fact he wasn't drinking at the time. Milo walked to a side of Pending he was unfamiliar with, not liking to travel any further than the shops and back. The houses in this part of town were more modern and compact than where Milo lived; they were wide and tall, semi-detached, and glancing through some of the windows, Milo determined they were even "cosier" than Hazel's. Narrow alleyways ran between the network of concrete which children would suddenly dart out of, kicking balls, stones, and sometimes, each other. The only colours besides mortar grey and brick red were the occasional and small patches of grass by the footpath which, for this morning, had become home of the ages 4-40 amateur rugby tournament. Milo arrived at Heidi's building, and dragged himself upstairs to the first floor to where she lived. Milo took a deep breath, noting the smell of something unfamiliar but not unpleasant, and knocked on the door. A second passed, and Heidi answered.

"Hello! You came," said Heidi excitedly.

Heidi stepped forward and hugged Milo as high up his body as she could reach.

"Nice to see you too," sighed Milo.

"Come in, come in," urged Heidi.

Heidi beckoned Milo forward as she walked back into her home, and the man followed. Heidi's home was a studio apartment with walls almost pure white, barring a large number of charcoal sketch drawings which immediately captured Milo's attention. The lines were thick and smudged with fingerprints, and most were of people. Clearly, these were individuals Heidi knew well, as their faces had been captured multiple times in varying angles and with great detail.

"Have you ever thought about paper?" asked Milo.

Heidi laughed, although Milo hadn't realised he made a joke. Milo continued looking at the portraits and discovered several repeating characters. An older couple, possibly husband and wife, were repeated most often, then a younger man, similar in age to Heidi, and a crowd of other faces, showing signs of fluctuating ages and varying racial characteristics. Milo must have counted at least fifty faces and thirty different people between them.

"Who are all these people?" asked Milo.

Heidi walked over sipping a mug of tea, handing a second cup over to Milo, which he accepted.

"Family and friends," answered Heidi. "Mum and Dad," she said, pointing to the older couple. "Brother, cousins, Uncle John, Mad Aunty Lin, school friends, old travelling buddies, everyone really."

Milo took in the faces a while longer. Everyone had such warm smiles that seemed so welcoming, apart from one woman who Milo guessed must have been Mad Aunty Lin. Milo sipped his tea; it was strong, and went some way to explain Heidi's boundless energy, although today, Milo noticed she seemed to be more relaxed than she had been before. Milo took another sip of his tea and went to place his mug down on a table, before realising that there were none.

"Oh, sorry," apologised Heidi. "I haven't got a lot of furniture."

Milo looked around a room containing exactly one piece of furniture: A futon covered in all manner of rugs, blankets, and cushions; it was more akin to a failed textile factory than a bed. Milo glanced around the rest of the room in search of somewhere to put his mug; the smell he noted previously was revealed to be an incense stick, slowly crumbling as it burned to dust,and there also stood a full sized mirror in the corner, framed in wood with peeling black paint. Milo soon discovered a set of fixed shelves that would suffice as a table, but he quickly became distracted by their contents. The shelves contained artefacts Milo recognised from books of different cultures: Yards of wool from sheep sheared in the ice flats, feathers from birds which lived in sweltering climates, polished stones of coastal seabeds, crystals from volcanic rocks, statues with their tits out, and all manner of cultured items.

"How much have you travelled?" asked Milo, becoming genuinely curious.

"Honestly, not a lot," confessed Heidi. "A lot of these were gifts from friends who explored. I've only seen maybe a quarter of these cultures with my own eyes. Oh, this is my favourite." Heidi picked up a short blowgun made from some kind of woven grass. It was very thin but incredibly sturdy. "I was given this by a friend I made in the desert. She's an assassin."

Milo flinched for a moment; he was going to question the fact that someone doesn't just become friends with an assassin, but soon realised who he was talking to, and concluded that statement to be quite possible.

"But, no," continued Heidi. "None of this stuff has any real memories tied to it. I just *really* want to see them for myself."

Milo smiled a little bit.

"That's no matter," said Milo. "It's nice you have something you're passionate about."

Heidi smiled as well.

"Oh, I just remembered why I invited you here," burst Heidi, as she rushed over to a small box by her bed and pulled out a set of pencils. "Do you mind if I sketch you?"

Milo was surprised by the suddenness of the request, flattered though he was.

"Sure," said Milo.

Heidi instructed Milo to stand close to the mirror. Heidi found an empty space on the wall where both Milo and the view behind him reflected in the mirror was visible. Milo suddenly became conscious of what his arms were doing, and stood with them by his sides, feeling incredibly awkward, although Heidi barely paid him any attention. Besides cursory glances, Heidi communicated very little; it was clear to Milo that she was very focused in her work, which he found quite admirable, and the absence of sound around the woman was almost alien to him. Even Heidi's bangles, which normally rattled like snakes in a saucepan, had been removed, apart from one, which was made from some form of stretchy rubber. Heidi swapped between pencils, leaving the tools she wasn't currently using tucked into the rubber bangle around her arm. Milo tried to glance at his picture from around Heidi, although the moment he had the nerve to do so, Heidi announced, "Finished!" Milo couldn't quite believe it; only a few minutes had passed and yet the picture was indeed complete. It would be fair to say that from an outsider's perspective, Heidi had been very kind in her depiction of the slowly ageing man, more than once bitten by a vampire called stress and less than once did any kind of modelling.

"What do you think?" asked Heidi.

Milo spoke before he had a chance to think about a response. "It's amazing."

Milo looked at the drawing in awe, and he felt his heart flutter for a moment; Heidi watched his face, and smiled at the result.

Some time passed at Heidi's home. The two of them talked about the cultures of the world through discussion of magic items, as well as the items on Heidi's shelves, seating themselves on the floor like children round a campfire. When the time came, Milo declared he should return home to get back to his reading and writing, knowing full well regret had been retired for the day. As he walked home, he paused for a few seconds having realised something he didn't expect: He hadn't hated the experience. As much as Milo didn't enjoy admitting it, Hazel was right, which was a pleasant change of pace from Pending's usual residents, who spent most of their time asleep on snooker tables, causing fires, and painting the pub walls.

The next workday arrived and Milo was sitting at his desk, skimming over some documents that Rob had happily proofread for him. It was something close to half an hour after work started when Heidi walked into the office. The rest of the staff, glancing up, then quickly back down at less important (but higher paying) matters, apart from Milo who looked at Heidi, smiled, and nodded at her. Heidi made her way over to Milo's desk and started rummaging around in her shoulder bag.

"Hold on. I have something for you," said Heidi.

Milo leaned over in anticipation, trying to look inside her bag. A few seconds passed, and Heidi produced a piece of paper, folded over. Opening the paper revealed the finished portrait of Milo, although it took the man a small amount of time to recognize himself, as he was unfamiliar with his own smile.

"Thanks," said Milo.

"You're welcome," beamed Heidi.

Milo looked at the picture a minute longer as Heidi walked away. He stood the picture against the inside of one of his desk walls, tightly in the corner where it was hard to be seen from outside eyes, not done so because he was ashamed, but because it might look egocentric if he had a picture of himself at his own desk.

Milo's eyes moved back to his work, and he smiled.

***

As the workday came to a close, Milo wasted no time escorting himself to the pub. The man sat down on the rock-solid barstool, and brushed away a piece of mould that had dropped from the ceiling as Hazel made herself known to him, wasting no time with questions.

"So," started Hazel, "how was your trip to the gates of oblivion?"

"Alright. I admit it. I was a knobhead. Heidi is perfectly nice," confessed Milo.

"Good to hear. The usual?"

"Please."

Hazel poured a highball glass full to the brim of a deep red liquid; a brand of whiskey known as "Tomorrow's Problem," before placing it on the bar in front of Milo.

"I think you're going to be good friends with Heidi," asserted Hazel.

Milo was doubtful. "Why do you think that?"

"A woman knows these things. Twenty years without a new friend; you're probably overdue some good fortune."

Milo dismissed the whole point; it was barely an argument worth having. Heidi said her goal was to explore the world, so no doubt the time would come sooner rather than later when she would pop off again. Milo slowly soaked in the atmosphere of The Devil's Neckhole, while his clothes also soaked in the suspicious patches of liquids that formed around the bar, but the man didn't care enough to be bothered.

This was the life Milo wanted: One of complete tranquility, with nothing changing in the slightest.

Milo was content.

CHAPTER TWO

Rookie Error

Magic in the world of Flatrock is a funny old business. On one hand, anyone can perform magic, as it only requires the user to know a special word from the language of God, but on the other hand, what's the point? The only people who can truly master magic are those of incredible intellect, and it's unfortunate that people of incredible intellect will tell you that practising magic is a waste of time. Unless you wanted to become a performer (and by proxy, a waiter), there is no need for frivolous tricks. Of course, the possibilities are limitless if you could learn the right words: The ability to make someone immortal, or destroy entire nations, with little more than a sentence, stands on the tip of your tongue; such a shame politicians had managed to do the same thing without magic for millennia. The world is already quite taxing without divine trickery, and after God revealed himself to be somewhat of a pillock, few people wanted anything to do with him. Magic is not taught in schools; the curriculum is instead taken up by equally useless tasks like algebra and the life cycle of a poo (although teachers would rather you refer to the latter as agricultural studies), so those who perform magic are usually self-taught. While it is true that wizards could spend their time tutoring apprentices, it is not common. Since learning magic is an incredibly difficult skill, mages take pride in their craft, not to mention it gives them a competitive edge over other wizards, so sharing their talent is rare. While in your world, there is a phrase that states "a magician never reveals their secrets," in Flatrock, the phrase is slightly elongated, and states "a magician never reveals their secrets because they're all arseholes." This is a story of one such person who, more than anything, wanted to learn magic. That person, coincidentally enough, was also a bit of an arsehole.

Heidi had moved to the town of Pending a little over a week ago, and she was still yet to become accustomed to what the town had to offer. Pending was a fairly well-known town; it was most famous for being next to a city called Dorcoast. Dorcoast was a port town and important trade route for the region, and as such, a lot of business flows through Pending, but anyone with common sense didn't stay long. Where Dorcoast was a civilised place with culture brimming from its borders due to the sheer quantity of produce from around the world that was traded there, the only culture you'd find in Pending would come from a yogurt. It was undeniable that Pending had a certain life to it; it's just a shame that life was mostly bugs collecting around a dung heap. Today, however, was market day; a day where everyone puts on their best fake smiles in a shallow sales tactic to make people buy from them. Heidi was finding market day quite enlightening, to say the least; there were of course some rather pleasant stalls like Butcher's bakery and Baker's butchery, but for the most part, it was normal townspeople selling used and hand-me-down products. Books, jigsaws, clothes, ornaments, second hand bicycles (the second hand still being attached), and all manner of knick-knacks littered the streets. Pending town centre, located on the far west side of town, had a collection of small cafes, banks, and far more than the necessary number of hairdressers. Heidi hadn't made the effort until now to explore the town thoroughly, so this was all new to her. The stalls were basic wooden tables with red and white pinstripe canopies made from cloth, donated by the town's council to give the trading economy a sense of professionalism; it was such a shame that tone wasn't so easily conveyed by the salespeople.

"Buy something, will ya!" shouted a merchant from across

the street to Heidi.

"Sorry. I don't want anything," replied Heidi politely.

"I've got things the likes of which you've never seen!" boasted the merchant, holding up something that to Heidi, looked like a dead rat sewed on to a live chicken.

"No, sorry, I'm just window shopping."

"I sell windows too," argued the merchant, now lifting up a pane of glass nearly as large as himself.

Heidi gave a courteous wave before turning around and avoiding eye contact with the man, still determined to sell her something. Once Heidi was convinced she was out of sight of the man, walking past a stall she genuinely wanted to visit to do so, she ended up about a hundred paces away from the market, so sat on a bench for the time being. Heidi let the weight of her hair swing her head backwards, and she stared up into the sky. The weather was clear, and the clouds were pure white with not a single sign of life to be seen; it was quite tranquil. Heidi became lost in the moment, and meditated on her entire surroundings. As much as people will joke about Pending (and trust me, there are plenty of jokes to make), Heidi was finding the town to be rather satisfying; that feeling lasted about three seconds as a sudden bellowing exploded from Heidi's left side, shocking her awake. Heidi quickly turned to see a small group of people gathering by a fountain.

"Do not be shy ladies, gentlemen, and the otherwise questionable. This show is free of charge for anyone with a love for magic."

Heidi heard the voice well, despite being a fair distance from its source; it was an oddly deep voiced man, roaring like a lion mid-castration. Heidi couldn't discern the voice's owner, so sped towards the fountain (although it was called the fountain, water didn't flow through it, so it was more like a stagnant paddling pool with a statue of some birds on top.) There wasn't a huge crowd, so Heidi found it easy to discern why everyone was so invested, and there she spied a young man presenting himself to the audience. The man wore (what had once been) an immaculate jet black waistcoat, white shirt with the sleeves rolled up to his elbows, and a yellow handkerchief poking out from a breast pocket. With his short black hair, clear skin, and trimmed eyebrows, the man's face was groomed like a prize-winning pig.

"People of Pending, I shall not waste your time any longer," announced the man, who was exaggerating himself greatly. "Oh, but where are my manners? I haven't introduced myself. You may call me Vincent, and I shall be your host into the world of illusions."

The magician threw his left hand in his trouser pocket and produced a red ball, then met eyes with a tall man in the crowd.

"Tell me, sir. What am I holding in my hand?" asked the magician loudly.

"A ball," replied the man confidently.

"No, I'm actually holding two balls." The magician produced a second ball from between his fingers, seemingly from thin air. "I'll ask you again. What am I holding in my hand?"

There was a small pause.

"Two balls," replied the man.

"No, I'm actually holding three."

The magician produced another ball from between his fingers and Heidi started to wonder how he was doing this (as was the man being asked the questions, who was slowly becoming red in the face.) Of the little Heidi knew about magic, she was sure it required that the person using it say strange words out loud to create the effects, but Vincent was talking normally every time the magic was occurring.

"I'll ask you once more or else I'll have to find someone who can count," joked the magician. "One final time, sir. What am I holding in my hand?"

The magician turned his hands around to show there was nothing hidden. The man counted at least a dozen times, and was certain there were three balls in Vincent's hand.

"Three red balls," answered the man, now feeling like his intelligence was being offended.

"I'm not holding any balls at all. It's an apple."

The magician turned his hands around and the balls slipped down his fingers, leaving an apple in the palm of his hand. Vincent then took a bite from the fruit to prove it was the genuine article. Heidi was astounded; she had no idea how Vincent was performing these illusions, not even caring about the irritated gorilla that had just barged past her.

"What a load of cack!" exclaimed the man, storming off, and counting on his fingers all the while.

The entertainment continued for a short time, and every new enchantment seemed to baffle Heidi to no end; a whole repertoire of vanishing, conjuration, restoration, and levitation flew by in quick succession, and before Heidi even realised it was happening, Vincent was standing just a few inches away from her with his hand out.

"Excuse me, Miss," asked the magician. "May I borrow one of your bangles?"

Heidi paused to think for a second. "Only if I can get it back."

"You have nothing to worry about," comforted the magician.

Heidi wore multiple bangles on most days which meant she released a rhythmic jingle whenever she moved her arms; undoubtedly, Vincent found it hard to miss the human keychain. Heidi removed one of her gold bangles and handed it over.

"As you can see, one normal metal ring, and a second from the crowd," said the magician as he gently knocked the large rings against the side of the fountain. "Now these rings," the magician bashed the two metal rings together, "don't like each other very much."

"I know the feeling," shouted a man everyone had believed to have walked away.

The magician ignored the heckle. "However, if you let the rings get to know each other slowly," the magician rubbed the two rings together, "they become inseparable."

The magician dropped the ring in his right hand, the one that belonged to Heidi, and it was connected to the magician's own metal hoop. Vincent invited Heidi to touch the bangle to test his statement, and pulling on the loops showed they were as stuck together as a teenager's bed sheets. "Now the interesting thing about these rings is that they're much more difficult to separate than they are to get together, but when they do leave each other," the magician dropped his own ring and let it hang from Heidi's bangle, which she was still holding. While Heidi kept hold of the rings, the magician struck a match, then placed the naked flame under the lower ring, which exploded into fire and light and retina damage. As the fire disappeared, a yellow tulip was left resting inside the hoop of Heidi's bangle, "they leave the other a gift," ended the magician.

Heidi was shocked, initially because there was a fire two inches from her hand and she damn near pissed herself, but now, she was in awe; she examined the flower for scorch marks, but not a petal looked out of place, nor was her bangle damaged in any way.

"Thank you my beloved audience, and thank you to my glamorous assistant. I must leave you here, but if you want to see more, you can watch me performing at the Dorcoast Stage Theatre for two nights starting tomorrow. I'd love to see you there. Goodbye!"

The magician sauntered away from the fountain and disappeared behind a house on the street corner. Heidi looked at the flower, still baffled how it appeared from a flame without a single burn, let alone the other number of sorcerous acts the magician had performed. Heidi was ecstatic, and felt she needed to tell someone about this.

Heidi abandoned the markets and went to the pub she knew best: The Devil's Neckhole. Heidi didn't drink, but the majority of the people she knew in Pending did. Heidi was still young enough to be happy over long periods of time without exhausting herself, and as such, alcohol wasn't yet a temptress. It was fairly early in the afternoon, so Heidi knew there wouldn't be many people about, except the two she most wanted to talk to. Heidi pushed open the light wooden door of the pub to see those two people, Milo and Hazel, sitting by the bar. Before Heidi had a chance to say hello, she saw Milo drinking some unusually extravagant drinks, while Hazel was pouring them.

"Hey, guys," said Heidi. "What are you up to?"

"I'm testing a couple of new cocktails," answered Hazel, "but Milo isn't exactly giving me any feedback to work with."

Milo was a heavy drinker, but he could manage it; he did however like to push his boundaries, and Heidi could tell he was feeling more than a little dizzy today.

"So, what do you call it?" asked Heidi, examining a glass containing one part red liquid and ten parts noxious fumes.

"Haven't decided yet," answered Hazel. "I usually name them after whatever effect it has on someone."

Hazel had several unique cocktail recipes under her belt, including the Builder's Brew, a sure-fire way to get hammered; the Hooker's Bra, because most people end up on the floor; and the Grammatical Error, women who drank this are often known to miss their periods. Hazel crouched down to look at Milo's face, who seemed half asleep.

"I'll probably call this one Euthanasia," muttered Hazel. "Anyway, is there anything I can do for you?"

"Have you ever been to Dorcoast?" asked Heidi.

"Once or twice," answered Hazel. "Full of posh pricks."

"Ah, well, there's a magician doing a show there tomorrow. I wondered if you wanted to go?"

"Ha ha ha ha ha!" burst Milo, who had suddenly woken up. "You don't want to go with Hazel, do you?"

"What's wrong with that?" asked Heidi.

"Do you know why they call her Hazel?"

"Why?"

"She's nuts."

Milo burst again, laughing at his own joke until he became delirious. Hazel resumed the conversation with Heidi, doing her best to drown out Milo's wailing.

"Flattered as I am," started Hazel again, "I don't particularly find magic very interesting."

"Aw, that's a shame," sighed Heidi.

"Excuse me. I'm still here," shouted Milo.

Heidi needed a minute to adjust to the sudden change in volume before speaking. "Do you want to come to a magic show?"

"Of course I would. Unlike Hazel, I fit in very well in Dorcoast," said Milo, unknowingly drooling on his own left hand.

"Awesome! You can show me the way there."

"Be careful what you wish for," muttered Hazel. "He'll only complain the whole time."

"Does everyone keep forgetting I'm here? I can hear you, you know," complained Milo.

"It'll be fine," reassured Heidi. "I'm sure we'll have a great time."

"We *will* have a great time!" shouted Milo. "You know, Heidi, you're one of my best friends."

Hazel whispered into Heidi's ear, "The competition isn't fierce."

The following day, Heidi and Milo found themselves travelling through the city of Dorcoast. After experiencing culture shock from the culture thunderstorm that was Pending's market stalls, Heidi was apprehensive about an entire market city just a few miles down the road, but she was entirely wrong. Where in Pending, most shops would be closing by dusk (mostly because the managers had run out of patience), shops in Dorcoast stayed open, and the employees smiled not as a cheap marketing ploy, but because they had experienced happiness some time within the last millennia. The roads were winding, complex as a philosopher with more nooks and crannies than a grandmother's face, each one holding a seemingly new piece of lore about the world through the people who walked between them. Dorcoast was full to the brim of boutiques, museums, art galleries, monuments, historical buildings, and even a fountain that worked. Heidi could scarcely believe the number of different cultures that had settled there, and barely had the time to appreciate the small percentage of the city she could see. Dorcoast was a meeting point for every civilised community in the world, and people from Pending were allowed to visit. This was the place of Heidi's dreams: A city of traders who had seen every inch of the world, and will again; she felt she was standing on the road to anywhere when she walked through Dorcoast. Milo, meanwhile, acted like he was walking through no man's land with an elephant on his back.

"How did you convince me to come here?" complained Milo.

"Uhh, I didn't," replied Heidi.

Milo thought back to when he agreed to see the magic show, but there was a blank space in his recollection sandwiched between one memory of Hazel saying, "This will be fun," and a second memory of himself face down in a storm drain with a hedgehog nesting on his cheek.

"Is it really too late to go back?" complained Milo.

"We're nearly at the theatre. You might as well watch the show," said Heidi. "Besides, I thought you liked magic?"

"I like the history of magic and magic items because they shaped the world," declared Milo. "Stage magic consists of some prat who thinks they're the centre of attention speaking gibberish and producing crap out of thin air. Toddlers can do the same thing." Milo looked up to the sky and groaned. "I could be doing something productive right now."

"What *would* you be doing right now?" asked Heidi.

Milo thought for a second, then another few seconds. About a minute passed as Milo tried to think of an answer that didn't involve the word "masturbating." Milo kept silent.

"I didn't want to come on my own and I am grateful you're here. Just try to be open minded and you'll have a good time," asserted Heidi.

Milo paused and put on a market smile. "You must be the most patient person in the world to deal with a knob like me."

"If you know you're being a knob, why don't you do

something about it?"

"I won't. I'm too much of a knob to try."

"Come on. Just for a few hours. Do it for me," begged Heidi.

Milo looked at Heidi; she was as excited as a teenage boy seeing a boob for the first time. He didn't have it in his heart to say no.

"Alright. I won't be a knob for the rest of the day," assured Milo.

"Is that a promise?" asked Heidi intently.

"I wouldn't call it a promise. I'd call it a harsh challenge."

Heidi and Milo soon arrived at the location of the Dorcoast Stage Theatre. The theatre itself was not huge, especially compared to the buildings around it, but modest nonetheless. Standing by a narrow river, the theatre was two stories tall, huge glass panels for walls on the front side, with a bar (heavily populated, as you might expect) on the top floor. The two of them were ushered into the auditorium and they sat on seats as comfortable as a stripper's lap. The stage was a semicircle, with dark violet chairs on tiered platforms all the way up, looking directly at the stage. As they walked to their seats, Milo was keeping eerily silent.

"Are you alright?" asked Heidi.

"I am now," replied Milo, holding a dangerously strong drink he bought from the bar.

A few minutes passed, and with approximately half the theatre seats left empty, the theatre lamp lights suddenly shut off. The stage lights rose up slowly, glowing bright orange fires on the stage. Stage technicians closed and shut the flame guards in rhythm to create a tidal current of fire. Darkness fell upon each side of the stage with deliberate pattern, making the light appear as if it was creeping away. Between the flashes of fire, a face could be seen appearing and disappearing, dancing between the dusks and dawns of the stage when *bang!* The lights flooded the stage, and there, standing with the unavoidable presence of a tombstone in an old folk's home, was Vincent.

"Ladies, gentlemen, and the otherwise questionable. My name is Vincent, but you already knew that. If you didn't, you might be in the wrong place."

"Oh, for cack's sake!" cried a man in the crowd. Heidi recognised the voice as the angry man from the fountain. Vincent gave the man as much attention as a spare prick at a wedding as he stormed off, and continued the performance.

"Now, isn't this a nice crowd? I'm a bit nervous, if I'm honest," rambled Vincent. "Of course, they say if you have stage fright, you're supposed to imagine the audience in their underwear, but I'll be honest, looking at some of you, it'd be best not."

The audience chuckled, except for Milo, who had already made up his mind on hating this show.

"You, sir," said Vincent, "with the face like a dying horse."

He was talking to Milo.

"What's your name?" asked Vincent.

"... Milo," he replied, half darting his eyes, looking around at the people now staring at him.

"Milo, and what do you do for a living?"

"Journalist."

"Oh, I'm going to have to be kind to you. Who do you work for?"

"The Bystander"

Vincent paused for a beat. "You know, for a journalist, you don't like to use words very much, do you?"

The audience chuckled again. Milo didn't again.

"Well Milo," started Vincent, "I'd like to warm up my magic muscles to start the show. Would you mind coming up on stage for a moment?"

Milo froze, and he would have stayed frozen if it wasn't for Heidi nudging him to stand up.

"Give him a round of applause, ladies and gentlemen," urged Vincent.

Milo stood up awkwardly as the people around him clapped. It took Milo longer than he would have liked to get past the other audience members, as he tripped over at least three handbags in the process, but the man eventually made his way onto the stage.

"Now don't worry, Milo, this is a very simple spell," comforted Vincent. "I have a standard deck of cards. I would like you, my good sir, to pick any card, and sign it with your name. Once you've done that, place the card back into the deck and shuffle them."

Milo followed his instructions without talking, as he already had more attention than was comfortable for him. Milo couldn't possibly have felt more out of place if he had an erection at a sexual harassment seminar.

"Thank you very much," said Vincent, patting Milo on the shoulder. "Now, are you confident you put your card back in the deck?"

"... Yes," said Milo.

"Are you sure? Would you mind turning out your pockets?"

Milo put both his hands in his trouser pockets, then pulled out the contents and realised there was something extra in there. Bent slightly against his keys was the card Milo had signed.

"You didn't put the card in the deck," accused the magician. "Let's try again. Put your card in the deck." Vincent opened the deck of cards and Milo placed the card back inside. "Now is the card back in the deck?"

Milo rolled his eyes, knowing exactly how the next minute was going to play out. "Yes, I put it back in the deck."

"Would you mind lifting up your right foot," asked Vincent.

Milo lifted his foot and didn't even bother feigning surprise as he saw his card reemerge.

"One more time, let's put the card back in the deck," asked Vincent, clearly enjoying playing with the crowd.

Milo complied again, and again, and again. Every time, the card reappeared in a different place, surprising the crowd, and slowly chipping away at Milo's patience. After the fifth time he was asked, "Is the card back in the deck," Milo would have replied. "You know what, I don't think it is. Would you like me to help you pull it out of your arse!"

Like I said, he would have done that, but there was a crowd watching, and there was no chance of Milo consciously drawing more attention to himself (not to mention Heidi's request, but that was now the least of his worries.) After concluding the performance by spitting the signed card out of his mouth, Vincent thanked Milo for his contribution, and the assistant marched quickly back to his seat, tripping over at least four handbags in the rush. As Milo sat down, Heidi nudged his arm as if to say "Good job," but the message was misinterpreted as "Wow, you looked like a twit."

Vincent's show continued with extraordinary feats of wizardry; his hands moved with gentle yet exaggerated precision, like a pervert at a melon market. The crowd shouted adoration for the levitation, exhilaration for divination, and jubilation for transmutation. Meanwhile, Milo sat agitated, frustrated and very, very intoxicated. Milo wanted to shout; he knew something no one else in the auditorium seemed to realise, but he remained silent. Some time passed, and following a particularly dangerous segment involving a rat, a chicken, and some knitting needles, the show was concluded. The audience applauded and cheered while Milo gave a sarcastic three slap volley, all the while twitching in his seat and waiting for the first socially acceptable moment to stand up and storm out. When the moment arose, and Milo knew there were no handbags en route, he escorted himself to the exit, until he remembered he had visited the theatre with Heidi, and was polite enough to wait for her outside.

"That was awesome!" burst Heidi, as she and Milo made their way back to Pending.

"It was… different," replied Milo.

"Come on, you must have had a favourite part."

Milo scrambled inside his head for a response that wouldn't be too heavily criticising. "The lighting was nice," said Milo eventually.

"You hated it, didn't you?"

"I said I wouldn't be a knob for the rest of the day. I'm glad you enjoyed it."

Heidi could sense the hidden feelings in Milo's voice. "Alright, you can go back to being a knob."

Milo, for a split second, felt elation; it was quickly replaced by a five-hundred-word essay on why he hated the show; he thought it was childish, mindless, some lowest common denominator act that he wouldn't even recommend as torture for fear the performer might make some money from the deal.

"Well, I liked it," contested Heidi.

"Good for you," replied Milo aggressively.

"But you have to appreciate his skill, and let's be honest, it's not like either of us can perform magic."

Milo erupted, realising one key point he completely missed in his rant. "It wasn't even magic!"

"It wasn't?" asked Heidi, puzzled.

"He was doing sleight of hand tricks. If it was real magic, he would have said some magic words, and definitely could have done something more impressive than spitting a playing card out his mouth."

Heidi paused for a moment to take in the new information, and compared it to what she saw on stage. "He's really good at it if he managed to trick everyone like that."

"He didn't trick everyone. I saw how it was done," snapped Milo again.

"Did you really?" asked Heidi, one half interested, and another half plotting.

"Yes."

"So you could recreate it?"

"I bet you I could."

"Then at work tomorrow, I'll bring in a set of cards and you can prove it," offered Heidi with a smirk.

"I will prove it," vowed Milo, returning the evil grin.

"I look forward to it," ended Heidi.

The next day, Heidi arrived at the office uncharacteristically early, and with her, she had brought a deck of cards; these weren't the usual set of suits and numbers that were the standard playing cards, having been decorated with various odd-coloured animals and wildlife, but they would serve the magic trick just fine. Filled with feverish excitement, Heidi pounced on Milo the second he had passed as much as a toe through the front door.

"Hello there," chirped Heidi. "Care to show off your talents?"

"I would care, thank you," replied Milo with a grin to match Heidi's confidence.

Heidi presented the short deck of cards to Milo, and he took them. Milo had not prepared for this challenge; as he said himself, he saw how it was done. The man knew in his head this was going to be as easy as a girl who had just drunk a Grammatical Error. Milo quickly examined the cards, then shuffled the deck and presented them to Heidi.

"Take a card, sign it, and put it back in the deck, then shuffle it," said Milo confidently.

Heidi followed the instructions, and took her time about it; she picked a random card from the deck, signed it close to her chest so Milo couldn't see what the illustration was, and placed it back in the deck before shuffling. As Heidi shuffled the cards, a shadow of doubt flew into Milo's mind; he couldn't remember if shuffling was supposed to be part of the act, and now he had no way of finding Heidi's card. Heidi handed the cards back, and Milo hesitated before taking them. A brief moment passed as Milo scrambled to remember what Vincent did next. Milo slipped a card from the bottom of the deck into his hand, hoping for the very small chance that it was the right card, and patted Heidi on the shoulder in a way that looked as if he had never touched another human before. Milo knew he had to slip the card into Heidi's pocket without noticing, and in bringing his hand down, one corner of the card slipped into her waistband, and sprung back out again. Heidi saw the card land on the floor.

"Not as easy as it looks, is it?" mocked Heidi.

"Wait. Give me another chance," asked Milo.

Heidi agreed, and the act was played out again. Heidi took a card, drew a quick scribble, placed it back in the deck, and shuffled it. Milo took the deck back and tried again, taking the bottom card again, and distracting Heidi with small talk, tried to slip the card into her pocket. Unfortunately, Milo brushed into Heidi's arm and the bet was lost again.

"One more time. One more time," begged Milo.

Heidi was happy to play along again and recreated the scene a third time. This time, Milo changed tact. After the card was hidden in his hand, Milo said, "Would you mind checking your pockets."

Heidi checked her pockets. "It's not there."

"Sorry. I meant check under your foot."

As Heidi looked down and lifted her feet one at a time, Milo slipped a card from the deck and tried to lodge it in a thick lock of hair. Heidi's hair made up half her body height, so the tampering was unnoticed.

"It's not there either," explained Heidi.

"Oh, what's that in your hair," said Milo with the acting quality of a child explaining to his mum why his brother had a gaping head wound.

Heidi ran her hand through her hair and knocked the card loose. Heidi picked it up, and to no one's surprise, it was not the card she had signed.

"You can't do the trick, can you?" asked Heidi.

Milo wouldn't admit it, but the evidence was stacked against him.

"Just face it, Vincent was a very good fake magician. I'm not saying you have to like him, but he can do things you can't," ended Heidi.

Heidi sat down at her desk, while Milo felt well and truly shafted; in the grand scheme of things (or even the small scheme of things), all that had happened was he was mildly embarrassed in front of someone who didn't care a great deal about someone's lack of fake magic abilities. This kind of outsider looking in perspective might have been useful to Milo if the rest of the day was anything to go by.

Milo spent the early evening with Hazel at The Devil's Neckhole, which was not unusual; what made this encounter out of the ordinary was that Milo wasn't drinking. Standing at the side of the bar with Hazel before the nighttime cacophony, Milo had been practising the same trick over and over in order to get it right. As it turned out, performing a sleight of hand trick when the most complicated thing you've ever done with your fingers is separate an egg yolk is actually quite difficult.

"Take a card from the deck and sign it," instructed Milo to Hazel.

Hazel took a card for what felt like the hundredth time that day and wrote her name on it.

"Now put it back in the deck," said Milo, opening the deck, and Hazel doing as she was told.

Milo, as he was closing the deck, managed to slip the card Hazel placed down into the palm of his hand. Milo patted Hazel on the shoulder and tried to slip the card into her pocket, completely missing and dropping it on the floor along with eight other cards all marked with Hazel's name.

"Are you ever going to give up?" asked Hazel worriedly.

"When I do it correctly, I can give up," insisted Milo.

Hazel sighed. "Why do you care this much?"

"Because I said sleight of hand was easy and I want to prove a point."

Hazel looked again at the mass of cards on the floor, and raised an eyebrow at Milo.

"I'm not trying to act smart," argued Milo.

"That was abundantly clear," replied Hazel.

Milo was becoming increasingly frustrated with himself; until now, he paid little attention to learning magic, and even less to researching imitation tricks, but suddenly, it was at the forefront of his mind.

"Sleight of hand tricks aren't impressive," badgered Milo. "Real magic takes time and skill."

"Well, you can't do either, so this Vincent guy is still the winner," disputed Hazel. "May I make a suggestion?"

"Why should I listen to anything you say?" snapped Milo.

"First of all, it's polite," snapped Hazel in return. "Secondly, I actually have an idea. Why don't you try saying the magic words."

"I don't know any magic words!"

"The magic words are please and thank you. Ask the man if he'll teach you."

"Why would he teach me?"

"Considering you're no good at teaching yourself, it's your best option."

Milo spent a moment contemplating, knowing he really didn't have many options; there was practice, which was already showing to test Hazel's patience, or beg like a dog to Vincent. Giving up would have been another option, but that hadn't crossed through Milo's thick head.

Milo that evening, remembering the promotional poster that said Vincent was performing for two days only, decided to try and meet with the man after his next and final show in Dorcoast. Milo didn't arrive at the theatre until halfway through the act, so his only chance was to catch Vincent before leaving the building. As an interviewer for a reputable newspaper, Milo knew proof of his job had the ability to open a couple of locked doors when it came to minor celebrities; it wasn't something he practised often, but had worked in his favour in the past; this was no exception. After finding the back door and showing off his credentials, Milo was able to blag his way into the hallway outside Vincent's dressing room. While Milo was unarguably not the most charismatic in the world, it's well documented that if you lie with enough fake confidence, people will believe you (ask your local politician for more information.) While the front of the theatre was presented with a professional attitude, if a little small, the backstage was not so charming. Exposed gas pipes connected the stage lights, dented scaffolding was held together with parcel string, and each door creaked like mice had been sewn into the hinges. Stagehands rested idly on the walls, many of whom not even questioning Milo's presence, waiting for the moment they could pack up and sod off home. While Dorcoast may have been the more attractive place to visit, behind the scenes, everyone had a little bit of the Pending personality. Some time passed, and the audience applauded their last for the evening. Milo headed over to the stage side and waited for Vincent to walk off. Vincent played the crowd for applause, smiling and waving with great enthusiasm, before turning around to walk off stage, where his smile dropped like a man three sips into a Hooker's Bra. Milo rushed over to Vincent before he had an adequate chance to leave.

"Excuse me, Vincent," started Milo. "May I trouble you for a minute."

"No, you can't," replied Vincent, barging straight past.

"I want to ask you a few questions."

"I want to go to my hotel."

Milo tried to keep up with Vincent as he walked faster and faster towards the door. "I need you to teach me part of your act."

"Sorry. I don't teach magic," said Vincent.

"But you don't do magic," blurted Milo.

Vincent stopped walking and turned around to face Milo; he gave no indication that he recognised his former assistant, which may have been for the best. Vincent didn't speak, only waited for Milo to start again.

"I know it's all fake," whimpered Milo.

Vincent smirked. "Well done. I assume you're a man who has experience with people who fake it."

"Are you trying to insult me?"

"Trust me, I'm not trying."

Milo was becoming ever more frustrated, but he needed to keep his mind on track with the thing that originally made him frustrated.

"I want to know how you do that card trick you opened your show with," asked Milo assertively.

"I'm not training you," reasserted Vincent.

"I'll pay."

"How much?"

Milo opened the content of his wallet.

"Deal," said Vincent.

Milo produced a pack of cards from his back pocket and gave them to Vincent, who gave a brief glance through the deck and furrowed his brow.

"Why do half of these cards say 'Hazel' on them?" asked Vincent.

"Not important. Can you just show me the trick?"

Vincent recreated the trick, exactly as he did before, explaining every step of the act as he went, although there were some issues involved. First problem: As the trick was designed to be performed on stage in front of an audience, certain body language that was used seemed unnatural in one-on-one conversation. Second problem: Milo was absolutely cack at executing instructions. Several attempts had only asserted the fact Milo hands would find more use as a cannibal's lunch than as appendages. Vincent did not have the patience to wait for Milo, as he would be dead some time before Milo succeeded.

"Look, mate. I haven't got all day. Can I give you some advice?" asked Vincent, as he sorted through Milo's deck of cards and organised them into two piles, handing only one of them back to Milo. "Just do what I do."

The next day after work, with new found confidence, Milo invited Heidi to The Devil's Neckhole to demonstrate his trick. This time, however, Hazel was a witness to the upcoming spectacle as well. Milo pulled out his now diminished deck of cards, and presented them to Hazel.

"Please, Hazel," started Milo. "Pick a card from the deck, but don't show it to us."

Hazel paused for a split second as this trick seemed to be partially different from the five-hundred practice attempts, and paused again when she picked a card from the deck, only to be quickly interrupted by Milo before she could say anything.

"And would you sign the card with your name," asked Milo quickly.

Hazel tried again to speak, and was interrupted a second time. Hazel stopped trying to protest and followed command. Heidi looked on in expectant curiosity as Milo seemed to hold more control over the situation than he had before (which comparatively, wasn't difficult).

"Now place the card in the deck," asked Milo, and Hazel complied. "Heidi. Would you care to shuffle the deck for me."

Heidi shuffled the small deck of cards and looked at them curiously for any obvious markings, but found nothing out of the ordinary other than the fact that the deck was half its usual size. Once shuffled, Heidi passed the cards back to Milo, who then fanned out the deck and presented them to Heidi.

"Pick any card from the deck. Whatever card you pick will be the one Hazel signed."

Heidi deliberated for a moment before taking a random card from the deck. Heidi lifted the card slowly, looked, and saw it was indeed a card signed with Hazel's name.

"Congratulations," said Heidi. "You can do magic tricks."

"I thank you," celebrated Milo, taking a mocking little bow.

Hazel did not show any sign of being impressed, only staring at Milo with contempt.

"Would you care to show us how you did it?" asked Hazel disdainfully.

"I can't do that. It would ruin the mystique," replied Milo, suddenly imitating his teacher's confidence.

Hazel sneered. "Did you somehow become more of a knob?"

Milo didn't seem to care about Hazel's usual volley of insults; he had proven that sleight of hand tricks were possible for anyone, and all that was required of him was to practise for an entire evening, harass a stage performer, and to empty his wallet.

"It's weird though," said Heidi. "She also signed this card."

Heidi revealed a second card she had picked up, similarly

autographed by Hazel.

Milo shat himself.

"How did you get that card?" asked Milo, losing all sense of victory.

"I can't tell you that. It would ruin the mystique," mocked Heidi.

Milo had been defeated again. Intentionally or not, Heidi had seen through his ~~clever~~ ruse. Milo admitted that Vincent had talent, and that creating a deck of cards all pre-signed by Hazel was the magician's idea again. Though he apologised, Milo held one thing to heart out of this whole experience.

He still hated the magic show.

***

Milo, Heidi, and Hazel stayed in the bar for some time; it was a quiet night for the pub, and most of the patrons still had all their teeth, so the atmosphere was relaxed. Milo absentmindedly shuffled the deck of cards over and over while stuck in a strop as the two women chatted idly.

"Anyway, Heidi," started Hazel. "Besides the people," she gave a quick glance over to the grieving Milo, "how are you enjoying Pending."

"It's great," remarked Heidi. "I've never seen so many wild animals."

"I said besides the people," joked Hazel.

Milo was a bit puzzled. "What's so special about the animals? There's just foxes and raccoons around here. Haven't you seen those before?"

"I have, but in zoos. I've never been anywhere where they just run wild."

"And that's a good thing?" questioned Milo.

"Is it a bad thing?"

"They're considered pests. You'll get diseases from them."

Heidi paused for a few seconds.

"Excuse me, I'm just going to wash my hands," muttered

Heidi.

Heidi got up and walked to the nearest washroom, although using the ones in The Devil's Neckhole would rarely make you feel cleaner. As Heidi tiptoed over the quagmire to reach the wash basin, Milo and Hazel continued the conversation.

"What an idiot," blurted Milo. "Who goes around stroking wild animals?"

"Wasn't she handling your playing cards?" asked Hazel, as Milo was shuffling them.

Milo paused for a few seconds, now noticing a brown mark on the cards he hadn't before.

"Excuse me, I'm just going to wash my hands."

CHAPTER THREE

Atheist God Botherers

Religion on Flatrock is a very interesting topic, it being a world where God is proven to exist, but everyone hates him. Technically speaking, there are no religions in the current day, but there are still groups that follow certain beliefs in a religious fashion. People now generally follow the beliefs of patrons. A patron is a person who existed in history and represents certain beliefs through their actions during life, such as giving to charity, helping the homeless, buying prostitutes for ugly people, and so on. You must fulfil one of two qualifications to become a patron: Prove yourself to a large number of people that your actions have had a great positive impact on your cause, making you worthy of historical importance, at which point, local governments and councils will debate your patronhood; or alternatively, have a lot of money. The churches, temples, cult leader basements, and the such that existed before God's reveal were converted into places to worship these patrons and learn from their teachings, and by this method, you could be part of multiple religions. It might be worth noting that several questions throughout theological study have yet to be answered: Why are we here? Is there an afterlife? Do sin and punishment exist? All these and more were forgotten topics while people were telling God to piss off. This story begins in Pending's church. Most places of worship, including Pending's church, are relatively modern buildings. As you might expect, after the discovery that all previous religions were false, riots were held worldwide, resulting in the destruction of many religious properties, but the places of worship had to later be rebuilt as there was nowhere to host the coffee mornings. Whether you use the term church, temple, or cult leader basement is irrelevant, as the words in this age of Flatrock are interchangeable. Legally speaking, they are referred to as "houses of patronage," but this phrase is usually reserved for pedants/arseholes. The church in Pending is dedicated to Roland, Patron of barrels, which may sound stupid to your ears, but rest assured, there are stranger patrons in the world, such as Olivia, Patron of fiction; Kennedy, Patron of erotic fiction; and Samuel, Patron of erotic non-fiction (who lost his patronhood after being arrested). The Church of Roland is managed by only a priest, who frequently asked volunteers to help, but it is generally believed in the local area that whoever wanted to work in the church had to be an idiot.

Heidi was working there today.

"Father Sullivan? I'm Heidi. Heidi Watson."

"Ah, yes, thank you for coming by," greeted Father Sullivan softly. "Here's a broom. Sweep the floor," he added bluntly.

Heidi was thrown a broom, quite possibly second hand from a stable, before she had even walked through the front door.

"Nice to meet you too," muttered Heidi, as Father Sullivan walked away.

The church from both outside and in was not ornate, or even very large, yet oddly tall, which allowed Heidi's voice to echo from the ceiling to her own amusement. The church only had capacity for fifty or so people at most, although more was rarely needed. The building was a circle pinched at the front like an arrowhead, with the centre being filled with hardwood single chairs pointing towards (what could generously be called) the altar. The church had plain glass windows constructed into the top of the building, set in the join between the walls and the ceiling, and because the sun is positioned in the same space every day in Flatrock, the light shone at exactly the right angle to blind Heidi while she was working (the windows had curtains, but they were too high up for anyone to reach.) Father Sullivan, who had disappeared into the sacristy seconds after commanding Heidi, was a portly man, but not so much that you wouldn't trust him with a freshly baked cake. With his greying hair, messy beard, and unmistakable aroma of cheap beer, Father Sullivan was the very picture of an uncle who had given up on trying. Heidi pushed the chairs to the side of the room and set to work on the floor; while she was sweeping, half of Heidi's mind was set on the job in hand, but the other half stared at the blank walls, wondering something to herself. When Father Sullivan reemerged from the sacristy, Heidi made sure to get his attention.

"Why aren't there any pictures of Patron Roland?" asked Heidi.

"Our patron demands not the use of his image," proclaimed Sullivan with the gusto of an amateur dramatist. "This church is branded only with his teachings."

Other houses of patronage Heidi had visited during her travels generally had a sense of grandeur; statues and colourful paintings, a spectacle to look upon with your own eyes to make even the most leeching sermon appear substantial. It felt odd for Heidi to find one as minimalist as this, but considering this was Pending, a town where even the public toilets were missing a hole, it seemed believable.

"If you don't mind, I'd like to hear some of Patron Roland's stories," asked Heidi.

"Of course," said Sullivan sweetly. "Finish the floor," he added bluntly.

Heidi hurriedly swept up the remaining dirt, which was not easy, as the bristles of the brush had a tendency to fall apart if they so much as carried more than a grain of sand. Once the well laden layer of dust was swept from the church floor, Heidi called to Father Sullivan.

"Grab me a chair," asked the priest, brushing crumbs off himself.

Heidi looked on in dismay as the particles fell on to what was recently a clean floor, before grabbing a chair for Sullivan, and one for herself. Father Sullivan sat down slowly and purposefully.

"Do you want to know the origin of Patron Roland?" whispered Father Sullivan, leaning forward into Heidi.

"Yes, please," answered Heidi, leaning forward to hear him.

Father Sullivan cleared his throat.

"TWO HUNDRED YEARS AGO," exploded Sullivan, sending Heidi careening into the back of her chair, "when Roland of Wrendie walked our rock, just a humble carpenter boy of nineteen years old, he found a group of no less than forty people, troubled by grief. Roland asked of them their plight, to which the crowd responded 'Lo, stranger. We have twelve jars, full to spilling of the juices of our crops, but not a one or any of our fellowship can lift the jars more than a few feet at a time. We must arrive before the moon shines down on our village, lest we face our children going hungry.'" Father Roland shouted his sermon with the force of a tornado, with twice as much debris coming from his mouth; it was hard for Heidi not to be invested in the performance if nothing else. "Roland looked around the group, and found trees growing close by; he cut down an apple tree and shaped its trunk into sturdy boards. In a short matter of time, Roland had created two barrels, much larger than the jars. 'Pour your juice into these barrels' commanded Roland," and with that line delivery, Father Sullivan shot up from his chair. Heidi, enthralled with the performance, did the same without understanding why. "The crowd was confused," continued Father Sullivan. "'If we cannot lift one jar of juice, how do you expect us to move six at once?' Roland asked the crowd to put faith in him, and they did as he said. When the barrels were filled to burst, Roland fixed lids to them, and tipped them over. 'Now you can roll the juice to your village.' The crowd were shocked and amazed; Roland had saved them. Roland was invited to the village, and stayed for some time drinking the juice of the crops. Spirits were lifted, the village was merry, and through Roland's actions, they had learned to put their faith in the kindness of strangers. Praise to our patron, Roland, genius carpenter of Wrendie!"

Heidi listened intently, and was interested, although when the story concluded, she was slightly bewildered. Several items in the story seemed curious, such as the apparent stupidity of the crowd, the final lesson learned, and she was fairly certain the barrel was invented far further than two hundred years ago, but she remained courteous.

"That was... interesting," said Heidi.

"Interesting? It was marvellous!" declared Sullivan. "And his later life was even greater."

Heidi had clearly hit a passionate point of discussion for Father Sullivan, evidenced by the fact he continued to his next story without asking.

"After settling in the village and making his home there, Roland walked out to the nearby coastline. On the way, he met a sailor who was troubled. Roland asked if he could help, but the sailor responded 'Alas, my boat cannot keep its balance, and capsizes mere seconds after leaving the harbour. I must go out and cross the Tip Sea to get home, before my family worries for me.'" Heidi wasn't as captivated in the story of Patron Roland as she had hoped, in fact, she was more distracted by the fact she'd never heard of the Tip Sea before, but she couldn't bring herself to stop Father Sullivan while he was so engrossed with having a shouting competition with himself. "Roland looked at the boat, and thought for a second; he left the sailor, and returned with four empty barrels. Roland affixed the barrels, two each side, to the boat's hull. When the sailor pushed his ship out to sea, the boat remained upright, made stable by the buoyancy of the barrels. The sailor thanked Roland, and returned home. A year later, the sailor returned, bringing exotic fruits for Roland's village to feast upon, and spirits were lifted once more. Praise to our patron, Roland, repairman of sea vessels!"

Heidi listened again, but this time her curiosity was raised to a higher stage when she noted the common elements between each parable. Heidi had to pause for a moment to make sure she chose her next words carefully, ending the conversation, but still being polite. Heidi had maybe paused for too long because Sullivan responded, "Awestruck, I see. Allow me to indulge you with more tales."

"No, that's fine," exclaimed Heidi, but the sentence was drowned out by Father Sullivan, who was now gesticulating with his whole body.

"When Roland visited his home town some years after that, he saw a panicked man running towards him. Roland stopped the man and asked, 'Why do you run like a wild animal?' The man replied 'I have done nothing wrong, yet the town believes me a criminal. I need to hide as soon as possible.' Roland looked upon his cart and-"

"Did Roland have a barrel?" asked Heidi, predicting the pattern.

"Yes," answered Sullivan.

"Did the criminal hide in the barrel?"

"Yes."

Heidi thought if she had predicted the story's outcome, Father Sullivan would have stopped, but instead, he looked on with just as much enthusiasm as before.

"Forgive me if this is rude," started Heidi, "but Patron Roland seems somewhat predictable."

"Ah, but you don't know what happened next," countered Father Sullivan.

"Go on," said Heidi tentatively.

"After the scene had cleared, the panicked man, now calm and safe, revealed to Roland he was in fact a thief, having stolen fruit from a local vendor to feed his family. The criminal offered Roland half the spoils for his silence, but Roland invited the man to return to the village with his family. The fruits were shared equally, and spirits were lifted, as the village learned the value of helping a criminal. Praise to our patron, Roland, harbourer of fugitives!"

Heidi was confused by the supposed teaching of the last

parable. She was expecting it to be something along the lines of "even the dishonest can have a good heart," or "the poorest man can hold the greatest treasures." The message "helping a criminal" is not usually one that should be taken as a blanket term. Before Heidi thought too hard about it, she remembered she needed a way out of this theatrical bear trap.

"Alright, I've done the sweeping," declared Heidi quickly. "Anything else I can help with?"

"Go to the back room and organise the documents in the cupboard," asked Father Sullivan, his story teller/shouter disposition vanishing in an instant.

"Will do," answered Heidi, walking away at double speed.

The back room was also known as the church school; the church school was also known as the holding pen for children while adults went about their business. The holding pen had a large but low table in the middle where the children could distract themselves with activities like paper craft and paper obliteration. It was obvious to Heidi that this room had been in disuse for some time, as it had become the new natural habitat of mushrooms. Heidi opened a cupboard door to find what she assumed were supposed to be the documents, but they could have just as easily been toilet roll. Most of the papers were junk, old, decayed and dishevelled beyond use; to even burn the papers would be playing with fire (pardon the pun). Piles upon piles of invoices, textbooks, activity sheets for children, DIY furniture manuals, cocktails recipes, and a well-worn book written by a certain Patron Samuel polluted the cupboards. Most of the papers needed throwing away, but Heidi couldn't find a bin. Where was a barrel when you needed it? Heidi struggled to arrange the papers in a way that allowed for some kind of order, and the most she could hope for was to turn the mess into an organised mess before day's end. After emptying the entire contents of the cupboard onto the table in a collection of piles, half of which fell on the floor, making little difference to the amount of mess, Heidi noticed a particular piece of paper; the paper was not special; why it caught her attention was because it had her name on it. Heidi had to double check, which was not easy, as the entire pile was pasted together with some kind of approximation of chocolate fudge cake and what chocolate fudge cake looks like the following morning, but it definitely said "Heidi." Specifically, the papers were about a Patron Heidi, official Patron of Pending some thousand years ago. Heidi's curiosity was sky high, and she tried prying apart the records to learn more, but whatever amalgamation of cinders, caramel, and rat hair had made home on the paper prevented any information from being extracted. It was while Heidi was struggling with the book of bile that Father Sullivan walked in.

"Whatever it is, throw it away," commanded Sullivan in disgust.

"It's something to do with another Patron called Heidi. Do you know anything about her?" asked Heidi.

"I said throw it away, you pillock."

Heidi was quite upset. "But there might be some interesting stories in here."

"This place is the house of Patron Roland," argued Sullivan, "and any other patron's word doesn't belong here."

"You can't just get rid of another patron's history like it's nothing."

A vein in the top of Father Sullivan's head was thickening. "I'm sorry, but does Patron Heidi own this building? I think not."

"That's not-"

"Be quiet! I'm not paid to concern myself with any other patrons, so throw those papers away."

Heidi was caught slightly off guard by something in that last sentence. "Paid? I thought you were a volunteer like me."

"No. I have a salary."

"Who pays you?"

"Roland does."

Heidi was very confused. "I thought Patron Roland lived over two hundred years ago."

"Not the person, you div. Roland Brewery."

"Roland Brewery?"

"Yes! Is there an echo in here?"

There was an echo, but regardless, Heidi had to process the information for a moment. "How often do you preach philosophies?"

"Hardly ever. Nobody visits here," answered Sullivan.

"Then what do you do here?"

"Accounting, and when the season is good, ferment crops."

Suddenly, the confusing puzzle was starting to piece itself together.

"So, in your stories," Heidi danced around trying to sound rude, "when you said *spirits* were lifted-"

"I meant the alcoholic kind," answered Father Sullivan.

"And all the fruits?"

"Used to make the drinks."

"Right," hesitated Heidi, lacking confidence as she was suddenly filled with mixed emotions about volunteering at this church. "One final question, are any of your stories real?"

After Heidi was thrown out of the church for heresy, she left for home. On the way, she stopped by a bookshop (the closest thing Pending had to a library, because nothing good in life is free when you live in this town), hoping to find more information about whoever Patron Heidi was. Pending's only bookshop was not big, so under normal circumstances, it would not have been hard to find whether or not a book was in stock, but this was Pending. The bookshop was a mess, with no kind of categorization at all, and far too many books for the amount of shelves in the shop, so many were left in piles in the middle of the floor. Heidi was a small woman, even as small people come, but she would have needed to be a mouse to navigate the shitstorm of stories. There was one employee at this bookshop, an elderly woman who looked like she had died thirty years earlier but was still walking, who was no help to Heidi in finding any specific book. Hours later, Heidi had managed to find nothing; she might have better luck surveying in another town, but it was now too late in the day to travel, and she had work the following morning. The next day, Heidi went to The Bystander offices with more than a couple of questions on her mind, first of which:

"Why didn't anyone tell me the church of Roland was for a brewery?" asked Heidi.

"First of all, it's not a church, it's a house of patronage," objected Milo. "Secondly, I expected you knew. Roland is a brand of cheap drinks."

"There's no need to be so patronising," said Heidi (the term "patronise" is quite a confusing term in Flatrock. As well as meaning to talk down in a condescending way, patronising is also the term used when someone is officially appointed as a patron.) "Besides, I thought churches were supposed to be sacred."

"They are to some people, but in this country, houses of patronage are considered charitable organisations, which means they're subject to tax breaks. A lot of houses of patronage are owned by big businesses as tax havens."

Heidi grimaced. "Pending is a strange town."

"Not exactly the S word I would use," added Milo.

Heidi leaned back in her chair, still full to spilling with curiosity. "I don't suppose you know who Patron Heidi was, do you?"

"It's not my area of expertise."

"Figures it would be that way. Maybe I could ask Rob."

"You should *not* ask Rob!" insisted Milo, a bit too loud considering Rob was in the room.

"Why not? He knows a lot."

"He doesn't know social cues."

"But I want to know about Patron Heidi."

"And I want beautiful women to feed me grapes. Wait until the office closes and try the library in Dorcoast. They probably have some information in there."

"Fine, I'll wait," moaned Heidi.

One minute passed.

Two minutes passed.

Three minutes passed.

"I'm asking Rob," announced Heidi.

"No! DON'T!" screamed Milo, hurriedly standing up to grab Heidi, but missing by an inch.

Heidi sauntered over to Rob's desk; he appeared to be reading a book on the history of gate hinges when Heidi leaned over to him.

"Hey, Rob," said Heidi. "I need some help with something."

"Ah, Heidi. Do you want a glass of water?"

"No," answered Heidi.

"Did you want to hear the gossip concerning the boss' haemorrhoids?"

"No," answered Heidi with increased concern.

"Do you want the address of a good hairdresser?"

"... No," answered Heidi, now quite self-conscious.

"Do you-"

"I want to know about Patron Heidi," interrupted Heidi. "Can you help me?"

Rob froze at Heidi's sudden intrusion.

"Yes, that should be possible," answered Rob, eventually. "Let me just check my catalogue."

Rob pulled out a thick book from under his desk, which had a thousand bookmarks of various colours poking from every side. After heaving the cover open and examining several keys and indexes, Rob ran his finger along the side of the page, checking the titles and mumbling to himself all the while. The writing in the catalogue was tiny, and filled with words and numbers Heidi could barely read from just looking over Rob's shoulder. After some time, Rob smacked the tip of his finger on a particular line, noted the number next to it, and closed the catalogue, then went to his drawer filled to the brim with folders all filed under some kind of six figure sorting system. Heidi questioned why Rob wasn't working in the bookshop, before he pulled out a folder and opened it.

"Here we are," cheered Rob. "The history of Dorcoast and

surrounding territories houses of patronage, second revised edition."

"Awesome!" beamed Heidi.

"Let me read it for you."

"No, thanks, I'll read it myself."

Heidi stole the folder from Rob and thanked him again before returning to her desk. The folder was stuffed much thicker than it looked, and after wading through several documents concerning other Patrons of recent history, Heidi finally found the document she was looking for, and read it:

"In the market slums of a great kingdom, against the side of a bread stall, sat a young girl, begging for food. The shopkeeper paid no attention to the girl, who had stayed at the stall for days now. Some who bought from the market threw scraps at the girl, but it was not enough for a child to grow strong. Eventually, she became sick, and fewer people wanted to be near her. When the week had ended, and the townspeople had been paid for their labour, droves leapt to the markets, but by now, the girl was only days from death, and no one wished to waste good food on a corpse. There was one man in the crowd, poor, as the girl was, but strong enough to work. He bought a loaf with the wages he had earned, and as he was leaving, he saw the girl. The man leaned down and asked for her name, something no one had at that market. 'Heidi,' the little girl confessed. The man spent a moment to think, before handing the loaf to the girl. The nearby crowd insulted his poor judgement, and the man heard, but did not listen; he returned home with empty hands, and slept on an empty stomach. When the man awoke, a feast had been laid before him, with all the luxuries money could buy. On the table also lay a piece of parchment; it read 'Thank you for asking my name.'"

Heidi was enthralled, far more interested in what she read than anything Father Sullivan had recited (not that it was a difficult task). Diving deeper into the pile, more and more scraps of paper bore the name Heidi; further stories about sacrifices, heroics, and mysterious gifts. There were peculiar elements between the stories, such as never stating place names or time periods; nothing of this fabled Heidi's personal life could be found. All the stories were disconnected, only joined together by their common themes, and it was debated whether Patron Heidi was a real person or simply a character. Regardless of the answer, Heidi was elated. Soon enough, Heidi found the official title of the character: Patron Heidi, Patron of Gratitude. Heidi couldn't stop reading the stories over and over again to herself for the rest of the day, all of which she did on company time. Patron Heidi represented the want and need to show affection to those who have helped you, which makes it understandable why her popularity declined in Pending. Eventually, Heidi returned the documents to Rob.

"Are you happy now?" asked Milo.

"Yes. Very, actually," answered Heidi.

Heidi felt uplifted to know the story of the patron. Maybe it was the fact that Pending had a way of wearing down all the good in the world, but reading about a shining force, even if they existed a thousand years ago, was pleasant, and even more than that, inspiring.

"I want to honour Patron Heidi," announced Heidi.

Milo was mildly surprised. "Why?"

"She was a great person who did great things, and-"

"She shares the same name as you."

"That has nothing to do with it."

"It has a little bit to do with it," suggested Milo.

"Does it matter? I'm going to honour her."

Heidi was buzzing like a bee in the mating season, full of hope and ambition; there was just one ever so minor oversight.

"How do you plan to honour her?" asked Milo.

"… I don't know," confessed Heidi.

"Couldn't you do a portrait?"

"I don't know what she looks like." Heidi thought for a short while. "You could write an article about her."

"I hate to be pedantic," lied Milo, "but you seem to lack a fundamental understanding of what the news is. A legend from one thousand years ago isn't exactly striking the iron while it's hot."

Heidi wasn't ready to admit defeat; she would think of something; she just needed more time. Portraits were definitely her strongest skill, but that was impossible without a description of what she looked like. When she left work for home, Heidi lay in bed and stared at the ceiling, hoping for inspiration to fall from the sky. Heidi thought about her patron namesake again and again, thinking of her stories and acts of kindness. Then suddenly, she had it. If it was Patron Heidi's acts that made her stick out in Heidi's head, her face was not important, her message was. Heidi decided to paint the bread giving scene she read about from Rob's file. Heidi suddenly had a clear picture in her mind of what she had to make, and that it would feature on the wall by the side of the local park she walked past on the way to work. The wall was big, white as snow, and already had its fair share of graffiti, most of which was much less tasteful than what Heidi had planned; it seemed like the perfect idea.

It was not the perfect idea. For one, Heidi wanted colour paints, but pigments can be quite expensive, and she couldn't afford them, so she had to compromise for black and white. For two, the wall she wanted to paint on was in worse condition than she realised, having only seen the thing in the middle distance. Heidi also thought it unwise to paint a beautiful picture showing the generosity of people next to crude drawings of ejaculating penises. Nevertheless, Heidi lacked any other plan, and made the most of her scenario. Heidi tied her hair back and wrapped it into a bun before getting to work, initially painting over the previous graffiti, which was a more delicate task than she anticipated, as the plaster on the wall flaked if you so much as breathed on it too strongly. With a suitably white wall created, Heidi set to work tracing a basic outline on her canvas of crap. Heidi had never done a painting of this size before, and it took much longer than she expected it to, wishing she had also brought some kind of ladder with her. Heidi's only tools for this task were some charcoal pencils to sketch the scene, a selection of brushes for the paint, and a large bucket of water to rinse everything in. Once it had approached lunchtime, Heidi sat down on a nearby bench to eat, admiring the work she had managed to achieve so far. The wall was full of rudimentary sketches right now, but the basic shape was clear, and Heidi was more than pleased with her work. It was exactly the point in the meal when one feels most at ease that Heidi caught a glimpse of something she didn't want to: Father Sullivan. Heidi tried viciously to avoid eye contact with the priest, but it proved a fruitless endeavour.

"You, girl," shouted Father Sullivan.

Heidi begrudgingly looked up at the man. "Nice to see you too."

"Did you do that?" accused Sullivan, pointing at the wall Heidi had been sketching on.

"Yes, I did," answered Heidi.

"You have to remove it."

Heidi was quite irritated by this. "Why?"

"It's council property."

Heidi started to speak in a mildly aggressive tone, "It's no worse than any other graffiti on that wall."

"That's like saying murder is no worse than any other crime."

Heidi was becoming incredibly annoyed at this attack, as she was led to believe Patron Roland promoted helping criminals, but despite that fact, she did not raise this hypocrisy.

"You have no right to stop me," argued Heidi.

"I will stop you," insisted Sullivan.

"Then do it."

"I will."

The childish bickering went on for quite some time. Eventually, Father Sullivan walked away, and after an hour, he returned with a man from the local council; it was unclear whether or not this new person was someone of authority or simply a binman, but he was at least wearing some kind of insignia. Heidi, in the time that had passed, was already painting the outline of the scene when she was interrupted again.

"Tell her she can't paint filth on that wall," demanded Father Sullivan.

The councilman looked at the wall in mild confusion. "It doesn't look that bad."

"She should be fined for damage to council property."

The councilman became even more confused. "If anything, she made it look nicer."

Heidi didn't want to speak up against authority; she was gambling on Pending's local council being quite lax, which as bets go, seemed pretty safe.

"It's criminal damage. It doesn't matter what she paints on it," ranted Sullivan.

"Fine, shut up," demanded the councilman to Sullivan. "You, whoever you are," he said, pointing to Heidi, "you can't use this wall to paint on. And you," turning back to Sullivan, "don't come to my office again."

Father Sullivan acted like he didn't hear his chastisement, as he seemed to be subtly smiling to himself as he walked away, taking only a single glance back at Heidi. Heidi gripped her brush tightly and sneered; it was the most petty, vindictive, knobheaded act she had ever seen, and her tolerance was wearing dangerously thin. Taking a deep breath, Heidi packed up her tools and left the park, mumbling to herself if Patron Heidi was supposed to help people who acted in kindness, was there another Patron who would punish people for acting like tossers? She could live in hope.

Heidi had lost the best part of the day, and her motivation had taken a serious hit, but she still wanted to paint the scene. Heidi scouted out the rest of town for anything that could display the painting, making sure it wasn't a council owned property, but after spending somewhere in the region of an hour circling town, there didn't seem to be anywhere suitable. Heidi tried to retrace her steps through the streets of Pending in her head for anywhere that might even be half suitable, but (I must reiterate) this was Pending. It was walking through the streets in her head that Heidi had a slightly wild idea: Could she paint on a public footpath? It had the word public in the name, so that means it's not owned by the council, right? At the very least, it was worth a shot, wasn't it? Heidi wouldn't be able to finish the painting in one day, but she could at least start it. Heidi found a pathway that was big enough, had a fairly smooth road surface to it, and didn't have too many people walking over it. Heidi got to work tracing the outline of the picture, the same she had done on the wall; if anything, working on the floor was easier since Heidi didn't have to reach high up without standing on tiptoes. The biggest problem Heidi faced was people stepping over the art while she worked on it, but fortunately, most people walking past gave a wide berth, thinking Heidi to be some kind of mad woman drawing on the road. The task of making an outline was done much quicker the second time, but with the sunlight drawing to a close, Heidi debated with herself whether she should start painting, and finish her work very late, or go home and finish the next day. The wise choice would be to go home, which is exactly what Heidi didn't do, as she was itching with too much renewed enthusiasm, and was more than happy to let her sleep schedule suffer. Heidi leaned closely into the ground to try and keep within her own lines, which were not so easily visible on a surface that wasn't white. It was becoming dark, and Heidi couldn't see around her easily at this point, which is why it came as somewhat of a surprise to her when she heard someone shout, "Again!"

"Hello again," mumbled Heidi, not looking up from her painting to acknowledge Sullivan, who was standing over her.

"Do you think you can just paint anywhere?" questioned Sullivan.

"Do you think it's your mission to get in my way?" Heidi's patience with the man was reaching breaking point, thinking if Father Sullivan had been this passionate about cleaning his own church, this whole pathetic rivalry never would have happened.

"It's a public footpath, and you're the first person to have any problem with it. I'm not bothering anyone, so go away."

"It's an eyesore," argued Sullivan.

"It's not finished," countered Heidi.

"You know you're not supposed to be doing that."

"Oh, bog off," snapped Heidi.

Father Sullivan's nostrils flared up. "Maybe if you didn't fixate on trivial matters like that, you might be able to hold a job for more than a day."

With fist clenched, Heidi finally stood up to look Father Sullivan in the eyes. "And maybe if you learned the teachings of other Patrons instead of going out of your way to annoy people, you might have more than zero volunteers to clean the church."

As insults go, this was not incredibly smart, but it can be forgiven as Heidi has had very little practice. Regardless of the quality, it had an effect on Father Sullivan, whose face turned deep red, so confounded by the fact someone answered back at him. Sullivan glanced over to the ground, picked up the bucket of water Heidi had prepared, and threw it over the painting. Heidi screamed out as the water roared across the footpath, washing away the sketch lines and smearing the wet paint. Heidi was in shock at this, and didn't know how to react other than to tear up. Sullivan tossed the bucket to the ground and walked away. Heidi burst into tears in the middle of the street, which in fairness, didn't help the remaining sketch marks to stay intact. Anger and depression rushed through Heidi's blood and boiled it, but by the time Heidi returned to her senses, Father Sullivan was long gone. Heidi had taken a serious hit to her motivation, and she couldn't think straight. The only light available now came from the street lamps, so there was no way she could work effectively. Heidi packed up her things once again and left, wishing ever so slightly for a barrel that she could scream into.

Heidi spent the rest of her evening in The Devil's Neckhole, recounting the entire miserable chronicle to Hazel, who was more than accustomed to hearing depressed drunkards talk about their problems. Heidi eventually recovered from being a blubbering wreck to simply become weeping debris, angry at Father Sullivan for ruining her work, and upset at herself for breaking her composure in the first place.

"I can't believe I snapped like that," admitted Heidi.

"You're a true resident of Pending now," said Hazel.

Heidi spent most of her time staring out into nothing, forgetting where she was as she repeated the events of the past day in her head.

"I feel sorry for you, Heidi," comforted Hazel. "Normally in these circumstances, I'd get you a drink, but you're a herb, and won't have anything but water."

"Thanks for the thought," mumbled Heidi.

Hazel didn't easily tolerate seeing Heidi in distress, and wanted in any way to help, especially if it could be used to infuriate a ham-faced old man with a vendetta against fun.

"Do you still want to paint that thing?" asked Hazel.

"Of course I do. I'm going to honour Patron Heidi if it kills me," answered Heidi.

Hazel smiled; she was proud of Heidi for sticking to her ideals, and it meant a plot in her head might be enacted.

"Then take some advice from me," started Hazel, "play him at his own game."

"Throwing water over him isn't going to solve anything," said Heidi.

"Ha! Heidi, you're sweet, but let me tell you how it's done."

Quite a few days passed, and Heidi and Father Sullivan did not cross paths once in that time, the priest in fact forgetting completely the rivalry between the two of them had ever occurred. On this day in particular, Father Sullivan had been "working" in his church, calculating the overhead costs of buying lunch for all the employee that worked there. With that important piece of calculation completed, Sullivan left the church for a local cafe, opening the door wide and enjoying the unusually good weather of the day, only for it to be spoiled for him a second later. Looking across the road, a large wooden scaffolding had been erected, positioned directly in front of the church's main door. On that scaffolding was a huge cloth banner, and painted on it was a scene Sullivan half recognised. The painting was of a bustling town market, rushed with people, walls soaked in dark greys and black, and in the centre, painted in vivid colour, was a man sacrificing his only loaf of bread to a child wearing a hood over their head, obscuring their face. To anyone else, the scene would have looked beautiful; to Sullivan, this was one heck of a vengeful insult.

"Are you kidding me?" shouted the priest.

Sullivan stormed over to the banner, determined to tear it down. The painting was tied with rope firmly to the wood frame, and Father Sullivan had incredible trouble removing the knots, but refused to give up, using as much force as he possibly could, getting angrier and angrier with himself. It was in this fit of frustration that Heidi decided to show her face.

"Hey, knobhead," shouted Heidi. "What are you doing?"

"Do you think this is funny?" whinged Sullivan, still losing against the foe who couldn't fight back.

"Excuse me, that's criminal damage."

"What? No, it isn't."

"I think you'll find it is," said a voice slightly familiar to the priest.

Father Sullivan turned around and met eyes with the councilman he had disturbed a few days earlier.

"I'm afraid I'll have to fine you for damage to council property," said the councilman.

"Council property?" whined Sullivan.

"Is there an echo in here?" exclaimed Heidi.

"This painting was commissioned by Pending town council for the purposes of display. You aren't allowed to remove it."

Father Sullivan turned around to face Heidi again. "You got paid for this cack?"

"Actually, I volunteered," replied Heidi.

In the days between Heidi's mental breakdown and the day

in question, herself and Hazel had visited Pending council with a pitch to make a public art exhibition. Very few people were in total approval of the idea, except one, who Heidi had met the day before. The councilman who had seen her work on the wall was more than happy to give her a chance after seeing the quality of work (and after discovering from Hazel that it would really annoy Father Sullivan.) Pending council paid for the material, and Heidi worked for free in the privacy of her own home.

"This is outrageous!" shouted Father Sullivan.

"Please step away from the banner, you're getting spit over it," replied the councilman.

Father Sullivan stropped off back into his church, completely forgetting he was originally going for lunch. Heidi felt an amazing rush from performing this elaborate prank, and discovered she quite liked being an arsehole, but more importantly, she had finally been able to honour her patron namesake. Heidi was proud of herself when she saw people walk past and admire the painting for a long time to come, even if chances are none of them looked for the deeper meaning behind it. The person who saw the painting more than anyone however was Father Sullivan, who couldn't avoid it every time he left the church, presenting a constant reminder of his defeat in the pathetic argument; he found it very hard to lift his spirits after that.

***

Heidi decided to spend some time on the streets of Dorcoast, for the first time venturing out of Pending on her own. With a now proper understanding of the country she was in, there was no excuse for her not to try the local shops and delicacies. The roads and paths were dense with people, especially musicians who played no end of different instruments. Heidi recognised most of the entertainer's toolkit, but one brand new to her was the bagpipes; a sort of fabric squid that sounded like it was being killed and resuscitated over and over again. Heidi also wandered into a clothing shop; she noted people in Dorcoast dressed rather colourfully, which she admired. One of the disadvantages of travelling was the knowledge that your clothing had to be practical over stylish, and though she didn't regret it, Heidi wished she could dress like something other than a middle-aged man going through a rough patch from time to time. Heidi argued with herself about whether to buy a sky-blue shirt, before declaring, "screw it," and purchasing the item; she wasn't leaving Pending yet, and she wanted to look nice for the time being. As the day ambled towards dinner time, Heidi decided to find a food stall that sold local delicacies, though due to the multicultural nature of Dorcoast, almost every stand was foreign. Curries, kebabs, corn shells, raw fish rolls, and sugary treats that made your teeth rot just looking at them as far as the eye could see. It took some time, but in a back alley, Heidi found a place that sold fish and chips, which sounded so basic as a food stuff that Heidi was certain she was misunderstanding. Heidi ordered a small cod and chips, and exactly as was advertised, she was handed a piece of battered fish on a bed of unseasoned cooked potatoes. There was no herbs, spice, or flavour to the dish at all; it was simply white fish in crisp, greasy batter, but it seemed the locals couldn't get enough of it, so there must have been something she didn't understand. Before the daylight ended, Heidi looked out onto the boats; commercial vessels and visitors alike roaming around the first stretch of marketeers peddling their wares. Heidi soaked in the atmosphere; the hectic life of a traveller and the noises around it, while scary to her at first, were now piano keys playing a symphony; the footsteps, the commanding captains, even the salty sea breeze were sweet music to her nostrils. Heidi took deep breaths with her eyes closed, immersing herself in the organised cacophony that was the world travellers way of life, and smiled.

CHAPTER FOUR

Voluntary Captive

The town of Pending has an interesting origin; its founder, B. Goathead, was originally a significant political figure of Dorcoast. After the mass commercialisation of travelling and trading by boat, Dorcoast wished to establish itself as a trade route for the region; Goathead was in the minority of people against these plans, fearing it would bring people from less developed nations and change the landscape of society for the worse. It would be fair to say that Goathead had some basis for his argument, but it would also be fair to say that the man was a total moron. In my opinion, I believe Goathead's problem was that he was not a world traveller; he barely walked to the shops, and in his ignorant state, started a campaign to prevent the construction of dockland, which was supported by numerous townsfolk. This political movement soon became a physical movement, as everyone involved in the campaign decided to emigrate after they didn't succeed. Failing to recognise their own irony, they left Dorcoast to create a new town with the goal of surpassing Dorcoast in every way. After Goathead travelled further than he ever had before (about three miles), he set to work making a settlement optimistically named "Great-Town." History has proven that Dorcoast flourished from its plans where Great-Town, now called Pending, was nothing more than a piss stain in the ocean. Some people came to regret their decision, but wouldn't admit it; their stubbornness had got them into this mess, and their stubbornness would keep them there too. People pointed the finger at Goathead, but he didn't care, as he had the fortunate circumstances of dying shortly after founding the town. Pending's entire foundation was based on a fear of the unknown, empty-headedness, and above all else, spite.

If only Milo had known all this when he first arrived.

Let me take you back a few years prior to the previous chapters and show Milo in the light of his early adulthood. Having spent his first years of employment working as a housekeeper, a cruel irony considering it didn't pay him enough to own his own home, Milo left his motherland to pursue the career he truly desired, journalism. Using what he had saved up, plus a generous donation from his family, Milo travelled east to the aforementioned town in order to start his apprenticeship at The Bystander newspaper. Milo wasn't required to take an interview, which shows either great enthusiasm, or great desperation, but despite this, Milo was optimistic (and equally as desperate). The sun was glaring down on the dirt tracks he had ridden on for the past five days, and the landscape was surrounded endlessly by field after field, growing no more than wheat, oats, and bored farm hands. During his five day excursion, Milo was seated between a beached whale, and a gentleman who adored the sound of his own voice, which spoke in an accent Milo couldn't decipher for the life of him. The roads approaching Pending were quiet, slowly becoming emptier and emptier the closer they got to the town. At an hour before midday, the stagecoach driver shouted, "Alright, everyone. Sod off," and Milo sparked to life, as this was the first time in the best part of a week he could move both legs without kicking someone. Milo smiled as he jumped off the stagecoach, and with wide eyes, took in his new surroundings.

His smile faded fast.

It was hard for Milo to define exactly where the town ended and the countryside began, as the local wildlife used both as a toilet. Pending was a cheerless place, even in the lunch time sun; it seemed to be darker than the rest of the world; gloomier, drearier, soggier. People slumped through the streets like snails climbing molehills in the search of a good mountain. The buildings were not tall, and gave the impression they were slumping down, as if the cement had lost the will to live. Milo thought that if the buildings were alive, they would have committed suicide, although where they would jump from is another question. Milo tentatively wandered the streets to get a bearing on his location; he was supposed to go to The Bystander offices, but he was waiting for someone with half a smile to show up before asking for directions.

Milo was walking for a while.

Eventually, the nervous creeping was interrupted by a jarring voice calling out from across the street. "Oi, Oi, skinny boy!" shouted the voice that Milo hated instantly. Milo didn't turn around, assuming it wasn't for him.

"Hey, stick insect. It's rude not to reply," raised the barbarous voice again.

Milo spun to see where the voice was coming from, expecting to see someone shouting at a friend in some banterish manner; in actual fact, he saw only one person: A very tall, bulky, face like a bruised scrotum kind of guy.

"I said hello, wazzock," asserted the human-orangutan crossbreed, pubic hair beard rustling in the breeze.

"Hello," replied Milo, walking straight through the beast.

"Hey, hey, hey, why so unfriendly?"

Milo knew there wasn't a right answer to that, so kept on walking, but monkey-man quickly caught up and stood in his way again.

"Where are you going, skinny boy?" intruded gorilla-features.

"Currently, nowhere," said Milo with a resentment that wild animals can't so easily pick up on.

"You're going there in a big hurry."

"Yes, I am. Can I get past?"

Chimp-nose blocked Milo's path. "Hey, I don't think you

realise, but I get respect in this town," boasted the primate.

Milo found it hard to believe this creature could even gain the respect of a dog if he was holding a pork chop; he tried again to walk past, but found twenty stone of gorilla flesh to be quite intrusive.

"I'm a pretty big deal in this town," claimed the simian.

"Are you really?" huffed Milo, rolling his eyes in the belief that entertaining the animal might make it go away.

"Yep, I took down the town mafia."

"Did you really?" replied Milo in growing disbelief.

"I did really."

"Can you prove it?"

"Do you see any mafia around here?"

Milo looked around, knowing full well if there were any mafia, they would probably be hiding.

"No," replied Milo eventually.

"That's because of me. I really cleaned up this town," said the baboon, while standing in fox crap.

Milo was getting tired of this game. "Excuse me but I really need to-"

"HEY! DEVLIN!" shouted a voice like a banshee.

Milo looked around the beast apparently called Devlin, which wasn't easy considering how wide he was. Milo saw a woman running towards them, a little smaller than he was with all the burning spirit of a graveyard on fire; she stood an inch from Devlin yet a solid two feet from his face and stared with eyes like loaded crossbows.

"Stop bothering people, and stop talking cack!" ordered the woman.

"It's not cack!" contested Devlin.

"This town has never had a mafia. It doesn't even have a school."

Milo was caught off guard with the new knowledge, but didn't disbelieve it.

"If you would be so kind," asked the woman, faking politeness, "sod off, and don't come back."

Milo listened on; if words could bite, Devlin would be needing medical attention. Monkey-man crumbled under the weight of the voice and walked away, saying very little. The woman watched as Devlin stamped away, and when she was convinced there wouldn't be any more interruptions, she looked over to Milo.

"Are you alright?" she asked, brushing the long brown hair away from her eyes.

"Yes. Fine, thank you," said Milo.

"Don't worry. He couldn't hurt a fly, although not through lack of trying."

"Who was that guy?"

"Everyone calls him Big Boy Dev; he talks big, but acts like a child. I'm Jenny, by the way."

"Milo."

The woman stared at Milo for a moment. "You're new in town?"

"Yes, I just travelled in," confessed Milo.

"You on your way to Dorcoast?"

"No, I have an apprenticeship here."

"You want to work in Pending! You must be desperate."

Milo knew she was right to some extent; he hadn't imagined a town with a reputable newspaper looking quite so… unique.

"Do you think you could point me to The Bystander offices, please," asked Milo.

"Sure. Follow me," motioned Jenny, already taking the lead.

Milo was hoping to go alone to his new work; he didn't enjoy company so much, and of the people he'd met in Pending and knew on a first name basis, half of them weren't particularly kind. Jenny talked all the way while the two were travelling, and it was the first conversation in five days where Milo had spoken to someone and understood what they were saying. Jenny was interested to listen to Milo's life story, which, after cutting out the parts Milo considered boring, was only a minute and a half long. Jenny pressed for more information, which made Milo uncomfortable; he didn't like to talk about himself, and he wasn't used to quite so many questions; this may have been a bad sign for his job prospects, seeing how he was to become an interviewer. Milo noticed Jenny was somewhat out of place for this town; she seemed to hold herself better than anyone else in Pending; she wore vibrant clothing and jewellery, and had a more relaxed attitude. After half an hour, the two of them arrived outside a surprisingly nice (for Pending) bungalow.

"We're here," announced Jenny.

Milo didn't know what to expect, but a converted bungalow didn't seem like the usual place for a newspaper office; there was even an elderly woman tending the anarchic flower beds that bordered the garden.

"Do you need me to hold your hand up the pathway?" joked Jenny.

"I'm fine, thank you," replied Milo.

Jenny tapped Milo on the shoulder just before he was out of arm's length. "Are you free later today?"

Milo hesitated. "Um, I don't know."

"You will be," asserted Jenny. "Look for The Devil's Neckhole. You'll find me there."

Jenny flashed a smile at Milo before walking away with a confident stride. Milo decided to dismiss Jenny's body language and simply walked into the offices.

Milo's new job was official; he would be working at The Bystander for a one month trial period, after which, he would be told to get lost, or start living in Pending for the foreseeable future; neither of which were wholly appealing. After an hour-long induction concerning the contents of the stationary cupboard, there was nothing for Milo to do that day; he did have a new home, but he wouldn't be able to pick up the keys until the evening, so was at a loss. Milo resigned himself to wander the streets of an unfamiliar town filled with unfriendly people, uninviting houses, and an ungodly smell. There was only one lead for Milo to potentially follow: To take Jenny's instructions; he didn't know the address of The Devil's Neckhole, and asking for directions could be risky considering he didn't know what kind of establishment it was. Milo had several theories, the most realistic in his mind was a brothel; he knew in the old religions that devils implied some kind of sin, and a kind woman dressed in flashy clothing advertising somewhere to a slightly awkward man didn't reduce faith in his hypothesis. After an hour and a half, with nothing more than luck, Milo found the place Jenny had told him about. It was clear to see now that The Devil's Neckhole was a pub; the smell of stale piss gave it away. Closed blinds covered the windows: A tactic some worse off pubs used lest people realise the travesty that might dwell within. The door was bright red and lacked a handle; Milo paused for a minute to work out if there was a proper lock to the building, until he walked in and found a large rock just behind the door. It was relatively early in the day for such a crowd to be gathered there. A good few dozen ambled the pub's floor, certainly looking happier than the people outside, although that was probably because of the numbing effect alcohol can have on a person. Milo looked around carefully for Jenny, avoiding eye contact with anyone else where possible, but couldn't find her. Milo pepped himself up before walking to the bartender.

"Is there someone called Jenny here?" asked Milo.

"Can I ask for her sake who you are?" replied the barman.

That kind of suspicious language didn't fill Milo with confidence. Suddenly, the brothel theory became all the more likely again, and the pub was just a front. Milo answered honestly, but insisted he wouldn't move from the bar.

"I'll call her," said the barman, before leaning out a back door and shouting, "JENNY! There's a skinny kid called Milo looking for you!"

Even though he knew there was nothing wrong with it, Milo started to resent people calling him skinny, fearing it may well become his nickname if he stuck around. A moment passed, and Jenny walked through the door to greet Milo; she beamed at him, and bounced through the crowd. Milo noticed she was wearing different clothes than before, and thought she had done something with her hair, but hadn't paid enough attention to know what exactly.

"Told you you'd find the time," announced Jenny triumphantly.

"Yes, congratulations, you win," said Milo. "Was there a reason you wanted to meet again?"

"Does there have to be a reason? Maybe I want a new friend."

Milo wasn't wholly satisfied with that answer.

"Did you have a plan?" asked Milo.

"You're new here. Is there anything you want to know about Pending?" replied Jenny.

"Are there any museums?"

"Ha ha ha! Oh, you poor man." Jenny put her hand on Milo's shoulder. "You really are a long way from home."

Milo started worrying about what he had got himself into, both Pending, and meeting this woman.

"An antiques shop?" asked Milo tentatively.

"Are you serious? How old are you?" challenged Jenny.

"Alright then, what would you recommend?" contested Milo.

"No, no, we'll visit the antiques shop if you want. Come on, there's one not too far from here."

Jenny walked ahead without looking back, expecting Milo to follow, which he did. Only half a mile away from the pub, precariously located on the side of a narrow road, which the carts could barely fit through without Milo pressing his face against a wall, was a small terraced house. Milo had to crouch under the short door frame, although the ceiling wasn't much taller, and inside, presented in rows and rows were tables full of clocks, rings, lockets, pottery, crockery, and cutlery, with a little bit of rotten egg left on for authenticity. To the sides lay aged dressers, chairs, and beds with stains worthy of historical (and scientific) study. Suspended overhead (or to Milo, at eye level) was a metalwork sculpture of a chariot, presented predominantly for the day a person with more money than common sense walked through the door. The shop was cramped, but not so much so that the old-fashioned art of cat swinging couldn't be performed. Milo took great interest in the ancient paraphernalia, while Jenny wasn't sure what she was seeing of value.

"Dare I ask," mused Jenny, juggling a single pocket watch, "but why do you like this stuff?"

"I enjoy history. Everything has a story to tell," answered Milo.

"I don't think the history of a teacup is *that* interesting," said Jenny, snatching the crockery from Milo, which he'd been examining for the last three minutes.

"You didn't have to come along."

"Well, I can't exactly leave you on your own. Someone needs to hold your hand when crossing the road."

"I'm not a child."

"Arguable."

"I'm probably older than you."

"And have half the life experience."

Milo knew he had probably been beaten on that point.

"Very well then," started Jenny, passing the teacup back to Milo, and adopting a mocking tone, "enlighten me to the story of this piece of old tat."

Milo rolled his eyes, feeling the weight of the approaching uphill battle. "You see this stamp here," began Milo, pointing to a tiny picture of a wild cat on the base of the cup, "that's the mark of T. Thyme, who five-hundred years ago, was one of the greatest ceramicists of his generation. He was one of the early adopters of using tin-glazes, and was a phenomenal artist in his own right. In his mid-life, he was commissioned by Queen Martinette of Scortillia to make crockery exclusively for her, but when it was found that he had also made plates as a present for his brother's wedding, the jealous queen ordered all Thyme's work be destroyed, along with his workshop. Very few pieces still exist, and almost never in a full set. Simply owning this teacup would have been illegal a few centuries ago."

Milo focused on Jenny as she listened intently to the entire story, seemingly following every single word.

"Wow. Some stories are really boring," said Jenny bluntly.

"There's no winning with you, is there?" complained Milo.

"To be perfectly honest, I didn't even remember half the names you said during that speech."

Milo felt deflated. "Do you want to go somewhere else?"

"Well, yes, but don't leave on my account. It's nice you have something you're passionate about."

Milo would have stayed in that shop a while, but he knew his tour guide wasn't entertained, and there would probably be a chance for him to visit again later in the week.

"I'm done here. Where do you want to go?" asked Milo.

Jenny spoke an unintelligible syllable, then stopped herself; she thought for a moment, and grew a sly smile.

"I know what you'll like," said Jenny.

Jenny brought Milo to a significantly quieter part of town; the buildings there were ancient, almost primordial, but somehow not as disorderly as the rest of Pending. There was no pavement, only a web of beaten paths leading to houses, and it was also evident that this part of town was still lived in, if you could call a life in Pending living. Milo looked around, and from examining the materials and general size, he deduced these homes must have been built centuries ago. Most interesting was a stone table on the edge of the old district, which had inscribed on its form the words "The First Settlers of Great-Town," alongside a hundred or so names. Milo realised this area was the starting place of Pending, and pitied the poor souls. Jenny weaved through a few houses and down a dark pathway of the old town, and after a few minutes, she stopped.

"Here we are," announced Jenny.

Milo searched around, and it took him a moment to find what he was supposed to be looking at. Under the shadow of a cottage was a bell. The bell was suspended three feet in the air by a stone archway and a chain; on the ground beside it was a hammer, similarly chained around the arch. Both the bell and hammer were decorated with varying lines and crosses in some kind of purposeful decoration.

"This is a relic from olden ages. Some people used sacred bells to test the nature of someone's soul. Whoever hits the bell has their true character revealed," explained Jenny.

Milo was surprised. "I thought you didn't like history."

"No, I don't like looking at five-hundred-year-old teacups."

"Where did the tradition come from?"

"I don't know. I'm not a historian."

Milo examined the bell closer. He tried to ascertain if it was a religious or cultural relic; either way, something this nice had no place being in Pending. Jenny wasn't exactly in the mood for entertaining Milo's behaviour again.

"Are you going to ring the bell, or what?" asked Jenny.

"Why should I?" replied Milo.

"So we can read your personality. And you think I'm bad for not listening."

Milo lightly sighed, learning now it would be better to blindly agree than to contest anything. Milo picked up the hammer, surprised by how heavy a fully metal tool could be, and heaved the weapon over his shoulder. Using the weight as a driving force with his hand merely supplying grip, Milo struck the bell near its base, and it rang out.

"Go on then," said Milo, "what does that say about my personality?"

Jenny's lips started to curl up. "Well, it sounded very dull."

"Oh, you cheeky bitch."

Jenny laughed having fooled Milo with a trick even a toddler could have thought of.

"Did you do this just to make that joke?"

"Maybe. The legend is real though, or as real as legends can be."

"Why don't you ring the bell?" offered Milo, passing over the hammer. "I don't know anything about you yet."

"Alright then."

Jenny took the hammer from Milo, managing its weight far

better than he did. Jenny gripped with both hands and swung full force at the centre of the bell.

It rang out violently.

A short while later, Jenny led the way back through the poky streets of Pending and up a surprising tall hill, which Milo found odd. In most cases, towns were built on hills and mountains to make them harder for enemy invaders to attack during war time, but he had to ask himself who would want to invade a place like this? Some houses along the incline were constructed without proper consideration, and were built at a slight angle, but generally speaking, this wouldn't cause the owner any significant problem, assuming they didn't own anything that might roll. In a back street on the side of a housing block, Jenny presented to Milo a quaint little cafe. The cafe was some distance away from the town centre, which didn't exactly seem like a prime location, although that might not have mattered too much, as the establishment was only big enough to fit five tables (although the owner had a stab at pushing eight in there.) Jenny and Milo shuffled through the chairs to a pair of seats near the back, close to a broad window. The owner had tried to make a decorative motif inspired by daffodils, painting the walls bright yellow, although the inspiration may have come from buttercups, given how greasy the mugs were. Milo only ordered a cup of tea, but didn't drink it; there were some items on the menu that interested him, although he would have preferred those items to be written down, and not smeared on the specials board. Jenny was bolder and ordered a full meal, an act that Milo did not envy. As she picked up her mug, Jenny lifted it over her head and examined the bottom.

"What are you doing?" asked Milo.

"I was wondering if this cup had a story behind it," answered Jenny.

"It was purchased at a market and hasn't seen soap in years."

Jenny giggled. Milo felt reassured to know that Jenny also thought this place was a dump, but that piqued his curiosity.

"You know that this town is a load of cack, right?" asked Milo.

"The biggest load of cack in the world," announced Jenny proudly.

"Then why do you stay here?"

"Because this is my home. I grant you that some places might be cleaner, or safer, or have a proper place of education, but Pending is familiar, and familiar is comforting."

"Don't you believe familiarity breeds contempt?"

"No. I believe familiarity breeds contentedness," answered Jenny, unsure if contentedness was a real word.

"Isn't there something more you want out of the world?" asked Milo.

"Other than a peaceful life, not a bit."

Milo didn't agree wholly with the sentiment, but respected it. "Considering I haven't had as much of a chance to make myself comfortable, is there anything good about Pending?"

"Well, good is relative."

"Very well then. In relation to being stabbed in the foot, is there anything good about Pending?"

Jenny huffed and shrugged her shoulders. "Can't say there is."

Milo's faith for a pleasant future in Pending was not considered to be in very high regard, and he sighed. Jenny noticed this, and had an idea.

"Although," started Jenny, "there might be one place. Drink up and I'll show you."

"I'm finished," announced Milo, having had one sniff of his drink and no more.

Jenny led the way once more through the Pending streets. It was now close to evening, and the foxes were ready to do business on the streets. Milo was becoming weary of wandering around town over and over again; he was becoming familiar with some of the sights, but wasn't yet accepting of his new home. As sunset loomed, Jenny brought Milo to a curious block of houses; there wasn't any sense of fashion or practicality to their construction; it had protrusions of brick work, odd shaped arches and windows, varying coloured bricks, and a curved roof so close to breaking down, a light fart could have sent it over the edge. It seemed like the building was made from the leftover pieces of other houses, without any care or attention to how or if the pieces of this chaotic puzzle could fit together (Or, as an estate agent might say, characterful.) Walking through a passageway to reach a small door on the far side, Jenny knocked and waited.

"Who is it?" asked a gruff male voice on the other side of the door.

"It's me," said Jenny. "I have a guest."

A metal bolt clunked behind the wall, and the door opened. Behind it stood a gentleman of average height, big smile, and unmistakable aroma of cheap aftershave.

"Kenneth," said Jenny, wrapping her arms around the older gentleman.

"Nice to see you," said the gentleman, returning the favour. Kenneth looked towards Milo, who was still standing outside. "Does he have a name or do we have to give him one?"

"Milo," exploded Milo, before he could potentially receive a nickname.

"Nice to meet you, Milo," and the man hugged Milo as well. Milo felt uncomfortable, as he wasn't used to this level of affection from strangers.

Jenny beckoned Milo to follow, leading through to a narrow passage laid with a heavy carpet. The interior of the building was quite dark; due to the house's odd design, very little sunlight came through the windows, and anything that could had trouble reflecting off the moss green walls. In regular intervals, taxidermy animals rested in the halls of the building like vanguards. Despite having no proof, Milo had no doubt in his mind that the animals had not died of natural causes. A short walk through this maze brought Jenny and Milo to a moderately large room set with recycled bar tables and chairs. In a corner was a gentleman doing a word puzzle, and three women playing a card game while cackling like school boys who had learned a new swear word. In the centre lay a pool table, taking up the majority of the space, and on a dark windowsill lay many books and board games.

"Welcome to Pending Clubhouse," announced Jenny.

Milo was not so surprised to find a gaming club in this town, but he was curious why Jenny had brought him here.

"This is, without a doubt, the best place in Pending," declared Jenny.

"Why do you think that?" asked Milo, looking around a building that seemed just as unappealing as the rest of the town.

"Because games aren't about where you are, it's about who you're with."

Milo smiled at the sentiment, but there was only one problem with it.

"I don't know who I'm with," argued Milo. "Other than the fact your name is Jenny and you think a town with roads paved in dog dirt is comforting, I don't know anything about you."

"That's your fault for not asking me," countered Jenny. "Alright then. I'll do you a deal." Jenny rested both hands on the pool table. "Every ball you pocket is a question you can ask me. The interview ends if I clean up before you."

"Deal," agreed Milo.

Jenny arranged the pool balls and insisted Milo make the breaking shot. Two rounds passed and Milo potted the first ball.

"First question," said Milo. "Where do you work?"

"The pub we met at before," answered Jenny.

Another round passed and Milo potted another ball. "What's the most daring thing you've ever done?"

"I once told a woman she was ugly to her face."

Milo potted a second ball in his round. "What do you hate the most?"

"People who think they're better than they really are."

"Like Big Boy Dev?"

"Devlin is an arrogant prick weasel who couldn't be more self centred if he crawled up his own arsehole," shouted Jenny.

Several rounds passed with Milo potting ball after ball at somewhat impressive speed.

"What's your favourite game in the clubhouse?" asked Milo.

"Chess," answered Jenny.

Jenny meanwhile was not able to pot a single ball of her colour.

"Do you prefer cold or hot weather?"

"Have you already run out of good questions? Cold, if you really want to know."

Milo was surprised Jenny had challenged him to this game if she was so bad at it.

"Do you know any magic?"

"Do I look like I waste my time with that crap?"

Unless, of course, she wanted to lose.

"Have you ever had a nickname?"

"Some people call me Hazel."

"Why's that?"

"You need to pot another ball before you can ask that question."

Milo lined up for a shot at the eight ball, raising his cue to a high angle, as the wall was not providing him with enough space. Milo struck the cue ball, but whiffed the shot and fouled.

"My turn," chirped Jenny.

Jenny used her first shot to line up the cue ball. With the second shot, she struck a ball into the far corner pocket. With another shot, she pocketed again, and again, and again. Milo realised now he had been played for a fool. Jenny wanted to be asked questions, but there was no way she was going to throw the game as well. In a single round, Jenny had potted seven balls, leaving just the eight ball remaining. Milo mouthed the words, "you cocky git," and Jenny laughed. Jenny lined up the shot; a clear line towards the middle pocket; she tapped the cue ball lightly, and it rolled towards the target, nudging the eight ball, which ended its travel on the cusp of the pocket.

"Did you do that intentionally?" asked Milo.

"You only have one possible question left; do you want to

waste it asking that?"

Milo took the cue and tapped the final ball into the hole.

"Final question," announced Milo. "Why did you spend your afternoon showing me around Pending."

"Because," started Jenny, "it's not often a handsome man comes walking through town."

Milo was startled by the flirtatious turn the conversation had taken; people in his home town stereotyped him as someone who was never much good at talking to women. In reality, Milo struggled talking to anyone, and what they had between their legs made no difference. Jenny acted like it was nothing, and to anyone except Milo, it might have been; he awkwardly tried to dismiss the incident, acting calm as best as he could.

Milo and Jenny stayed at the clubhouse for an hour or so, and thoroughly enjoyed themselves. Kenneth checked in a couple times to see what was happening; it turned out that the clubhouse was his home, which he shared with his wife, and people were allowed to visit whenever they fancied, although anyone who took the mick would find themselves among the other taxidermy guests. Once the sun had practically vanished from the sky, Milo knew he had to leave and fetch the keys to his flat. The two friends walked in the same direction for a time until Jenny reached The Devil's Neckhole.

"See you around," called Jenny, as she walked away.

"Bye," replied Milo.

Milo turned around, smiling for a short time, until not a few paces in front of him stood a primate he recognised from earlier in the day.

"Hey," shouted Big Boy Dev. "I've been thinking about what you said."

Wow, thinking. Quite impressive, thought Milo, before deciding to try and avoid the whole encounter.

"I really don't have time for this," pleaded Milo.

"Well, I have all the time in the world," boasted Big Boy Dev.

"I believe you. When you only eat bananas and masturbate, I

don't imagine you have a busy schedule."

Milo very much had enough of Devlin, but insulting his intelligence was not going to get him very far, as the ape wasn't smart enough to realise when it was happening. Instead of returning with a witty line, Devlin threw one of his fists towards Milo's left cheek. The force of the punch had great strength behind it, and had the air next to Milo been able to feel pain, it surely would have hurt. Hazel clearly wasn't exaggerating when she said Devlin couldn't hurt a fly. Devlin grabbed Milo by the shirt and pulled at his collar before bellowing, "Do you think this is funny?"

Milo hadn't realised he'd started sniggering. Big Boy Dev really was so fascinatingly arrogant that Milo couldn't help but laugh at him. Devlin went to throw another punch at Milo's stomach, but the blow was cushioned somewhat by an intervening hand. Jenny's eyes showed unadulterated fury, but she had far more control over her actions than Devlin. Gorillas used brute force, but Jenny had dirty tricks; she removed a piercing from her ear a moment before entering battle, and used the needle to stab Devlin in the wrist he was using to hold Milo. Big Boy Dev dropped Milo, and he recoiled as he checked his arm for injury. As Devlin was distracted, Jenny punched him square in the forehead. The force itself was not immensely strong, but the shock was enough to make Devlin flinch.

"What did I say about not coming back?" ordered Jenny.

Big Boy Dev was cowering under the ringleader's command; he hesitated, until Jenny stepped forward, to which he ran away. In a fight, Devlin was certainly the stronger, but he was also the most cowardly, which generally put him at a disadvantage. Jenny turned around to face Milo before asking, "Are you alright?"

Milo was slightly stunned into silence, only being broken from his trance when he realised Jenny's hand was bleeding.

"Never mind me, you need a bandage," urged Milo, applying pressure to the wound. "Are you hurt?"

"A bit," replied Jenny.

Milo held Jenny's hand as they crossed the road back towards her home while he thought of what he could do.

"Do they have anything back as The Devil's Neckhole for your wound?"

"Whisky?"

"That'll have to do."

***

Milo sat across from Hazel in her living room as they played a game of backgammon. The room was silent bar the rhythmic pattern of dice rolling and counters moving, although Hazel started to wonder out loud.

"Do you ever regret coming to Pending?" asked Hazel.

Milo looked up. "Why do you ask?"

"Heidi seems to like it here. Don't know why though. I thought a foreign eye might shed some light."

"I'm content here. I didn't like it at first, but I've become used to it."

"Just playing devil's advocate here, but if you had the opportunity to go somewhere else, would you take it?"

"Probably not. There'd have to be a good reason."

Milo, over time, had adopted "Jenny's" attitude; familiarity did breed contentedness, and he was happy enough living his life as he did, inevitable liver failure aside.

"Speaking of my first time coming to Pending," started Milo, "do you know what happened to Big Boy Dev?"

"Last I heard, the mafia took him out."

CHAPTER FIVE

Every Day Is A Workday

As has been previously stated, Milo was the primary interviewer at The Bystander newspaper; not his only job, as the presence of an interviewer also required the attendance of someone halfway famous, which was uncommon for Pending. When not engaged in pretending to enjoy the company of people who achieved fame by being born pretty, Milo was a fact checker; a thankless job that most other newspapers wouldn't even consider employing, as presenting the truth can affect the editor-in-chief's agenda. Milo visited several notable celebrities through his work, including entertainers, sports personalities, and one man who ate fifteen live hamsters in a minute (although interrogation might be a better word in that last case). After some training in company procedures, Heidi was now considered fully capable of joining Milo to interviews for the purposes of drawing portraits of the interviewees, although training is a generous term when all that was required of her was to sketch while sitting in the corner, two tasks that Heidi already had some experience with. On this day in question, Milo was interviewing Donna Furst concerning a touring play where she acted as the leading lady. Milo had done research on Donna and the play she was performing in; one such article that drew Milo's attention was an old review of Donna's work that described her acting as "so wooden, even the worms wouldn't go near it." Another more generous review described Donna's performance as "brave," which Milo knew was journalist code for shit. The play was called Death Of The Oceans, a title which, to Milo's untrained eye, had sod all to do with that plot of the show, which was supposed to be a mystery come romance come waste of three hours. Early in the morning, Milo and Heidi made their way to where Donna Furst was staying for the duration of her tour, a small bed and breakfast in Pending named The Bard (although you could read that name backwards for a more fitting title). From the outside, you would be forgiven in thinking that The Bard was merely a bungalow with a sign in front of the door, but you would be wrong; the sign had fallen down. To say the bungalow had a distressed look is underplaying the amount of suffering this establishment has faced; the locks were broken, the windows were cracked, and the welcome mat had a dog turd on it. Milo tentatively opened the door and walked through into a thin hallway laid with a carpet so thick, it could have been a towel, if it wasn't for the mud set into the fibres. Milo made it known at the reception/desk in the middle of the kitchen that he was here to meet with Mrs. Furst, and he waited with Heidi until they were summoned.

A few minutes passed, and Heidi started to become quite fidgety.

A few minutes more passed, and Milo started to get annoyed.

A frustratingly long time passed, and after several other inquisitions at the reception, Donna was still not ready for her interview. After the fifth inquiry, Milo and Heidi heard from down the hallway, "FINE! COME IN THEN!"

The pair suddenly lost any sense of urgency, and would much rather have left there and then, but professional obligations have a way of persuading people, and the two of them walked to the room where the roar came from. Milo opened the door slowly, as if unsure what kind of creature could jump out, and when it was barely halfway open, the cat pounced on them.

"You're an hour early!" growled Donna.

"We're actually starting an hour late," countered Milo truthfully.

"Bah, I hate men who can't admit they're wrong."

Milo knew from that moment that this was going to be a long day, and even if he had started an hour early, that would be very little consolation. Donna Furst was an elderly lady, liver spotted and offal smelling; the acting work she may have got in her early years may have been attained solely based on her looks, but in her current state (or rather, currant state, considering her face looked like a dried grape), she was struggling in the cut-throat world of beauty being more important than talent or kindness, of which she possessed neither. Milo could see why Donna had taken so long to get ready, as she was wearing an elegant blue dress, which had very much the same effect as drawing a smiley face in a puddle of vomit. Heidi introduced herself in the more traditional manner to the actress, and Milo reluctantly did the same.

"Well, sit down then," commanded Donna.

The room had no chairs in it, besides the one Donna already claimed ownership of in front of a vanity dressing table. The room Donna was staying in was very small; the bed took up half the room alone. Milo sat on the corner of the bed, and Heidi crossed her legs on the floor.

"Shall we get started?" asked Milo.

"I think we should. You're already wasting my time as it is," hissed Donna.

Milo rolled his eyes and turned his attention to his notepad. "What attracted you to this play?"

Milo knew the honest answer was money, as it is with most actors, but he knew Donna would never respond in such a way.

"I saw this character," started Donna, "who was a lover, not a fighter. Something I would know much about having gone through four husbands..."

Milo looked down at his notebook and marked down the comments, also crossing off one of the squares on his interview bingo card. Since he had done so many interviews like this in the past, Milo would often become bored while doing them, so devised a bingo game he could play with the interviewees answers to give himself something resembling fun. When it came to actors, a particularly commonly used square included the interviewee avoiding a question about the show by talking about their private life, a square that was used much more often the worse a show might be, which Donna was able to fill with her first answer. Another often used trope is for the actor to say in some roundabout way how they relate to the character they play, even if said character happens to be a three headed pig creature from another planet, but the most tired phrase of them all was the answer to the question "what do you want people to take away from the play," to which the answer is always some variation of "people will leave the theatre with something of value," usually implying some emotional worth, but can also refer to cheap merchandise. Milo continued through his usual questions, which had all the rehearsal of a cheating lover, as Heidi sketched the actress as kindly as she could. A true to life portrait of Donna may not have been a good idea, as Heidi would rather not be scratched by the cat's claws, and chose to omit some of the larger crevices in her face. The portrait took much longer than it normally would have for Heidi, as she tried to include all of the actress' jewellery, the most striking of which being a large sapphire pendant with a white gold border; the jewel seemed quite sophisticated, which begged the question why Donna had it. At some point during the interview, Donna seemed to become agitated.

"Is there a problem?" asked Heidi.

Milo winced, hoping to get this interview finished in the minimum number of questions possible.

"This interview doesn't seem to be about me?" questioned Donna.

Milo was slightly dumbfounded. "Normally, actor interviews are used to promote a show they perform in."

"Hogwash! I know your tricks. I wasn't born yesterday."

"I'm very aware of that," said Milo, looking at the woman whose face contained more folds than an origami manual. "Would you mind if we continued the interview as normal?"

pleaded Milo as calmly as possible.

"Fine, but I'm not happy about it."

Donna hadn't been happy for the whole interview, so this was of no further grief. Milo struggled through the remainder of the interview as Donna would distractedly meander through her life story, fully contempt to ignore the reason this interview was booked in the first place.

After what felt like an eternity, Milo reached the end of his questioning. "Final one, Mrs. Furst. Why do you think people should come and see this play?"

Donna answered, "It's unlike anything you've ever seen before."

"Bingo!"

"Excuse me?"

"Nothing."

Heidi showed Donna the portrait sketch, and Donna seemed pleased enough, but didn't say anything by way of thank you. Donna had barely looked in Heidi's direction the entire time she was there, and had Milo not been talking to her, she may well have stared into the mirror. Milo and Heidi stood up and said their goodbyes, with Donna returning a badbye. The remainder of the day was spent at the office, polishing up Donna's portrait and writing up an article that could conceivably be considered entertaining to read, or at the very least, more entertaining than speaking to the subject, but Milo thanked the laws of fate that the ordeal was over.

For about a day.

The following morning, after the interview was published, The Bystander office was as uninteresting as it usually was; some people were working, others were gossiping, and one person was sleeping off a hangover from the night before, having been forced to watch Death Of The Oceans to write a review of it. The peace remained until there was a knock at the front door. No one ever knocked on the door to the office; if it was an employee, they would have walked straight in, and if it was the postman, they would leave whatever parcel it might be outside; there wasn't a procedure in place for who in the building would answer the door, so everyone looked at each other in confusion. Heidi, being the least experienced in the workplace, wasn't sure what everyone was so confused about, and took it upon herself to answer the call. When she opened the door, a goliath man in a police officer's uniform was standing there, who made no effort to waste time.

"I'm looking for Mr. Milo Point and Miss Heidi Watson," asked the policeman sternly. "Are they in this building?"

Heidi was very intimidated, if not for the thought she was about to be arrested, then definitely because this man was a certified giant. The policeman was built like a brick shithouse, in contrast to Heidi or Milo, who were built like shit brick houses. The uniform was pressed and pristine, navy blue, as was standard, with a slew of equipment draped across his belt.

"Milo," shouted Heidi. "There's someone here to see you."

Milo rose from his seat and walked to the door, having very much the same reaction as Heidi upon seeing the colossus.

"Is something the matter, officer?" asked Milo, knowing full well the man was not here for tea and scones.

"I'm taking you into questioning concerning a recent robbery. If you would please accompany me to the station where I will brief you further."

Milo and Heidi did as they were told and left the office immediately. During the trip over, Milo tried to ask what this matter was about, but the officer said nothing of the nature. The police station was one of the few buildings in Pending that had been well maintained, which was good, as the place was often busy; the building was previously a dungeon from an older age, and the majority of the structure was underground. Milo and Heidi followed the policeman, whose name they learned was Bill, down two sets of cold stone stairs into a small room where another policeman was standing guard. All the while, Milo was still trying to probe the policeman for information, becoming increasingly vexed. Bill instructed Milo and Heidi to sit down, and chairs were this time provided, making this police station a better holiday destination than The Bard Bed & Breakfast.

"I'm sure you'd be interested as to why you're here," said Bill.

"What gave you that idea?" huffed Milo. "Was it the six times I asked?"

Bill ignored Milo's sarcasm. "During a performance of Death Of The Oceans just outside of town, an expensive sapphire pendant belonging to the actress Mrs. Donna Furst went missing."

"And this concerns us, how?"

"When we asked Mrs. Furst if she saw any suspicious characters in the past day, she directed us to," Bill looked down at his notes, "'that troublesome newspaper interviewer with a face like a smacked arse, and the child he brought with him.' We believe she meant you two."

"Cheeky git!" blurted Milo.

Heidi watched Milo as he talked, and became increasingly nervous the more he spoke.

"Maybe we should be a little more cooperative," urged Heidi to Milo. "I'm sure this is a big misunderstanding and that there's no reason to get angry."

Heidi wasn't the only person to realise Milo's frustration, and Bill asked Heidi to leave the room to be interrogated later.

"Mr. Point, I'm sure you're a busy man," said Bill to the man who was never busy. "If you answer my questions regarding Mrs. Furst pendant, we can be out of here quickly."

"She's an old lady. Are you absolutely sure she didn't forget where she left it," argued Milo.

"Mrs. Furst was quite adamant."

"I'm sure she was adamant."

Bill was studying Milo's body language carefully. "Do you have some kind of grudge against Mrs. Furst?"

"She's a knob," replied Milo, it being the most cooperative thing he had said since arriving at the police station.

Bill took a deep breath and breathed out slowly, knowing Milo was going to be difficult. Bill opened his notebook to jot down anything Milo said.

"Mr. Point," started Bill, "can you tell me where you were yesterday evening?"

"At home," answered Milo.

"Did you have any interest in seeing the play Mrs. Furst was performing in?"

"I would rather shag a skunk up the backside."

Bill wrote down the quote, finding that his notebook was quickly becoming loaded with words he would have to omit when it came to the official report.

"You met with Mrs. Furst for an interview. Can you confirm what time this interview started?" asked Bill.

"Four hours past sunrise," answered Milo.

"Mrs. Furst claims you met with her an hour earlier than that."

Milo threw his hands in the air. "We arrived at The Bard at the agreed time, and she had me wait an hour in the reception with a thumb up my arse."

"Mrs. Furst also claimed you were talking to yourself by the end of the interview."

"No. I just shouted Bingo."

Bill was confused by this notion. "Pardon?"

"I play bingo with the interview answers to help pass the time. Here."

Milo pulled the notepad from out of his pocket and opened it to the last page that was used. Bill looked at the bingo squares and examined them carefully, noting particular interest in one that was crossed out.

"On this bingo card," started Bill, "you have marked off 'Leave the theatre with something of value.' Care to explain that."

"It doesn't mean literally," argued Milo. "It's an answer to a question I asked."

"Is it really?" replied the policeman with serious doubt.

Milo failed to keep the same etiquette he reserved for being an interviewer for when he was being interviewed, and spared no expense of passive-aggressive comments. The interrogation lasted longer than either of the men were happy with, and very little insight was gained from it. Heidi was brought in for interrogation later, answering as cleanly as possible to the man who could have snapped her in half as easily as snapping his fingers. Once both suspects were interrogated, they were brought into the same room.

"Thank you for your cooperation. It has been very... enlightening," noted Bill.

"I'm glad we could be of help," gloated Milo sarcastically. "Can we go now?"

"Miss Watson, you may leave."

Heidi thanked the policeman and stood up from her chair, expecting Milo would follow.

"What about me?" protested Milo.

The behemoth glared daggers at Milo. "Mr. Point, you are arrested for suspicion of theft, and you will be held in police custody for the remainder of the investigation."

"What!" shouted Milo.

"Please accompany me to your cell."

Heidi watched the scene in shock; she had no idea what had happened during the interrogation, but clearly Milo had done something a little more than act like a tosser. Milo argued more, which if anything, only served to summon more police officers to their location. Milo soon had no choice but to give up and walk to his cell. Heidi was ushered out the door, and she returned to the newspaper office somewhat nervous for her co-worker. Heidi didn't believe Milo stole this pendant, but that begged the question of where did the pendant really go? In the absence of any evidence to swing this investigation, Heidi bit her lip and made it through the remainder of the day.

The following evening after work, Heidi returned to the prison to visit Milo. The cell Milo was staying in was only one floor above the very lowest level of the dungeon, where they kept the more criminally inclined. Milo was expectantly miserable, lying in a bed, stewing in cold resentment for the situation he had been forced into. Milo was allowed a book, but only from a limited selection that was provided by the station; he was currently reading the novel version of Death Of The Oceans. The cells had been renovated from the times when it was a dungeon, now having a smooth concrete floor and painted walls, but still kept the iron bar door that was traditional in older prison cages; despite that, it was still a better holiday destination than The Bard Bed & Breakfast.

"Hello," greeted Heidi. "I told Hazel what happened. She said she'd visit as soon as she stopped laughing. How are you?"

"I've been imprisoned for a crime I didn't commit, I'm going to be behind on work, and this novel is cack. Overall, I could be better," answered Milo. It was clear to Heidi that in the day and a half that had passed, Milo had calmed down very little. "I imagine everyone in the office is talking about me."

"Actually, no."

"What?" Milo's eyes widened, more offended that no one was talking about him rather than the rumours he had expected.

Heidi continued the conversation politely, and kept the subjects as light as Milo would allow. After a few minutes, Heidi made it known why she wanted to visit.

"I just want to check," started Heidi, "but you didn't steal the pendant, did you?"

"Of course I didn't," protested Milo.

"Alright, calm down. I'm not here to accuse you. I'm offering to help."

Milo looked to Heidi hopefully.

"I heard the police don't have any evidence of a theft, so the pendant is probably lost. I plan to go out and look for it," explained Heidi.

"Why would you do that?" asked Milo.

"Because if you're innocent, this is injustice, and I want to stop it."

Milo was beginning to believe that having a friend with a functioning moral compass had its benefits, and was elated at the prospect of getting out of that place, plus if his theory that

Donna Furst really did lose her pendant was proved correct in the process, then all the better for it. That feeling lasted a total of three seconds after Heidi said, "There's just one thing I want in return."

Milo's smile dropped like a stone in a puddle of piss. "What is it?"

"I want you to ask me nicely," said Heidi.

Milo felt the rage returning to his bloodstream. "Are you kidding me?"

"If you weren't so angry in the interrogation, you wouldn't be here. Consider this part of your rehabilitation."

Milo noticed that this behaviour was unlike Heidi. "Did Hazel make you say that?"

"Maybe."

Milo winced and put his hands to his face, not that contemplation took very long, as there are very few places worse than prison. Soon enough, Milo looked Heidi in the eyes.

"Heidi, would you please help in proving me innocent," begged Milo.

"It would be my pleasure," answered Heidi.

With the pact made, Heidi left the prison to search for the sapphire pendant. The police said the jewellery was stolen during Donna's evening performance, so the theatre had been thoroughly investigated. If the theory that the pendant being lost was true, the next most logical place to look would have been Donna's room at The Bard. Heidi chose to visit during the night, when she knew Donna would be at the theatre performing. Heidi was not questioned when she passed the reception desk to reach Donna's room, and knowing the locks in the building were almost all busted, entering the room was easy. Something could definitely be said about committing something illegal to prove someone else innocent, but there is one principle that is important in any crime: You aren't in trouble until you get caught. As Donna's room was not big, Heidi believed the investigation shouldn't take too long, but that was not anticipating the sheer volume of clothes Donna had brought with her. Every available space in the drawers was taken up with over-decorated garments, not a single one designed with practicality, or even a reasonably sized pocket. Heidi plunged the depths of the silky swamp, making an effort not to disturb the scene as much as possible, finding several small wooden boxes throughout the dive. Heidi opened the first box and found a mass of Donna's jewellery; gold and gemstones to rival a king's hoard, assuming the king in question ruled over a fairly crappy country. Heidi picked out the boxes one by one in search of the pendant, but the sapphire was much larger than any of the tat that could be found in those small chests. Heidi moved from the drawers to the larger furniture, checking to see if any of it had fallen down the back of something, but with no luck again. Finally, the last place to check was a bookshelf over the bed. The shelf was positioned over the pillow of the bed, and the brackets keeping that shelf up were dangerously unstable, one screw away from screwing you up. Heidi stood on the mattress, and saw that the books provided were dusty, and half of them still had old library stamps, giving no illusion as to where they originally came from, but if the owners felt the dire need to steal books, maybe they could have chosen something a little more interesting than "The Complete History of Dental Floss." The books had a thick layer of grime over them, and had clearly not been opened in a long time. Heidi pushed the chronicles of cack to one side, and behind the very last book on the shelf was a wad of crumpled up paper; Heidi knocked against it and noticed it was oddly heavy. Unwrapping the paper, Heidi had found it: The elusive sapphire pendant.

Now this raised some odd questions:

Why was the jewel buried on this shelf?

Why was it wrapped in scrap paper?

Why wear something this heavy around your neck when you're at danger of osteoporosis?

Was this supposed to be a hiding place, thought Heidi. If that was true, then that meant the pendant was never lost, but if that was also true, that meant-

"What are you doing here?" growled a familiar voice.

Heidi turned around, pocketing the pendant quickly, before seeing Donna Furst standing in the doorway. The first principle of crime was in jeopardy.

"Hello," cried Heidi. "You're back early."

"Cretins don't appreciate art. Who are you?" asked Donna forcefully.

Heidi realised in that question that Donna didn't recognise her as the "child" from the interview, and used this opportunity to create an escape route.

"I'm a big fan of yours, Mrs. Furst," yelped Heidi.

"Is that so?" purred Donna.

The actress smiled delightfully, clearly she didn't receive praise of this kind from anyone other than herself.

"Yes, absolutely. Your play, it was..." Heidi paused to think for a moment, then remembered something. "It's unlike anything I've ever seen before."

At this perfectly parroted phrase, Donna smiled more. After the moment passed, there was an awkward lapse in conversation as Heidi and Donna stood staring at each other.

"Is there a reason you're standing on my bed," asked Donna.

Heidi panicked. "I'm very short."

Donna found the answer odd, but couldn't deny the statement was true.

Another awkward silence lingered.

"If you wanted to meet me, there are better places to do it than my hotel room," suggested Donna.

"Yes, you're absolutely right. I'll leave right now," informed Heidi. "Thank you for your time. Thank you. Thank you."

Heidi breathed a heavy sigh of relief upon escaping the cage. Donna was obviously startled, but through little more than luck, Heidi had made it out of the room without raising too much suspicion. Heidi leaned back on the wall, but was surprised when she felt something in her trousers poking into her.

Oh, right. The pendant.

Heidi had shoved the gemstone in her back pocket during the panic of being caught, and in proving Milo hadn't stolen it, she did. Heidi knew she had to give it back, but she couldn't be caught again. Mustering up some willpower, Heidi turned back and knocked on Donna's door.

"Not now, dear," answered Donna.

This was bad. Heidi had no way of giving the sapphire back without incriminating herself; she was still a suspect as far as the police were concerned. Heidi stood in front of the doorway and thought of a plan of action, but nothing came to mind. Reluctantly, Heidi returned home and mulled in the guilt of her own crime.

The following day at The Bystander office, Milo arrived in the later half of the afternoon; it turned out that a little earlier that day, Donna Furst had reported her pendant stolen again; this confused the police, as they hadn't retrieved the pendant to be stolen again in the first place. Embarrassed, Donna had to admit what she had done, and confessed to the crime of framing her interviewers for a crime they didn't commit (at the time). It was unconfirmed whether this was a vengeful act against her interviewers or some kind of insurance fraud, but what was confirmed was that Donna Furst was a dick. Donna was reprimanded and fined for wasting police time, and Milo was released with compensation for false imprisonment. When Milo walked through the office door, Heidi met him with open arms.

"You're back!" beamed Heidi.

"Yes, I'm fine thanks," replied Milo, surprised by this sudden burst of affection. "Are you alright?"

"I'm fine," said Heidi, who was not fine. "How did you get out?"

"The pendant was never missing and someone stole it for real. When it was reported, I was released. Thanks for trying to help regardless."

"It's no problem."

"No, I mean it. Very few people would have done that,"

thanked Milo. "You're a good person."

Milo's words were sincere, which only served to compound Heidi's guilt. Once she had regained composure, Heidi probed for more information.

"Were there any suspects in the theft?" asked Heidi.

"They didn't tell me," replied Milo.

Heidi fidgetted about, unsure exactly how to raise the subject to Milo, but slowly, words fumbled out of Heidi's mouth. "Hey, so, considering I got you out of prison, would you mind helping me with something?"

Milo was confused. "You didn't help me out of prison? The pendant was reported stolen, and you just went to look for…"

Milo's sentence trailed off when he put together exactly what had happened.

"You stole the pendant!" whispered Milo.

"I didn't intend to. I panicked," pleaded Heidi. "I almost got caught yesterday which means I'm probably a suspect."

Milo put his head in his hands and tried to block off the outside world.

"Please!" pleaded Heidi again. "Today's the last day of the performance. I just need to sneak back into her room while the show is on, but she came back early last night so I need someone on lookout just in case. Please, I'm asking nicely."

Milo had to give himself strength; he had only within the past hour left the police station, and didn't fancy going back there so soon. All the while, Heidi kept begging Milo, until he gave in.

"I want you to know this is a bad idea," stated Milo.

"It's the best I have," admitted Heidi.

Milo and Heidi made their way once again to The Bard, watching over their shoulders the whole walk over. Why was it so weird that the act of resolving a crime was scarier than committing one? The police were yet to come and question Heidi at the office, but the chances of them appearing were increasing by the moment. Heidi had already constructed a plan: Go back to The Bard the moment the performance was set to start, that way eliminating as much risk as possible of Donna returning too early. The operation had to be done quickly and quietly.

"We just want to be in and out," explained Milo. "Don't look anyone in the eyes, walk up to the room, throw the pendant in, and walk away."

"Understood," replied Heidi.

Milo and Heidi walked past the reception. This was the third time the receptionist saw Heidi in the past few days, and they might have mentioned something if it wasn't for the fact their paycheck was much lower than their level of caring. Milo positioned himself in a passageway where he could see both Heidi and the front door should Donna return early from the performance. Heidi kept walking up to the actress's room, and she paused for a second to psyche herself up. As quickly as she could, Heidi pulled the door handle, and without looking inside the room, tossed the pendant quickly through the gap in the doorway.

Thwip.

Smack.

"OW!"

Heidi started to walk away.

Heidi stopped suddenly.

Where did that "ow" come from?

Oh no, thought Heidi.

Heidi turned around and saw a half made up Donna Furst standing in the doorway, studying her prey with a now jewellery dented face. Heidi winced, and paused for slightly too long, allowing Donna to close the distance between them. Heidi ran away, and Donna chased. Milo, who had been looking the other direction, suddenly saw Heidi zip straight past him. Believing this was his cue to leave, Milo started walking away, until Donna also pounced past him.

He realised at that moment that they were screwed.

After paying bail for the crime of theft and premeditated

assault, Milo and Heidi were released from prison. The pair of them spent a day in cells, making absolutely sure the play, and by proxy, Donna Furst, had left town; it turned out that the actress never went to the scheduled final performance of Death Of The Oceans after the less than stellar audience reaction from the night before. After leaving the cells and going home, the two unfortunate journalists reminisced on their past few days.

"That must have been the worst person you've ever interviewed," said Heidi.

Milo replied, "Eh. Maybe top ten."

***

After the stress that had been the entire Donna Furst episode, Milo was more than eager to arrive at The Devil's Neckhole, and Heidi was pleased to join him. The weather was warm, so the front door was left ajar, which assisted Hazel giving instruction to Milo as he entered.

"Keep your head down," whispered Hazel. "Rob's in."

Milo instinctively looked down as he travelled; the man could move through that bar with his eyes closed if he needed to. Heidi, still not quite having a firm grasp on Pending traditions, decided to look over to Rob, and saw he was talking the ear off a not completely repugnant woman.

"Who's the person with him?" asked Heidi.

Hazel answered, "That's his wife."

"Rob is married!"

"She's deaf."

"Ahh." Heidi's sentence trailed off as she started to wonder if Rob realised he was talking to a deaf person. If Rob was married, would he even realise it? Heidi was only broken from her trance when Hazel raised a query.

"Speaking of husbands and wives, I don't think I've seen you with anyone since I first met you," said Hazel to Heidi.

"Actually, I'm asexual," announced Heidi. "It's quite lucky actually; it suits my lifestyle."

"I didn't know that about you," stated Milo.

"Well, when you don't have something, it doesn't really come up in conversation."

Milo had a hard time arguing that point.

"What about you, Milo," asked Heidi. "Do you have anyone special I don't know about?"

"Her name's Tequila," interrupted Hazel.

Milo exchanged an often rehearsed, "Oh, shut up," to Hazel before addressing the question. "No. I'm single. I gave up on relationships when I realised I needed to work on my personality."

Heidi thought that mentality was a tad cynical. "That's no good reason to stop trying."

"Sorry, but we aren't all lucky enough to be asexual."

CHAPTER SIX

Locals Wander Local Wonders

Question: Why do you think bank holidays were invented? Do you think it's because someone with a terribly important job needed extra time off so that they may be at the top of their game in regard to their occupation, or do you perhaps believe bank holidays are a generous gift from the government as a reward for your hard work?

Of course not.

Bank holidays were simply a demand made by a banker that they should be entitled to extra days off. The banker in question (who you will be unsurprised to hear was also a politician) forced the order through government, and enjoyed extra-long weekends until they died. The act did however spark some revolution, debating that giving only bankers extra holiday was an injustice. The usual moniker of the government - "Life is unfair" - didn't work as well as it usually did, and after a number of years, plus an even bigger number of broken windows, everyone now has the right to waste their time more than they usually would.

A national bank holiday was fast approaching in Pending, and as could be expected, the present company of Milo, Heidi, and Hazel were discussing how to spend their newly found spare time.

"I was just planning on staying in here," said Milo nonchalantly, while looking around The Devil's Neckhole.

Heidi had to ask, "Don't you ever go out of town?"

"It's hard enough getting him out of here," interrupted Hazel.

"I don't need to go out of town," answered Milo. "Things are boring in here; they'll be boring outside as well."

Heidi had become used to Milo's attitude, but it didn't mean she had lost hope that he couldn't be pushed out the door.

"Aren't you going to ask what I'm doing?" suggested Heidi.

"No," said Milo.

"I was going to see the river blossom festival."

Milo had become used to Heidi's attitude, and he had lost hope that she would stop talking if he ignored her.

"Go on," started Milo. "What's the river blossom festival?"

"How do you not know?" queried Hazel. "It's a local thing."

"I didn't grow up here, and you've never mentioned it before."

"I'm sure I have; you just didn't listen."

Milo could believe that.

"The river blossom festival was the whole reason I came to Pending," beamed Heidi, trying to bring the conversation back. "It's supposed to be the most beautiful sight in the country." Heidi's eagerness to discuss the festival was overflowing; she was practically jumping in her seat like an impatient child. "You should come along. It'll be better than drinking all day."

Milo was almost offended. "I hardly think so. I'm staying here for the bank holiday."

"No, you aren't," informed Hazel. "We're closed for redecorating." (Redecorating is code for health and safety violations need addressing.)

"I can just go to another pub," argued Milo.

"No, you can't. You're barred from most of them."

Milo's voice started increasing in volume. "Then I'll stay at home and read."

"You can read on the way," countered Heidi.

Milo was screaming, "Then I'm going to sit in my bed, crying and wanking."

"I'll buy you a hankie and a thick blanket," shouted Hazel.

"Why won't you go?"

"I travelled when I came to Pending and I hated it," revealed Milo. "I don't want to do that again."

"The river blossom festival isn't that far away; only a day at most," informed Heidi. "What have you got to lose?"

"My time."

"Oh, because you use that so productively," argued Hazel. "I'll come along too. I haven't been since I was a kid."

Milo remained steadfast in his stubbornness. "I'm not going, and that's that."

Heidi and Hazel were determined to change Milo's mind, if for no other reason than to win the pathetic argument. A few seconds passed before Heidi had an idea.

"Milo, I didn't want to bring this up," raised Heidi, "but we're having an intervention."

"A what?" replied Milo, not believing his ears.

"You need to take a break away from alcohol," stated Heidi, giving a quick glance over to Hazel who was more than happy to play along.

"Recently, your drinking habits have become more and more dangerous," added Hazel. "You have to prove to us you can stop."

"You can't do that," raged Milo.

"I'm the barmaid here. Do not forget the power I wield," warned Hazel, adding the menacing tone of a stage villain. "Unless you go to the river blossom festival, I won't serve you, and I'll make sure no one else does either."

Milo weighed up his options; he could just drink at home, but he didn't like to make a habit of that because he didn't like having to replace the broken ornaments. Heidi said this would only be a day trip, which would be manageable, or at least more manageable than being teetotal for who knows how long. There was also begging, but that stopped working on Hazel after she learned what Milo was like.

"You know I'll just complain the whole trip," stated Milo.

"What else is new?" asked Hazel.

"What will you get out of this?"

"Nothing. This is for your benefit."

Milo didn't believe that, but he loudly exhaled and gave in. "Fine. Let's go to the river blossom festival."

Heidi and Hazel both smiled, the latter more smugly than the other. Heidi left early, newly eager to prepare for this trip, while Milo slumped across the bar and decided to prepare in his own way.

"Triple whiskey, please," asked Milo.

A few days passed, and the bank holiday had arrived. The weather was uncharacteristically fine, which in Pending, was a bad omen. Milo was advised by Heidi to bring food, a couple sets of clothes for if the weather changed, and some decent walking shoes. The food wasn't an issue, as Milo ate it most days, but a change of clothes would have been superfluous, as he only had one costume: shirt and trousers; the colour and quality may have differed, but each one was the same. A similar statement could be made about Milo's shoes, as he only had two pairs: one that he normally wore, and another that would do in a pinch; Milo was wearing the second pair. As Milo arrived at the agreed meeting spot, he was caught off guard by two things: Initially because Heidi had actually arrived earlier than him for a change, but mostly because she seemed to be tending a goat.

"What is that?" asked Milo.

"It's a goat," answered Heidi slowly, feeling the answer to that question was obvious. "You really don't get out much, do you?"

The goat was large, its horns curved like scimitars, and to use the phrase "unkempt" would be generous. The goat's long hair brushed gently against the grass; just low enough to collect the fox turds on its locks. Fortunately, the goat was brown, so it didn't show up too much.

"His name is Ramsey, and he's pulling the wagon," said Heidi, pointing to a miniature carriage no longer than Milo's legs.

"That's a small wagon," said Milo, stating the obvious.

"It doesn't need to be big," replied Heidi.

Milo couldn't work it out, so he had to ask, "Why have we got a wagon?"

"It's for putting your bags in while we walk," answered Heidi.

Milo was putting pieces together now; for some reason, despite being told he needed walking shoes, he thought he would be travelling in a stagecoach, and walking only part of the way. It was now very clear that Milo was walking the whole distance for a day's trek, which was going to make his crying and wanking plans slightly more challenging. A short time later, Hazel appeared, having received *and* understood the memo. Heidi meanwhile was more prepared than she seemingly ever had been; she had a map, hiking poles, and clothes clearly purpose made for trips like this.

"Are we ready?" asked Heidi, pumped with enthusiasm.

"Yes," answered Hazel in a normal tone.

"Yes," answered Milo, half deflated.

"Let's go!" shouted Heidi, excitement shooting from her like a cannon.

With their willingness fully accounted for, the three of them set off. It was uncommon for people in Pending to venture outside of town; the group didn't encounter anyone else making the same trip, and that was mostly because the Pending mentally involved the phrase "Why would I go over there when all my shit is here?"

For Heidi, this was quite new to her; while yes, she had seen grassland before, there was a serene beauty in seeing the subtle changes of flora different locales offer. The trees were huge, spreading out their branches in some chaotic dance, and the fields laid out over the rolling hills furnished the scenery with calming yellows and pinks.

For Hazel, this was somewhat nostalgic; she had childhood memories associated with running through the fields, being chased out of the fields, trying to set fire to the field because she was angry. Good times, she thought to herself. Hazel diverted a large portion of her attention to the world around her, just as Heidi was.

For Milo, this was a reminder of why he hated travelling. Granted, Milo wasn't in a cramped stagecoach like he was when he first arrived in Pending, but walking wasn't much better, as his choice of shoes were falling apart like a marriage with too much honesty. There also wasn't a great amount you could do while moving that was proactive; at best, Milo could read, but when you're walking, you need your eyes to make sure you don't trip over anything and turn your face into a plant pot. The three of them moved along for an hour or so before Heidi caught sight of someone in the distance riding some kind of ship.

"Woah! What's that?" asked Heidi.

Milo looked over to the canal and saw a man steering a long, thin boat down the waterway.

"It's a narrowboat," answered Milo. "Haven't you seen one before?"

"No. Are they common?" asked Heidi.

Milo had to process for a moment that something coming from this country could possibly be construed as exotic. "Fairly common. The rivers here are quite small, so people made boats in that shape to accommodate. I guess other countries don't have the same problem."

"What are they used for?" asked Heidi, giving in to her inquisitive nature.

"Some people live in them, but a lot of them are still used in trade."

"In trade?" chuckled Hazel.

"What do you mean by that?" asked Milo.

"Oh, nothing. It's just you sound like a textbook."

"Saying 'trade' is a perfectly valid word in that context," chastised Milo in a raised voice.

"It is, but most people would say 'selling things.'"

"I'm not most people!" shouted Milo. "Most people aren't most people."

"Wait, wait, wait," jolted Hazel, raising in pitch. "What do you mean by that?"

"What's so confusing?" amplified Milo again. "You know

what I mean, don't you, Heidi?"

"Don't bring her into this, she hasn't done anything wrong," said Hazel, pointing to the girl who was doubled over in laughing fits.

As soon as Heidi had calmed herself down enough to make coherent sentences, she said, "I think I get it. You're saying how everyone has something weird about them that most people don't."

"There! You see," shouted Milo. "You're the idiot here."

"No, no, no," argued Hazel. "My point still stands that saying 'trade' is weird. Even people who work in trade probably don't say trade."

"Fine. We both win," ended Milo.

There was half a moment of silence before Heidi spoke again. "Have you ever worked in trade?"

"No," disclosed Hazel. "I've worked the bar since before I was allowed to."

"Ah," said Heidi, before realising the content of that sentence. "I've worked as a waitress, dishwasher, box packer, librarian, artist for commission, and now a portrait artist. What about you, Milo?"

"I've only had two jobs," announced Milo. "Cleaner for three years, and working at The Bystander for about twenty."

Heidi smiled. "I guess you two must like those jobs since you've stayed with them so long."

"No," replied Milo and Hazel in unison.

Heidi was caught by surprise.

"I have zero transferable skills for a workplace," admitted Hazel, "but I know how to pour drinks, and that's enough to pay my bills."

"I thought I wanted to be a journalist," admitted Milo. "When I was a child, I fancied being an archeologist, but I thought it would be more realistic to try and become a writer."

"Wow, even as a kid, you were pragmatic," joked Hazel.

The rambling conversations carried on for a while until it

was around midday. The travelling trio sat down on the grass and relaxed their muscles, suddenly having the realisation of how tired they really were.

"I just remembered why I haven't been back to the festival in so long," moaned Hazel. "This is a lot of walking."

"Do you want to borrow my hiking poles?" asked Heidi.

"No, don't worry about it."

"Are you sure?"

"No," ended Hazel.

While those negotiations were taking place, Milo tried to take a parcel of food from his bag, but Ramsey hadn't understood the message that they were stopping. Milo hiked his bag off the wagon, which was a mistake, as it allowed the goat to speed up. Milo ran and forced the goat to face the other direction, before pulling some grass from the ground and attempting to feed it; this seemed to work, although Milo now had the goat's saliva covering his hand, and he was about to eat lunch. Milo, using only his off hand, unwrapped his food, and ended up half crushing his rations in the process. When Milo eventually managed to sit down, wiping his hand on the grass to clean it, he started eating.

"What have you got there?" asked Heidi.

Milo was eating a baked potato with the insides removed, mashed, and mixed with cheese, gherkins, and pickled onions, before being stuffed back into the potato skin, which he conveyed to Heidi. The snack looked as appealing as a cinderblock to the crotch, but Heidi was curious nonetheless.

"Is that a food from around here?" asked Heidi.

"Actually, it's from my home country," revealed Milo.

"Oh, I've never asked you about that. Where exactly are you from?"

"The country is Veezee. I'm from a city called Laskia."

"What's it like there?"

"It's not very different from Pending; they have the same language, roughly the same weather; the only major differences are the skin tone and the brainpower."

Heidi and Hazel chuckled, before finding their own food. Hazel had a large cheese and pickle sandwich, while Heidi picked out something more interesting; it was a sealed bread parcel stuffed with sausage pieces stewed in tomato and paprika sauce, and a soft biscuit layered with jam and crumble pieces.

"What are those?" asked Hazel with hungry eyes.

"It's a sausage bun, and the cake is called a crumble coin. You can't get them anywhere except my home country."

"Can I have a bit," asked Hazel, not hiding her intent.

"Sure," said Heidi, handing a piece of the crumble coin to Hazel. "Do you want to try some?" asked Heidi to Milo.

"Sure. I don't usually eat sweet things though," answered Milo.

Milo and Hazel both took a bite from the confection, and it was delicious. The softness of the cake, the sharp sweetness of the jam, and the crunchy topping came together in some kind of beautiful cacophony.

"Hang on," started Hazel, "if you can only get these cakes where you come from, where is this one from?"

"I made it," revealed Heidi.

Hazel's eyes widened. "Why didn't you tell me you could cook before?"

"It never came up," countered Heidi. "When you travel, you have to learn to cook a little bit, and I made those cakes with my grandma when I was a kid. Also, they're much better back home."

"What was the name of your home country again?"

Heidi chuckled, and Milo himself was quite surprised at how much he enjoyed the food. After she had finished eating, Heidi stood up and started pacing, eager to start travelling again. Once Milo and Hazel had finished their lunches, urged on by Heidi, they agreed they had to continue walking, throwing their bags back on the wagon (after catching it again). It was getting to be mid-afternoon when the group finally saw another traveller going in the same direction, although they were too far away to say hello. The other traveller had been wealthy enough to afford a horse, and Hazel was intensely jealous; she was so distracted about the tiredness she was suffering, it hadn't even crossed her mind that she would have to walk back as well. A while into the afternoon, when everyone was quiet enough to have their own thoughts swim around their heads, Heidi vocalised one of hers. "I've been meaning to ask for a while, Milo. You study magic items, right?"

"As a hobby, yes," answered Milo.

"When we met, you said magic items played a big role in history, and I've been trying to learn about every culture there is. In that case, how come I haven't come across magic items since school?"

"There could be a couple of reasons," started Milo. "For one, magic items are as rare as rare can be, and the majority of them aren't in the public eye. A few are owned by wealthy tycoons, but no one knows where most of them went. There are theories about it; they were either destroyed, buried, or stored away by some government agency because of the damage they did to societies. There's also the fact that not all accounts are trustworthy; I don't know for certain that all the magic items I've researched ever existed. But the final point, which is the most plausible reason why you don't know about magic items, is that you don't read very much."

"Hey! That's not true," argued Heidi. "I read travel books. I just prefer to see history with my own eyes."

"My point still stands," affirmed Milo.

"Didn't you say you worked in a library earlier?" asked Hazel.

"Yes, but I didn't read every book," countered Heidi. "It wasn't even a library in my home country, so there was a language barrier."

"Don't you learn the languages of the places you go to."

"Yes, but I never stay long enough to be fluent."

"How many languages can you speak?" asked Milo curiously.

"I'm fluent in my native language and yours, then there's three others that I can speak enough of to get by."

Milo was surprised; it had never even crossed his mind that

Heidi spoke a different language in her home country, and he couldn't help but compliment her on it.

"Thank you," said Heidi.

"Isn't all the travelling and having to learn new languages a bit of a faff?" asked Hazel, who was just about managing to stay upright.

"I don't think so."

"But there's got to be problems with travelling though. Everyone thinks an orgy is fun and games, but someone's got to do the catering."

"Well, there can be," admitted Heidi. "The first time I went travelling, I stayed in an awful place, and I didn't know any of the language. Back then, I was also a lot shyer. To be honest, people terrify me a little bit, and I can't deal with confrontation very well, but I'm getting better. I think living in Pending has helped a lot because everyone's so shouty."

Milo thought about that statement. "I think that's called exposure therapy."

"I think it's called trial by fire," added Hazel.

"The reason I travel though is because the world is a much bigger place than you will ever realise. Every country has its own history, landmarks, food, festivals, music, loads of stuff. I want to see as much of it as I can. My mum says that my curiosity outweighs my common sense."

"I think I agree with her," said Hazel wearily. "How much further to the festival?"

"It is..." Heidi stood on her tiptoes to get a better view of the horizon, "close," she confirmed, before running forward with glee.

Hazel smiled, and pushed herself forward, as the river the supposed festival took place at lay just a few minutes in front of her. The surrounding area was starting to become dotted with figures off in the distance, and it was dawning on Milo that while the word 'festival' was used, there weren't the usually expected food stalls, or children destroying the atmosphere. In reality, many people had come to the river, but no one was making a big fuss about it. It also dawned on Milo that he never once questioned what the river blossom festival was, or why it was celebrated, but he didn't think now was the best time to bring it up. The river in question was not, in any evident way, significant; it was maybe a few metres wide, and there weren't any trees or buildings near its bank. Milo soon realised there wasn't any sign of society outside of the random travellers; there wasn't even a bridge to cross over.

"When does it start?" asked Milo.

"Soon," said Heidi, trying to estimate the time.

Milo and Hazel sat down by the wagon, too tired to worry about what Ramsey was doing, while Heidi stood near to the bank and looked upstream. Milo wondered what exactly was going to happen, and what Heidi was looking for. Milo had never been hiking like this; the thought hadn't even crossed his mind, but he was struggling at this moment in time to see the point in it. Meanwhile, Hazel had taken off her shoes and was massaging her feet. After a while, just before you could reasonably say night was drawing in, Heidi shouted, "It's starting!"

Milo got back on his feet, while Hazel propped herself up against the wagon to gain a better view of the river. Initially, there wasn't anything out of the ordinary, besides maybe the odd leaf floating down stream, but it wasn't until those leaves got closer that Milo realised he was actually mistaken.

The leaves were flower petals.

Slowly, floating at the mild pace of the water, several pink flower blossoms meandered past Milo's vision; only a few to start, but within minutes, more and more petals cascaded down the river. Before long, the water was no longer visible under the congregation of delicate blossoms that glided on the water's surface. Not a single word in those minutes was exchanged between the three people; all of them awestruck by the ballet before them. Milo was shocked that something so serene and beautiful was just a few miles away from the shithole he called home; he realised that there was so little of the world he had seen; he barely knew the local area.

"Where do they come from?" Milo had to ask.

"No one knows," replied Heidi.

That answer was enough for Milo, as he decided to sit by the water's edge and simply observe. The presence of anything else disappeared from his mind, and later he would remark to himself when was the last time he had felt this way, to which the answer is that he couldn't remember. Minutes passed by until the moon started to eclipse the sun, and the remaining river blossoms washed past. Milo needed a minute to return to his senses, before he stood up and went back to the wagon, still existing in some cosmic state of tranquility. Milo lifted his bag from off the ground, and with a gentle heave, placed it back on the wagon.

The wagon's wheel broke off.

And Milo returned to reality.

***

Heidi had prepared for the worst, and brought with her some camping equipment; there was only enough for one, but she offered to give Hazel the bedroll, she being the one who was complaining the loudest. The night sky on Flatrock was pure black, as the moon blocked out any starlight, but a campfire had been set ablaze, and the three people were relaxing close to its comforting flame.

"Do you always walk this much?" asked Hazel to Heidi.

"Sometimes, yes." answered Heidi. "Not everywhere can be reached by cart, so you have to do what you can. I once met a tribe of people who do nothing but walk endlessly. Besides sleep and foraging for food, they're always moving. That's a little extreme for me though."

Hazel's eyes widened in fear; she'd rather chew her legs off than walk forever, though the last comment Heidi made did make her think.

"If the river blossom festival was the reason you came to Pending, does that mean you'll be leaving soon?" asked Hazel.

"Not yet," replied Heidi. "I don't have the money to start moving again. I'm fine for the moment though."

The pair prattled on for some time, while Milo was in a deep half-conscious state, still reminiscing over the river blossoms; the girls just thought he had fallen asleep early. The river blossom festival was dream-like, as if he had hallucinated the whole thing; it was a sensation Milo didn't recognise; his heart was fluttering, and he felt a gentle tingling in his throat. It was a feeling Milo didn't recognise, but he knew he had felt it before; it was a song lyric on the tip of his tongue, or an itch on the end of his penis.

Oh, that's it, thought Milo. This is happiness.

CHAPTER SEVEN

Too Late To Turn Back

As it was offhandedly mentioned in the last chapter how Heidi came to be a traveller, I think it would be worthwhile going into detail about what exactly happened on that fateful first excursion. I am doing this for two very good reasons: Firstly, self-reflection is an important piece of therapy that everyone should do, and in showing you someone's starting point so that you may compare it to later in their life, you may be better informed and less hesitant to do the same process to yourself.

The second reason is schadenfreude.

Heidi's homeland is that of Grenbourg: A country most notable for starting a rather embarrassing war; if it wasn't humiliating enough that they lost in quite spectacular fashion, the political leaders of the time had to bite the bullet and admit that mass genocide was *not* the best international policy. Since then, many museums and monuments have been created as a testament to the loss of life, but it felt like a moot point considering most people were already acutely aware that genocide was bad. With the war being the only significant event to happen in Grenbourg as of recently, anyone visiting was usually there for the previously mentioned museums and monuments, making it the ideal tourist destination for anyone who likes to be depressed.

Heidi was wandering around town with her friend, Franchezca. Town centres are the teenage equivalent of the pub for places where you can meet up with friends and moan about life. Grenbourg's towns had been renovated and remade over and over again in the name of efficiency, with everything old stripped down for the brand new; the end result is a town with less personality than a politician. Normally a town has something special about it, like an aged historical building, or at least some kind of communal area in the shape of a duck, but Grenbourg was one big country of perfect organisation, like it was constructed entirely out of set squares. Heidi, at this point in time, was in the very early stages of adulthood; out of education, but not fully employed; unsure how adult life worked, but not old enough to realise no one knows how adult life works. With no real objective for the day, Heidi and Fran were simply wandering past shops and thinking out loud.

"Is there anywhere around here that sells second hand shoes?" asked Heidi.

"Of course there isn't. You don't wear shoes on your hands," replied Fran sincerely.

From any other person, that might have been witty, but if you know her, Fran was anything but. Franchezca could best be described as all beauty, no brains; a lot on the face, but nothing between the ears; a few beers short of an accident; I think you understand. Franchezca had wavy brown hair, a willowy figure, and wore clothes that in contrast to the browns and greys of Grenbourg, looked practically radioactive. The two girls kept walking through town, idly chatting amongst themselves when Franchezca said the words, "I got that job in the lawyer's office."

"That's great for you," said Heidi, slightly depressed, but enough for Fran to notice.

"Are you alright?" asked Fran.

Heidi shuffled, slightly nervous. "I don't know if I want to get a job."

"No one wants a job. It's just something you have to do."

"I know, but I really don't want one."

"What are you going to do instead?"

"I don't know. Everything feels weird, and nothing interests me anymore."

Heidi had reached the bothersome crossroad of life where you have to choose what to do before you really have the knowledge and experience to make an informed decision; what she chose was likely to inform a large portion of her life, and she didn't exactly want to waste ten years finding out she hated everything. Heidi's brother had joined the army (they rebranded themselves a humanitarian movement following the war), and the rest of her school friends were already employed. Heidi had spent her later years of education studying art, but getting a job in that industry was nigh on impossible, especially in a country where free expression had been replaced by perfect right angles. Franchezca saw the uncertainty on Heidi's face and thought for a moment.

"How about we go on holiday?" suggested Fran. "A big holiday in another country." Heidi looked at her friend, unsure if this was a stroke of genius or another one of her brainfarts. "It will take your mind off things, and you'll come back with a fresh head."

Heidi didn't discount the possibility, but she hadn't been totally convinced. "Is that a good idea?"

"Are you doing anything?" disputed Fran.

"No. That's the problem."

"Then we should go!" asserted Fran excitedly.

Heidi thought about it; she did like the idea of going on holiday with Fran, but she was still cautious. Heidi had never been to a foreign country, and she only had a vague recollection of language classes in school. If she was going to say yes, Heidi needed at least a little more information.

"Where would we go?" wondered Heidi out loud.

"What about Udonia?" suggested Fran. "I went there before, and it was great."

Udonia was a country bordering Grenbourg, so it wouldn't be far or very expensive to travel to, but there was a reputation with the place. Udonia was a country where laws regarding alcohol and drugs were so relaxed, the police stations were fitted with reclining chairs, and Heidi knew a few people who had taken advantage of that fact.

"I don't know," said Heidi uncertainly.

"Do you have any better ideas?" asked Fran.

Heidi knew if she was good at coming up with ideas, she wouldn't be having this conversation about going on holiday at all; she would be in a job she liked and everything would be great. As it happened, Heidi didn't have any better ideas, and as questionable as some of Franchezca's decisions can be, she did trust her.

"Alright, let's do it," said Heidi, losing her inhibitions.

Fran hugged Heidi suddenly and dropped her again, instantly pumped full of energy. Led by Franchezca, the two of them hurried around town to find supplies for the trip. Heidi wasn't in any way curious about what Udonia was like; she only really enjoyed the fact she now had a forward plan, and no matter how brief the feeling would last, she wouldn't have to think about work, and her lack thereof. It seemed things were good, but little did Heidi know her entire life was about to be shaken up.

Within a week, Heidi and Franchezca were on an airship to Udonia. Airships had been invented out of necessity: a necessity to avoid the newly implemented road tax. Using a balloon filled with hot air, and steam to power a propeller, the airship is by far the most dangerous and inefficient way to travel in Flatrock, but because of the road tax laws in Grenbourg, it's slightly cheaper than a stagecoach. The major disadvantage with airships is that they're so large, you need a square mile of land just to park the beast; it also takes half a day just to inflate them, and they can't be used in strong winds unless you don't mind crash landing, but despite these glaring flaws, someone had managed to make a business out of them. Heidi looked around the seats and saw there were a lot of passengers on the ship; this was clearly a trip that many people took. Heidi looked around at the passengers on this journey, and made internal judgments about the kind of people who go to Udonia.

Heidi saw a man with a spike through his nose and felt slightly uneasy.

Heidi saw a woman seemingly wearing belts instead of clothes and became concerned.

It was when Heidi saw a man with a spider tattooed over his entire face that she started to worry.

Heidi spent some time face down reading a phrase book; she had never been outside her home country before, and never needed to know another language until now. It was a few minutes into the trip that Fran noticed what Heidi was doing, and asked, "Why are you reading that?"

"Aren't we going to need to know the language?" asked Heidi.

"No, they speak the same language as us."

"Are you sure?" asked Heidi, already pretty confident she knew the correct answer.

"I'm sure. No one spoke that language last time I came."

Heidi put faith in Franchezca instead of her better judgement, and closed the book before staring out the window. From this altitude, Heidi saw the ocean for the first in her life: A completely unrestricted body of water, free to move and flow wherever it wants without any expectation. Lucky knobhead, thought Heidi. After she had finished being passive aggressive to bodies of water, Heidi suppressed her feeling of jealousy and tried to sleep; the wind was blowing in the wrong direction, and this airship ride was going to take a while.

After a day, Heidi and Fran arrived in Udonia. Heidi pulled herself out of her chair and stretched her legs before being shoved along by the crowd into the open air of a new country. After leaving the ship, and taking the overlong walk it takes to get out of the field the airship landed, Heidi was smiling, optimistic of the new adventure she was about to embark on, and she looked with wide eyes at her new surroundings.

Her smile faded fast.

Heidi stared into the barely restrained chaos that was

Udonia. The town Heidi saw was twisting and unorganised, not so much drawn freehand, more drawn broken-hand. All the road signs and shop windows used the local language, and it wasn't overly clear what those shops sold. Fran commented about a woman standing in one shop's display, holding a weird shaped pipe in one hand, and an unopened chocolate bar in the other, presenting them like prizes. Heidi thought the woman was just crazy, until she saw three more nutters doing the same thing.

"This is different," muttered Heidi.

Even Fran admitted the country looked slightly different than she remembered; living mannequins are not something you simply forget. After the duo broke out of their stupor, they remembered the first item on their agenda was to find a hotel. Fran took the lead, walking through random streets and circling around and around until something vaguely hotel-like presented itself. Heidi, relying on something other than luck, tried to use her phrase book, but playing snap when each word had its own garish font was not easy for her; it was also incredibly distracting when people's pets wanted to cuddle up to her, especially when those pets were crocodiles.

The two of them looked vigilantly for a hotel, but they saw nothing of the sort. It was only when night was drawing close that Fran spotted something; it wasn't a hotel like it was written in the phrase book, but it contained most of the same letters, and looked at least somewhat similar to a hotel. Heidi wasn't prepared to see just how disorderly this country could get at night, so took the chance and dived through the door. The building had the hallmarks of a usual hotel: reception desk, people with backpacks, fungal smell; it seemed like what they were looking for. That being said, it was difficult to feel lucky when Heidi had just stepped in a gooey puddle of je ne sais quoi. While her friend was distracted, Fran walked up to the front desk.

"Can we have a room for two people, please?" asked Fran.

The woman behind the desk looked slightly puzzled, so Fran repeated herself, but with no better reaction.

Then Fran tried again, but louder.

It wasn't until Heidi removed whatever it was on her shoe that she realised what was happening, and it wasn't until after Fran started aggressively pointing that Heidi jumped in with her phrase book. Heidi motioned to a sentence that conveyed what they wanted, and the matter seemed to be sorted relatively easily. While the receptionist was sorting out keys and papers, Heidi said to Fran, "I thought they all spoke our language."

"Maybe she's just a bit thick," replied the woman who once glued her hand to a cat.

The receptionist handed over two keys and directed the women upstairs. The keys had the numbers "11" and "12" crudely painted on them in green, and Heidi realised in the confusion that they had accidentally ordered two separate rooms. Heidi was slightly annoyed that they had probably overpaid, but in fairness, the rooms were cheaper than expected. Heidi and Fran walked up the nearby staircase and looked for rooms eleven and twelve, but there was only one door. Technically speaking, they found a doorway; the door was missing, but that was not the issue. Heidi and Fran walked down the corridor and tried to see if there were corners they could turn, but there was only this one doorway.

"I think we have to stay in here," stated Fran, pointing through the hole in the wall.

Heidi looked in and saw a flood of bunk beds, half of them polluted with some of the most vile smelling people she had ever had the privilege of sharing space with. The room had dark blue painted walls, although the higher parts of the lodging were cream coloured; evidently the place had been painted over with a colour that is less likely to show the stains. It was at this moment that Heidi realised this wasn't a hotel.

It was a hostel.

Heidi wondered why they had been given a key considering the lack of door, until she saw two beds with matching numbers, and safe boxes fitted and screwed down underneath the bottom bunk. Heidi had been acutely aware that her possessions might be stolen if she wasn't careful, but the fact she had a safe box didn't fill her with the hope it probably should have. If there wasn't a safe box, she wouldn't have thought anything of it, but because there was a box, that implied theft was a problem, and if theft was a problem, that would be the first place the thief would look. Heidi was so engaged by her double bluff dilemma that she completely didn't notice Fran leap onto the top bunk and yell, "Bagsy!"

Heidi wasn't sure what the etiquette of a hostel was; whether she should say hello, or at least try to, but opted against the idea in the end. Heidi (in this period of her life) knew she wasn't the most confident person in the world when it came to meeting strangers, and it didn't help that the residents of this hostel had some odd idea that their faces didn't have enough holes in them. Fran meanwhile couldn't care less about the fact that strangers were hanging underwear off the end of her bed (six pairs of pants in total, owned by seven different people.)

"We should get some food" thought Franchezca out loud.

"Good idea," said Heidi very quickly, keen to leave the somewhat claustrophobic atmosphere.

The two of them walked through the streets, Heidi only now remembering she didn't enjoy outside the hostel either, but committed to her mistake. Heidi hadn't paid a lot of attention to the town while looking for a hotel, not exactly able to focus while sharing the street with man-eating reptiles. It was only now that Heidi had a little more freedom to explore that she started to appreciate the constant twists and turns of the streets. Around every corner was something she had never seen before, for better or worse. The sculpture of a long-ago worshipped God atop a mountain that had stayed upright for thousands of years was magical; the building decorated with chicken carcasses, slightly less so. As Heidi strolled through town looking for a place to eat, she did start to understand the layout of the city; there was somewhere in the region of a shit ton of rivers flowing through the streets, and the buildings had to be made in a way that compensated for nature's drunken meanders. Heidi was more relaxed than she previously had been, though she did feel like people were staring at her; whether that was due to her being a foreigner, or her grandad's recent invasions efforts remained unclear. The two women eventually settled on a restaurant that looked pleasant enough, but more importantly, it had the courtesy to put pictures on the menu.

"Fran, are you sure people here understand our language?" asked Heidi, completely unconvinced by her previous argument.

"Yes, I never had a problem the last time I was here," stated Fran again.

Evidence was stacked high against Fran, but before Heidi could present her argument, the waiting staff came over and took their order. Heidi ordered a stew similar to what was common in Grenbourg's restaurants, while Fran was more daring, and ordered "something." It's hard to use a word other than "something," as neither woman could pronounce the name, and when the dish came out, there was no way to discern if it was an animal, vegetable, or mineral. The dish had a shell-like outside, soft doughy innards, and was served with a cream and cranberry sauce, but "something" remained the most apt word for it. Fran was generous enough to offer Heidi a piece, if for no other reason than to discern the "something's" identity, but it didn't help. Admittedly, Heidi enjoyed it a lot more than her stew; the doughy part felt like bread, and had the smell of cheese, but tasted like crab or chicken. Whatever "something" was, it was good. Heidi and Fran had organised to stay in Udonia for only two nights, and as they were eating, they discussed what they should do with their limited time. A few ideas were thrown onto the table, but it wasn't until Fran suggested, "We should go to a bar," that a true debate was had. Heidi was somewhat terrified by the prospect of going to a bar. Back in Grenbourg, there were very strict laws about entering pubs and bars until you reached a certain age, as it was expected you'd need to defend yourself, and both these women were underage, at least for their home country. Heidi had never drunk alcohol;

Fran had, and the aftermath was disastrous, fire acting how it does. Heidi wanted to make a conceited effort against the plan, though she was not naturally argumentative.

"Are you sure?" asked Heidi, it being the best argument she ever had.

"We've got to have some fun on our holiday," argued Fran, "and our parents probably expect we'd go anyway."

"Yours might," contested Heidi.

Fran ignored the insult and continued her plea. "There's a place I really want to go to that my parents wouldn't let me last time I was here. I don't think it's too far from here either." Heidi gave a look that didn't show any sign of being convinced. "Come on. Nothing bad is going to happen."

Heidi didn't like what might be some famous last words, but in the manner of fairness, nothing had gone horribly wrong so far. Yes, the country was weird, and she was planets away from her comfort zone, but nothing you could technically call "bad" had occurred as of yet.

"Alright," whimpered Heidi, whose will had been bent so many times by this point that you could tie knots with it. "Let's see what this bar is like."

Fran hugged Heidi over the table, and before long, the two of them were wandering the streets yet again.

It didn't take long to find the bar; how could you miss it with its cannon balled roof and ear shattering music. There was every chance that the building used to be a cart stop, as there was a large sector to the side for tying down horses, although the area was now mostly used for the comatose patrons to make a human pyramid. Every single window had a different colour and style of frame to it, as if bits had broken, then been replaced with whatever could be found at the time; it was like a patchwork doll, and smelled like the kind of toddler who might own such a toy.

"Are you sure this is the place?" asked Heidi, hopeful it wasn't. "It looks dangerous."

"Definitely," affirmed Fran over the sound of a bottle

smashing. "It looks slightly different to the last time I was here, but this is it."

Heidi looked at what she would hasten to call a building, and recounted the conversation from a few minutes earlier.

"You never explained; why didn't your parents let you come here?" asked Heidi, confident the correct answer was common sense.

"They said I was too young," answered Franchezca.

"But it *was* legal for you to drink in this country last time you came?"

"I don't think so," said Fran. "I was only four."

Heidi was stunned. "What?"

"I was four years old last time I came to Udonia," repeated Franchezca as if it wasn't a big deal.

"But that was nearly fifteen years ago!" shouted Heidi.

Suddenly it made sense why Franchezca had a memory of this place completely different to the reality: she had only just graduated potty training academy when she was last here, and her parents would have done all the heavy lifting as far as cultural barriers were concerned. Of course Fran didn't have any problems last time she was here: she was a baby. Heidi instantly wanted to back away, but before she could react, the excitable Franchezca was already dragging her inside.

Heidi looked around the new environment and determined that "Bar" must be short for "Barbaric." Heidi could feel the sound bounce off her forehead as the uproaring populous of the building screamed along to some untranslatable folk song. The place was lit with torches rather than lamps, and the flames were covered in violet stained glass which caused the bar to radiate a ghostly purple. The people themselves were finding difficulty in keeping their balance; even the tables and chairs were struggling to stand on their given legs. This bar was a total mess of insanity and madness.

And this was early in the evening.

Franchezca made her way to the barman and ordered drinks on Heidi's behalf. After a minute, two bottles of piss water (Pronounced "Peeswuter" in this country) appeared in Franchezca's hands, before giving one to Heidi. The drink was obviously beer, and if for nothing more than to take her mind off the world around her, Heidi decided to take a big swig.

It tasted like vomit and disappointment.

Heidi and Fran sat in the bar for a while, neither of them entirely sure what they were supposed to do. They tried chatting as they usually would, but the sound of "Flobadob ab da Fluufmurtles" (as they found out the band was called) over-screamed anything they could say. The band, consisting of a singer, a drummer, and a large tube smacker, had to be among the worst sounds Heidi had ever heard; the double percussion coupled with a singer who screeched the lyrics gave the impression of two men kicking an injured fox for half an hour. The "music" eventually stopped, but it seemed to only invite the somehow less professional singers to have a bash at the same kind of thing. There were game tables of some description around the bar, but they were the most inhabited places in the building, and Heidi didn't want to go near them. Heidi took another sip of her beer; the only reason she was drinking at all was because one negative experience took her mind off the other one, and as Heidi's brain returned to the realm that she had found herself in, she realised that Franchezca had gone.

Heidi panicked.

Heidi thought she had blinked and the world had changed; like a child suddenly losing a parent. Heidi shot up and scanned the crowd, but her miniature height could barely see over most people's shoulders. Heidi had to plunge into the cesspool and find Fran before anything bad could happen to either of them. The bar had an upstairs and a basement level, so Fran might as well have been on another continent for all the ground Heidi had to cover. As Heidi ran through the bar over and over again, she realised she was gaining attention, her face popping in and out of people's vision every other second. Time seemed like such a nebulous concept for Heidi, completely absorbed in the mission of finding Franchezca. Heidi was only taken out of her trance-like state when a rat scurried over her hand as she rested it on a nearby windowsill. Heidi shrieked, piercing through the crowd, which seemed, more so by luck than anything, to summon Franchezca from the shadows.

"Heidi, what's wrong?" asked Franchezca, who seemed to be dancing with a group of strangers.

"Fran, I hate it here," confessed Heidi. "It's noisy, it's dirty, and I think I lost one of my shoes."

"Don't worry about it," suggested Fran, unhelpfully.

Heidi realised in the way that last sentence was said that alcohol seemed to have taken hold of Franchezca, and her co-ordination was wavering, but Heidi felt she could still get through to her friend.

"Fran! We don't speak the language, and everyone stares at us. Neither of us know what we're doing here!" argued Heidi.

"We came here because of you," countered Fran. "This was to take your mind off work."

"Yes, that's true. I'm not thinking about work, because I'm too busy thinking about in what state the police will find my body. I want to leave."

"But I'm having fun."

Heidi believed she had been very forgiving to Fran considering she let herself be convinced time and time again to go along with this plan, despite all the obvious warning signs.

"I want to go back to the hostel," shouted Heidi, surprised the words were coming out of her mouth.

"You can. I won't stop you," mumbled Fran.

"We need to go back together. It's not safe on our own."

"You're being crazy."

"I'm being careful."

"Oh, bog off!" yelled Franchezca.

Heidi turned red and grabbed Franchezca by the shoulders. "I trusted you knew what you were doing, even when I was sure you didn't. Now I'm stuck in a foreign country in the middle of night surrounded by people who look like pincushions. This is all your fault!"

Heidi stormed out of the place, which is hard to do with any gravitas after you've lost a shoe and your feet are off balance. Heidi walked out of the bar, and had there been a door fitted to the place, she would have slammed it; this had been one of the worst experiences of her life (bear in mind she was still young and didn't have a broad perspective of the world yet), and she was utterly distraught.

Anyway, bring on day two.

As much as she wanted to, Heidi couldn't leave the vicinity of the bar without Franchezca; regardless of whether the streets were safe to walk on their own, Heidi had to make sure Fran came out of the building unscratched. Heidi still hadn't found her shoe, and with all the rivers around town making the streets wet, she was doing her best flamingo impression to avoid getting her foot damp. An hour passed awkwardly for Heidi, ashamed of herself for shouting at Fran, and paranoid of every Tom, Dick, and Harry that passed by her standing spot. After well past midnight, Heidi heard a familiar voice coming from the coma pile. Heidi turned the corner cautiously and saw Fran stumbling around with the grace of an elephant on a greased hill.

"Are you alright, Fran?" asked Heidi.

"Heidi? You're more taller than I remember," said the woman whose chin was six inches from the floor.

"Can you walk?" asked Heidi, certain there must be some conscious mind behind those horrifically intoxicated eyes.

"Did you see the giraffe earlier? It was wild!"

Fran's words were slurred, but it wasn't drunkenness; not like the other drunks in that bar; this was something extra.

"Fran. Are you alright?" repeated Heidi. "What were you doing in there?"

"Watch out, Heidi!" shouted Fran.

Fran pushed Heidi to the side and wrestled with something Heidi had trouble seeing.

It turned out the reason Heidi couldn't see anything was

because there was nothing there.

It was at this moment Heidi had a horrific revelation.

Udonia wasn't just famous for its drink.

Udonia was famous for its drugs.

Heidi grabbed hold of Fran and looked her into her eyes; they were scarlet with veins.

"Fran, what happened in there?" asked Heidi, panicking.

"There was this guy," started Fran in a moment of clarity, "he had a fish on his head, and he was handing out these cakes and I ate one of the cakes and it was good but I think it was too good because everything looks worse than I remem-"

Before Fran could finish her sentence, she was vomiting on Heidi's one good shoe, then passed out on the floor. Heidi reached down quickly and slapped Fran gently on the cheek.

"Fran, speak to me!" yelled Heidi worriedly.

After a moment, Fran slowly reopened her eyes, looked at Heidi with the kindness of a mother, and said to her, "A man in a wheelchair called me an idiot, but I don't think he had a leg to stand on."

Fran fell asleep from exhaustion.

Heidi mustered up the strength and carried Fran all the way back to the hostel, where they both woke up late the following morning. Fran had to sacrifice the top bunk, as Heidi was exhausted from carrying the woman halfway through town, and in that situation, she couldn't care less about the immortal laws of Bagsy. Fran was recovering from a hangover, as well as whatever cake it was, and Heidi watched over her while taking care of the blisters she had amassed. Fran's eyes slowly opened.

"Morning," said Heidi, technically during the afternoon.

"Ow!" muttered Fran.

"Do you remember what happened last night?" asked Heidi.

"I think so. I got way too drunk, and there was a moment where I thought I was hallucinating, but I think it was just my mind playing tricks on me."

Heidi dismissed Franchezca's brainfart and gave her some

water.

"Sorry for shouting at you in the bar," apologised Heidi.

"I'm sorry too," said Fran. "You were probably right about it being dangerous."

Interesting use of the word "probably," but Heidi was just happy to have the matter resolved.

It was fair to say Heidi had not enjoyed her trip to Udonia, and it was in this moment of self-reflection that she realised this trip was nothing but delaying the inevitable decision she would have to make about her employment. Heidi sighed, accepting defeat at the hands of a cruel yet mundane world, and went back to watching her friend. After a short time, a woman walked over and knelt down in front of Fran's bed.

"Is she satisfactory?" asked the woman in a stunted accent.

"No, she's sat in a bed," said Heidi, completely mishearing the question.

Heidi realised this woman wasn't a local as she didn't have the prerequisite number of ornaments in her face; it was also obvious that the woman was from a country much further away than Grenbourg. This woman, who was checking on Franchezca, was definitely a few years older than Heidi, but not by many; her clothes were worn down and ragged, and she wasn't what traditional standards would call clean, but she seemed to be the most friendly person Heidi had come across so far.

"She should drink this," proposed the woman.

The woman produced a flask and poured its contents into a small cup; the liquid was light blue and smelled of sour lemons.

Fran drank from the cup.

Fran immediately spat it out over Heidi.

At this point, Heidi was numb to the pain; what was one more drop of piss in this toilet of a situation, and she wiped herself clean.

"It's a medicine. You need it," explained the woman.

"Thank you," said Heidi.

"You are welcome. My name is Ulga. Are you travellers?"

"No. This is just a holiday."

"Very brave holiday," said Ulga with surprise. Heidi sighed at the acknowledgment that, even to an outsider, this was a bad idea. "Is this your first time away from home?"

"Yes," admitted Heidi. "What about you? Where do you come from?"

"I am from Hamani."

Heidi was shocked by that fact. "That's on the other side of the world!"

"I am big traveller."

Heidi thought for a moment. "Of all the places you've been to, how does this country compare?"

"It is interesting. There is no other country like this." Heidi looked over at her comatose friend and decided there was probably a reason for that. "Have you explored here?"

"I didn't want to. I don't think it's safe."

"Let me come with you then. I can show you interesting places."

Heidi looked over at Fran.

"Do not worry about her," assured Ulga. "She is safe here. We will bring her soup on way back."

Fran wasn't in any kind of state to answer questions at that time, but if the argument at the bar taught her anything, Fran did have Heidi's best interests at heart, even if her methods and final conclusions were misguided. Heidi left Fran to sleep while she went with Ulga to see whatever was interesting in Udonia, hopping the entire way in a sick-sodden shoe. Heidi trusted Ulga knew what she was doing; it would be hard to know less than Franchezca did, but Ulga seemed warm and caring. At some point Heidi didn't remember, she was holding on to Ulga's hand like a child, and once she realised it, wasn't sure if it would be more awkward to let go or keep holding on. After some time hobbling up a steep incline, Heidi noticed she was looking face to face with the god sculpture she had seen atop a mountain yesterday.

"Here we are," stated Ulga.

Heidi, seeing the statue up close now, realised it was much

more than a sculpture of an old god; it was a whole scene. Standing at the feet of the effigy was a stone table with treasure, food, and flowers arranged delicately, while statues of normal looking people in robes examined the items.

"Do you know who this is?" asked Heidi.

"No idea," confessed Ulga. "It looks nice, though."

Heidi had to admit that close up, the sculpture was immaculate. Standing towers and towers above Heidi's head, the stonework and detailing on every inch of the statue was immeasurable precise, almost as if someone from Grenbourg had made it, but it lacked the absence of free spirit that hallmarked Heidi's home nation. Heidi stared up at the colossus until she lost track of time, only being broken from her daydream when a small creature started climbing onto the table. The animal was a small, plump, brown speckled thing, almost like a tortoise or large cockroach, but what stuck out to Heidi was that it had a shell.

"That's the thing I ate!" shouted Heidi in excitement.

Ulga turned around in confusion. "What do you mean?"

"I ate one of those things in a restaurant yesterday, but I had no idea what it was before now."

Ulga looked at the climbing critter, then back to Heidi in some distaste.

"Is something wrong?" asked Heidi.

"That animal is almost extinct," explained Ulga.

Heidi suddenly felt immense guilt at her contribution to damaging the local ecosystem, but Ulga comforted her with the fact that it wasn't her fault. Heidi stayed at the statue for a while, and the occasional tourist passed by her, but no one stayed for more than a few minutes, while Heidi lost her entire afternoon theorising the history of the monument. As daylight started to slip away, Heidi and Ulga returned to the hostel, bringing Fran her much anticipated tomato soup. Heidi had ended the day very differently to the previous one: She wasn't the slightest bit fearful for the first time since arriving, she discovered something genuinely interesting, and, most thankfully, nothing bad had happened to her shoes.

The following day, Heidi and Fran boarded the airship back to Grenbourg. Fran had made a full recovery, or she thought she had before the transport started moving. A day's travel is not fun at the best of times, but try it while doing your best not to acknowledge the blood red pool that is caused by eating too much tomato soup. Once Heidi was home, she found books on her parents' shelves, and visited her local library for information regarding the statue back in Udonia. As it turned out, the sculpture was of an old god named Bilbrun, and represented a religion characterised by free spirit, and its followers were expected to live life for themselves. According to legend, Bilbrun flew around the world and collected treasures from foreign lands, before bringing them home and giving them to the community. When God let slip that he existed, and the whole world rioted to destroy all religious iconography, Udonian people, probably too high to realise what was going on at the time, left the statue up, and it remained one of the few truly ancient monuments of the world. For some reason, the name Bilbrun gave Heidi a nagging feeling in the back of her head, and upon checking, she realised she had heard the name at school during history classes, but in the legend she was taught, Bilbrun was actually a trickster thief, not a hero. Heidi realised that in the cultural divide between Grenbourg and Udonia, they had created completely different interpretations of the same basic story. Once Heidi realised this, she began trying to cross-reference the legend with other countries, and then new stories with other cultures, and then she became engrossed in completely different sights and scenes portrayed in the library books.

Before Heidi had realised it, she had spent the entire day reading about other countries.

There were civilisations Heidi had never heard of in school, and even these library books were disappointingly brief when it came to the finer details of international culture. Even Udonia, which Heidi knew by reputation, had a completely different side to it when she did the proper research. School had done very little to broaden her mind about the world outside this prison of protractors called Grenbourg, and Heidi wanted to see the entire world.

That was what she was going to do; Heidi was going to be a traveller.

The logistics of it could be worked out in time. Heidi had found her purpose: To learn about this weird and interesting world for herself.

***

Heidi lay on her bed, staring wistfully at the blank ceiling and thinking back to that trip she took with Fran all those years ago. Fran was getting married last time Heidi had heard from her, but how much else had changed in her life? How long had it been since the pair talked face to face? Heidi was drowning in a sense of longing nostalgia that can come when left alone with your thoughts for too long. No, thought Heidi. Think positive. Look to the future. Where am I going to travel to next? Heidi thought continuing south was the best idea since she was already close to the southernmost point of the continent, but she preferred the warm climates of the north, and thought about the golden deserts she had passed through before. No, thought Heidi again. That's in the past. I want something new. Heidi took a deep breath and exhaled; she was having a hard time fighting the longing urge to return home and see her old friends and family. Eventually, Heidi caved into her emotions and sank into sentimentality; she missed her parents, her brother, Franchezca, Uncle John, Mad Aunty Lin, everyone really. One of the hardest parts of travelling was the goodbyes. Heidi glanced around her flat looking for a piece of paper and a pencil, and she started writing her thoughts down in a letter addressed to her old home.

"Hey. I wanted to let you know I'm still doing well. I'm still in Pending, and it looks like I might be here a while longer. I got to see the river blossom festival at last. It was so much better than it looks in any of the paintings. I also discovered that some people in Pending live on small boats called narrowboats, and they just float downstream their whole life.

How are things back in Grenbourg? Has Fran got married yet? Even though I work for a newspaper, I don't hear a lot of international news. I want to know how everyone is, so please write back to me soon. It's kind of lonely being so far from home.

Hugs and kisses.

I miss you.

-Heidi."

CHAPTER EIGHT

Home Away From Home

Alcohol: Probably God's biggest mistake in creating Flatrock. Alcohol is created when certain organic materials like fruit decompose under specific conditions. Decompose, if we should define it, is a word that can also mean decay or rot, and most creatures were created by God in a way to make rotten food taste bad to avoid harmful bacteria and toxins from entering their bodies; the same is true of alcohol, which tastes bitter and burns your throat. Unfortunately, the sense of giddiness from ingesting alcohol greatly outweighed the flavour. The love of alcohol became so ravenous, that people tried to create ways to make the effects more potent, which is why the chemical is almost always in liquid form in the modern age. People were so busy trying to get drunk that they didn't even think about creating glass receptacles to keep it in until thousands of years later. Alcohol quickly became a multicultural phenomenon, used as a way to celebrate, relax, and (less popularly) to clean. Some cultures in Flatrock have even created a twisted sense of pride with how much of the toxin they can ingest without vomiting, going as far as to create drinking games and have competitions. Alcohol was discovered early in the development of intelligent life on Flatrock (although the definition of intelligent is up for debate), so it's difficult to say in this age how much alcohol has affected society, but with almost every culture indulging in the pastime of shit-facery, it's fair to say the impact is large.

There are five stages of drunkenness, which I shall illustrate with a story involving Milo. Milo was at The Devil's Neckhole, and it was populated by the usual class of bigots, barbarians, and broken-hearted berks, swimming in their seas of self-destruction. Milo entered the building sober; this is considered the first stage. While sober, you are running at your maximum mental capacity, and any mistake you make can only be blamed on yourself.

The second stage you experience is tipsy. Being tipsy is the awkward tightrope people walk when drinking; everyone aspires to be tipsy, as it's a state in which you still have most of your senses about you, but are buzzed enough to reap the benefits of alcohol. Milo started with half a pint of brandy, having developed quite the tolerance after spending half his lifetime enjoying liquid anarchy; this took him to the point most people desire to be. The problem with tipsy is that it's hard to maintain, and over time, you slowly become more sober, so for someone to stay tipsy, they have to drink alcohol of the right potency at regular intervals to stay buzzed. If you drink too fast (which happens more often than not), you fall off the tightrope and land in the not-so-safety net of stage three: Drunk.

While it's possible to go from stage two to one very easily, dropping from stage three is nearly impossible, and only stages four and five await you. Milo's next drink was ouzo and limoncello in pints, a combination he called "cheeky lemonade." This turned Milo from the mild-mannered mess he usually is into captain catastrophe. Milo screamed and shouted, laughed and cried, told people he loved them then told those same people he hated them, the usual range of emotions that any sober person would consider some kind of mental disorder. Another side effect of drunkenness is beer googles: The condition in which alcohol makes you attracted to someone you would normally consider a "Grade 'A' Minger." Even Milo, whose interest in the opposite sex was comparable to the amount of interest a politician shows the homeless, found a woman who had taken his breath away.

No, wait, he was being strangled.

He didn't know what had triggered the reaction; maybe the off handed comment about her dress looking like a fox scraped along the road from the back of a diarrhetic horse, but he wasn't sure.

Maybe she was just a knob.

Milo acted in a similar fashion for the rest of the night, acting like a wasp without a sting, or a sociopath without a political party to join. There was no working brain function behind Milo's actions, like so many drunks, which is how they end up in stage four: How did I get here?

Stage four usually happens the morning after drinking, the moment you say the question "How did I get here?" Some people wake up in an unfamiliar bedroom, others, a park bench.

Milo woke up in a basement.

This definitely wasn't his home, nor was it anyone's he knew. The only light in this cellar was through cracks in the boards of the ceiling, which reflected off barrels and boxes that Milo was surrounded by. Milo's world was still rocking side to side, he couldn't walk straight, and was close to vomiting; he didn't often carry last night's dizziness through to the morning, and concluded his age must be affecting his ability to stave off hangovers. There was a chilly breeze in the basement, unusual, but Milo had bigger problems to worry about. Milo stumbled up the ladder that led to what seemed to be a trap door, and swung it open.

Oh no, he thought.

This building didn't have any ceiling; Milo was staring up at the sky, the walls were only a few feet tall, and everything was made of wood as soggy as a hooker's pants. Surrounding him were about half a dozen people dressed in thick jackets and trousers, and almost everyone had a full beard. Milo wanted to retreat back into the cellar, but someone had already seen him. The man, much bigger than Milo, didn't say anything, just watched like a pervert does a crack in the bedroom curtains. Milo tentatively emerged from the cellar fully, and felt a chill breeze against his face. Now standing at full height, Milo could see clearly where he was.

Milo was in the middle of the ocean.

At some point last night, Milo travelled all the way to Dorcoast and boarded a merchant ship, and judging by the cold expression by the now full crew looking at him, he hadn't been invited. Milo stood still in the middle of the boat for a while until one of the men shouted to him.

"Co kun duer hawn?"

Oh no. They didn't speak the same language.

Milo didn't even recognise the language.

Milo had no idea where he was, where he was going, and how to communicate to the few people who might help him. This is stage five of drunkenness: Regret.

Milo had to think what to do. Speaking was useless. Writing was useless. He was useless, but that was beside the point. After a while, Milo decided to rely on the internationally recognised language of miming things you think would correspond to words.

Milo waved his hand once as an attempt of a greeting. The crew of the ship kept staring and didn't respond.

Milo pointed to himself and shrugged his shoulders. In his mind, this would tell the crew he was lost, but that much was already clear.

"Do you understand me?" tried Milo.

One of the crew shouted, "Tuncup!" After a minute, a man emerged from what Milo assumed were sleeping quarters. Milo was confident this new man was the captain; he could tell because he wore a hat. The man who had shouted spoke a bit more to the captain, hopefully explaining the situation. When that was finished, the captain spoke.

"You look like you've just walked in on your parents having it off," said the captain. "What are you doing here?"

"I don't know," answered Milo. "I think I boarded your ship by accident. Can you take me back to Dorcoast?"

"No."

Milo wasn't expecting such a direct response.

"What?" asked Milo.

"We're not going back that way," confirmed the captain.

Milo's eyes widened. "Really?"

"We're travelling home to Nunca. Tomorrow, we sail north."

Nunca was a place Milo could point out on a map, as it wasn't very far away from Pending; the issue was that Nunca was an island, and the only way of returning was by boat.

"Can you not go back now?" pleaded Milo.

"I'm on a schedule. You can find your own way back," asserted the captain.

"Isn't there any other option?"

"I could throw you overboard."

Milo swallowed. "It's always nice to have a choice."

Milo sat on the deck until the boat docked at Nunca. His only possessions were his wallet, which didn't have a lot left in it, the clothes he was wearing, and a serious case of seasickness. Milo was incredibly nervous; he had no way of getting back to Pending any time soon, which meant he desperately needed to find food and shelter, which could be difficult considering he didn't understand the language, and mime can only get you so far. In terms of Nunca itself, Milo only knew what he read in history books: The island was invaded some centuries ago during a small war, but in a twist of fate, despite the occupiers of Nunca losing, when treaties were officially drafted, the victors accidentally made no mention of the island. The losing side kept their mouth shut, and by all international rights, were allowed to keep the territory. Not a bad deal considering the original war was only concerned with a slightly unfair trade deal, but this information was ultimately useless unless the job Milo went for was a primary school history teacher. After several hours, well past midday, the boat docked on the pier of Nunca. The sailors immediately worked on moving the stock of items from below deck while the captain started talking to someone who probably worked in trading. Milo knew he couldn't let the only person who would understand him slip away, and decided to ask for help.

"Excuse me," started Milo, "but can I ask a favour?"

"You want a lot of favours today, don't you?" replied the captain, not turning around from his business.

"I need somewhere to stay. Do you know where I could go?"

The captain thought for a moment, then for a split second, Milo thought he saw him smile, before quickly suppressing it.

"Look for a place called Gunkar's Fafia, it's about a mile that way," answered the captain, pointing into town.

"What is Gunkar's Fafia?" asked Milo.

"Gunkar owns the place. Fafia means hotel," answered the captain.

Milo became slightly relieved he at least knew that he had a bed for the night. The sailors all disbanded shortly after the conversation, and now Milo was in a more stable headspace, he could see exactly where he was. The first thing Milo noticed was the buildings; every one of them was brightly painted and decorated, like it was some kind of competition to see who could do the most damage to house prices in the local area. The town immediately from the pier opened up into a plaza, with stalls and sellers all around, although the smells of freshly baked bread and cakes that usually fill these kinds of markets was overwhelmed by the smoked saltwater fish. The shops seemed to be closing, so Milo ran to one that was still trading; he tried to buy something, but his money was no good. Milo was directed through some elaborate hand movements (one of which was definitely the sign for wanker) where to exchange his currency, but by the time that was done, it was becoming dark, and the shops were all gone. Milo kicked a wall in rage, and had he wished to hurt his own toes, it would have been the most productive thing he had done all day. Pending's and Nunca's weather were very similar (cold and crap), so Milo made haste to reach Gunkar's Fafia as fast as possible. On his jog, Milo felt like he was being watched the whole time; this island didn't seem like the kind of place to attract tourists or foreigners, and Milo's naivety was frightfully obvious. Overall, Nunca felt less modern than the mainland; there weren't any street lamps to light the paths at night, and the clothes people wore looked very basic; function was prioritised heavily over personal taste, much like alcohol. Milo thought the captain needed a better sense of direction, because it was definitely more than a mile before he reached the hotel he was looking for. Gunkar's Fafia was a tall block of flats, but every building on the island seemed to be that way, so that wasn't very surprising. The hotel was painted pink and adorned with hearts, like it was a present for the most obnoxious little girl in the world. Outside seemed to be some kind of price list, and Milo was so grateful that numbers were still written in the way he understood. Milo thought his best option was the cheapest, and he could afford a single bed room for three nights. Milo walked into the establishment and was almost knocked off his feet immediately, having smelt what was uncannily similar to the market he passed before. Knowing a beggar can't be a chooser, Milo walked up to the receptionist, pointed on the board what we wanted, and handed over the money. The receptionist smiled and gave Milo a key, before saying something he didn't understand and pointing at the stairs. Milo walked up the stairs and found his room, and for a split second, he wished he hadn't. As well as being quite gaudy and having unidentifiable stains all over the place, he really didn't like the fact that he could taste the air. There could have been a murdered body in that room, and it would only be the third thing Milo would complain about. Milo lied down on the bed and tried to make himself comfortable. After about five minutes, a woman walked through the door. Milo didn't realise he'd have to share the room, especially considering there was one bed, but he had paid now and there was little to do about it now.

"Buna," said the woman smiling.

Milo gave a courteous nod, not knowing what she said.

"Uni alm Tola," added the woman.

Milo repeated his action.

This woman was not tall or short, nor fat or thin, but looked strong. Her clothes seemed somewhat expensive compared to most of the town's folk, enriched with coloured ribbons and patterns, and it was odd to Milo why someone who could afford to dress like that would be in this hotel. Her face and long red hair were also heavily made up, only adding to the confusion, but the woman was smiling, and clearly friendly, so Milo didn't believe there was any reason to worry; he thought if he could stay out of her way and make do with the bare minimum conversation, he would get out of this unscarred. Milo decided to move off the bed for the woman and sat down on a sofa to the side of the room, but for some reason, the woman followed and sat beside him, seating herself a little closer to Milo than was comfortable for him. The woman spoke some more words that Milo didn't understand, and grabbed him gently by the arm. Milo was beginning to worry that he had accidentally bought a room with a creeper; this wasn't how people acted in Pending. Milo was at a level of discomfort that rearranging the cushions was not going to help; he considered the possibility that this was some kind of Nunca tradition, or maybe the culture was just radically different, but up until now, it didn't seem like the island had been so weird. This was one of those moments where Heidi's experience with foreign cultures would have been really helpful, but she wasn't here, and this situation didn't seem like it would resolve itself unless Milo did something.

"Can you understand me?" asked Milo nervously.

The woman clearly didn't, and she continued to cuddle up to Milo. Milo sat stock still with eyes wide, worried any movement could provoke a reaction, but this kind of thinking generally only works when attacked by a grizzly bear. It wasn't long until the woman started kissing Milo on the cheek.

Milo was extremely worried now.

The woman tried to turn his head so they were facing, but Milo resisted. Unfortunately, this woman really was strong, and succeeded soon enough. The woman tried kissing Milo on the lips, but he didn't return the favour. When she realised, she backed away and looked at Milo confused.

"Kun bom?" the woman said.

Milo put up his hand as if miming to stop.

The woman tentatively started holding hands with him.

Both of them looked incredibly confused.

Milo backed as far to the other end of the sofa as he could and tried to mime he wanted to be alone, but the message didn't seem to be getting through. Milo then tried to explain he would sleep on the sofa, and the woman could use the bed, but this confused the woman more. Eventually, the woman stopped the discussion and commanded Milo to focus.

The woman pointed at Milo.

Then the woman pointed at herself.

Finally, she pounded her fists together.

Milo suddenly clicked things into place.

This was a brothel.

"I'm sorry, I think there's been a terrible mistake," said Milo, suddenly forgetting the language barrier and backing his way to the door. "I'm going to leave now. I hope you have a good day. Bye-bye. Bye. Bye."

Milo walked through the door and the second it was closed, he bolted into the street. Milo's face was flush with embarrassment, and he swore profusely; he was *not* going to stay for three nights. Milo was in such disbelief about what had happened that he completely forgot that he no longer had anywhere to sleep, nor did he have the money to pay for another hotel. When Milo calmed himself down a long time later, he found a field away from civilization, and tried to sleep on a dry patch of grass.

The next day came and Milo barely slept at all; the night was too cold, and every half an hour or so, he had to go for a walk to warm his body up again, only to get another half hour sleep. On the positive side of things though, being awake for so long gave

Milo more thinking time, and had developed a plan to get back home. The price of a ferry ride back to Dorcoast wasn't cheap, but what was cheaper was international post. If he could send a letter to Hazel, she could send him the money to get back, and repay her when he returned. Milo also knew he needed a job to get the funds, and if needs be, he would live rough until he could get home; basic food would suffice, and Milo was forever tentative of hotels thanks to yesterday. Speaking of which, Milo also spent ample time wondering how to take revenge on that boat captain the next time they crossed paths, but one step at a time. The biggest issue with this plan was actually finding a job. His primary skill was in writing, which isn't exactly helpful in a country that uses a different language. Preferably, Milo needed something that meant he could stay quiet; maybe a library? Actually, a library could be good for something else, thought Milo. Milo thought maybe he could find some kind of phrase book, or language dictionary; there must be one somewhere. It was no good looking up job adverts when he didn't know what he was signing up for; he definitely didn't want to be on the other side of the bedroom in another Gunkar's Fafia. The list of objectives was this: Find a library with a phrase book, then find somewhere that advertised jobs, like a newspaper or shop window.

Crap, thought Milo.

Milo let out a big sigh when he realised what his mission entailed; he had walked the streets over and over again, but still didn't know what half these buildings were. He was tired and couldn't read the signs, but he was desperate; Milo needed to find a library. Milo felt he only had one choice: Trial and error. Milo searched for every building with a sign, looked through every window he could, and walked through every door that wasn't locked; this wasn't the best idea considering some people had their homes in the same building complexes as some businesses, so more than once walked in on a family having breakfast. The families were often scared to hell, but Milo was so tired and infuriated that any cause for embarrassment was superseded by the stronger emotions; if Nunca didn't have any fairy tales to frighten children, he may well become one. The fact that every building was a block of flats didn't help matters, as Milo had to climb and descend every set of stairs, but getting through this situation was all that needed to be done; when it was over, he would never have to look back. After several hours, walking in on pet shops, home catering companies, and one person who dared to combine the two, Milo found a library.

Now to take a guess where the correct book was.

There were categories, but par for the course, these foreigners insisted on writing in their own language. Milo went to every shelf in turn, chose a book, opened it, and if there wasn't any word he recognised, he moved to the next section. Rob would probably know what most of these books were, or at least understand the cataloguing system, but Milo realised if he was starting to miss Rob, he really was desperate to get home. After a good while, Milo had in his hands the book he was looking for: A word-to-word dictionary. The book was in alphabetical order of the local language, so reverse engineering what Milo wanted to say would be too time consuming, but it would be enough to translate job adverts. Milo walked up to the main desk and put the book in front of the librarian .

"Due kun habben lindersh map?" said the librarian.

The librarian put out her hand as if wanting something. Milo was a bit confused, considering libraries back home gave books for free; maybe he had walked into a bookshop accidentally, but he couldn't see any price labels anywhere. Milo opened up his wallet and looked at the remaining change he had. Milo tentatively took half the coins out and handed them over. The librarian looked at the coins and then back to Milo.

"Co on unpe?" said the librarian with a confused tone.

Milo clearly hadn't paid enough, and bit his tongue before handing over the remaining coins. The librarian looked at the money for a moment, counted them, and handed the book over. Milo was relieved; he ran out the door and downstairs to find the nearest newsagents.

It was only a few minutes later that he realised she probably wanted a library card.

Milo literally had no money at this point, spending everything on a prostitute he didn't sleep with, and a book that was free. He hadn't eaten anything for the last day besides a half-finished apple, and a twig (which lacked proper seasoning). It was around the middle of the afternoon by the time Milo found a shop with what seemed to be adverts in the window; most of them were advertising businesses, and were properly printed, but there were others that were handwritten, which in Pending, would be simple household jobs. Milo opened up his new dictionary and worked on deciphering the adverts. The first job Milo translated was for a "recreation attendant," but Milo didn't like the sound of watching other people be happy when he was only a few more poor decisions away from finding the nearest serial killer and asking them for directions. Another job was titled "sales assistant advisor's apprentice," which meant bugger all to Milo. Would he be helping the person who helps the person who helps someone buy things? This was something probably not worth remembering. One job Milo knew he had no chance with was for building work. Regardless of qualifications, Milo was incredibly skinny, and hadn't exercised his muscles to any intense degree since discovering masturbation; the only thing his body was truly good for was being a meal for a cannibal on a diet, so he decided against that job instantly. The selection seemed to be a bit crap, and nothing paid well by the looks of it, but Milo had to take something. There was one job that Milo was considering: A housekeeping position. The job was the worst paying of them all, but it came with live-in accommodation. As much as Milo swore he would live rough, he felt a cold coming on, and he would struggle to keep any job if he started looking any more like a tramp. Realistically, Milo was not getting out of Nunca quickly, and he needed a place to live. Milo noted the address, and walked towards the home; he knew it wouldn't take too long to get there having walked around the island enough times by this point to learn the street names, which felt more like a curse than a blessing. It was late in the afternoon when Milo came face to face with the bottom floor flat's door. Milo took a deep breath and tried to create something as closely resembling a smile that he could physically muster, but he was never good at hiding his true emotions, especially of the blinding rage variety. Milo knocked on the door and waited for a second before someone answered.

"Buna," said the red-haired woman Milo recognised.

It was the hooker he had met the night before.

Milo's painted smile washed away in shock. The woman, who's name Milo realised he had never learned, also recognised him, and glared him down with a completely stoic face, but it was easy to tell what she thought. This was the first time Milo had met someone who was annoyed because he hadn't slept with them; usually they were annoyed because he did. Milo didn't know the word for sorry (like most men), so tried to move to the job at hand.

"Husmel Jabu," said Milo, believing he said something along the lines of "housekeeping job."

"Slaba Un?" replied the woman.

Milo had no idea what the woman just said; he hadn't accounted for a job interview. Milo mimed to excuse himself and opened up the dictionary again, trying to work out what he just heard. It was while looking up the words that the woman stole the book and looked at the cover. Upon realising what the book was, the woman looked at Milo slightly despondent.

"Husmel Jabu," said the woman with proper pronunciation.

The woman bonked Milo on the head with the dictionary, like a teacher telling off a student. Milo rubbed his head as the attack actually hurt. The woman started paging through the book, and soon after, showed Milo a page, pointing out the word "name." Milo assumed this was a question so told the woman his name. The woman pointed to herself and said, "Tola," so Milo finally had a way to refer to her with a title that was a little more courteous than "that hooker." Tola then called out, and Milo saw a very small boy, about six years-old with blonde hair and snot crusting his lips, running out of a room far down the hallway.

Tola and the boy spoke, making passing glances at Milo, which made him nervous. When they finished chatting, the child looked at Milo.

"Uni alm Dodek," said the boy proudly.

Milo realised Dodek was the child's name, since his dictionary was already open on the right page. Milo wasn't good with kids, and even ignoring the language barrier, he didn't understand them past their love of anything sugary or nugget shaped.

"Uni alm Milo," said Milo, copying the kid as best as he could.

Dodek laughed at Milo for reasons that were unclear, but that was nothing new. Tola let Dodek go back to playing, and she led Milo into the kitchen. Tola's home was nice (in theory). Much like the street, the flat was basic, with the floor, walls, and ceiling all being varnished wood, but it was warm, and if it wasn't for Tola's frosty reception, it may have been comforting. Where it failed as a nice home was the mess. Granted, Milo knew there was a housekeeping job for a reason, but there's a distinct difference between having sticky floors, and not being able to walk without losing a shoe. Dodek's toys and clothes were littered about the place, and whatever slime children produced was caked on the walls. The one area of the flat that seemed to be nice was the kitchen. The kitchen had a wood burner crackling, with some kind of stew bubbling away on the stove, and the sugary smell reminded Milo how little he had eaten recently; he would have dropped his head into the pot if it wasn't for the fact he needed to be polite. The home was quaint; the kind of place an estate agent would describe as "Retro chic," which is code for "old fashioned, but not a castle." Milo and Tola sat at the dinner table, and Tola started writing something. Milo glanced around the kitchen while this was happening, and noticed an oak rack full of liquor bottles, which wasn't surprising. A mother's first priority is always their child; their second priority is wine. When Tola had finished writing, she handed over the piece of paper and the language dictionary, instructing Milo to work out the message. Translating in this fashion was very slow, but eventually, Milo worked out the paper said something along the lines of:

"I go to work at night.

You look after Dodek and clean.

If you hurt my son, they will never find your body."

Milo looked Tola in the eyes. She was dead serious.

Milo slowly nodded his head to show he understood, and Tola seemed pleased enough.

Tola examined Milo's outfit as well before writing on the paper a sentence that translated to "Do you have fresh clothes?" In the rush of the day, walking back and forth so much, Milo had completely forgotten he had slept in dirt last night, wearing the same clothes that he was right now. Milo couldn't smell himself, and until now, made no consideration to other people that he might be a walking pollutant. Milo shook his head to the question, so Tola brought him to a small room with nothing but a bed and a wardrobe in it; this was probably where Milo was going to sleep tonight, assuming he could do that with one eye open. Tola opened the wardrobe and gave Milo a box of clothes before walking out of the room and shutting the door. Milo couldn't help himself but collapse on the bed, staring at the ceiling and thinking about everything that led to this point. Milo was feeling guilty about this act of charity, especially considering the person giving it barely looked him in the eyes without murderous intent. It didn't help matters that Milo still hadn't learned the words for please and thank you yet, and he couldn't help but feel incredibly rude for visiting the prostitute's house he walked out on without giving a reason why he wouldn't have sex with her. Milo didn't mean to cause offence, if that's what this hostility was about, but that dictionary was not an adequate tool for learning a new language. Milo stood up from the bed, realising only at that moment he hadn't changed his shirt yet, and had covered the sheets in mud; he only had enough energy to huff at his own disappointment. Milo undressed to put on the clean clothes, and with how big they were, it was like wearing a three-man tent, before returning to the kitchen and finding the family. Milo bowed, not exactly sure how to mime thank you, and tried to smile. Tola looked at Milo annoyed and walked over to him. The man screwed up his eyes as Tola approached, not sure what she was going to do, before she sorted out his tucked in shirt collar. Milo sighed in relief; after seeing Tola go for his neck, he thought she was going to strangle him; she then pointed to the pot of stew and said something. Milo nodded, believing (hoping) he was invited to dinner. Milo sat at the table, where Dodek was already waiting. The child stared at Milo like he had a diamond the size of an apple on his face, but he tried not to pay the kid too much attention. Unfortunately, Dodek didn't like being ignored, and started pulling at Milo's sleeve. When Milo turned around, Dodek pretended to not be looking, staring straight ahead, as if a particular section of wall could be the most interesting thing in the room. Milo looked away again, and Dodek pulled his sleeve again. The routine repeated, and Milo stared at Dodek, who somehow kept a completely straight face. If Tola really did kill Milo, this kid wouldn't give away anything. Milo looked away again, and waited for his sleeve to get pulled. When Milo felt the tugging on his shirt, without even looking Dodek's way, he leant over and tapped the kid on his far shoulder. The child fell for the trick and looked to his side. Milo instinctively shouted, "HA!" and Dodek spun around to face the prankster. Milo turned away as if to deny it, but he wasn't as good at hiding his facial expressions as the miniature mod boss, and couldn't resist taking a quick glance at him to see his face. Before Dodek could retaliate, Tola had served up some kind of poached cabbage parcels. Milo hadn't seen any dish like this back in Pending, and when he cut into the parcel, the cabbage burst ~~like one of Tola's patrons~~, and chunks of beef flowed out. Milo wanted to dive in, but he let the other two take a bite first; that way, he would know if the stew was poisoned. It was at this point Milo started to realise he might be paranoid, and took a big bite of his meal. Milo wasn't sure if it was the flavour, or the two days without food, but it tasted amazing. The beef melted like chocolate, and the leaves of cabbage were coated in some kind of syrup that could turn athletes into slobs. As much as Milo loved the meal, and as hungry as he was, there was far too much on his plate to finish everything. When Tola saw Milo's plate still had food on it, and he wasn't eating it, she pointed at the plate and said something. Milo worked on the context clues and believed he was being asked if he was going to finish his meal. Milo held his hand up as if to say he had had enough.

Bad move.

Tola's nostrils flared, parental senses shouting that you must eat everything on your plate. Even Dodek looked at Milo as if to say "your fate has been sealed." Milo realised he had committed a faux pas, and forced himself to eat another mouthful. Tola seemed to calm down after that, but was still watching. Milo forced himself to finish the meal, not even sure if the food was reaching his stomach with how close it was to overflowing. The tension in the room relaxed, although the tension of Milo's stomach was at a critical point. One sudden movement, and chunks of dead cow would be covering the walls, and as the new cleaner, he would have to take care of it. Once Milo was confident enough that he could move without spilling himself, he washed the dishes while Tola and Dodek relaxed in the living room. Milo spied on the family, and saw they were both playing with some kind of castle building blocks, or Dodek was, while Tola made suggestions that would make the structure not look like the content of Milo's stomach. The two of them seemed content, and Milo didn't want to intrude, so he retreated to his room, feeling out of place, and stayed there until the morning. Milo heard Tola leave at one point, and thought he should check on Dodek, just in case he'd been stabbed so he'd know to run as fast as possible. Luckily, the child was fine. It crossed Milo's mind if Dodek knew what his mother did for a job, or if it was even taboo in this country, but best not find out lest he have to explain the birds and bees, especially considering he'd have to convey it through mime. It soon became late, and after settling his overwhelmingly gassy stomach, Milo fell asleep.

Milo woke up fairly early, but being a guest, he didn't want to leave his room until someone else was awake. After hearing someone move about, Milo left his bedroom, and found Dodek in the kitchen, who was standing on a chair with his hand in yesterday's casserole pot. Tola instructed Milo not to wash the pot yesterday, but didn't give a reason; he now saw that Tola had let some more cabbage parcels soak in the stock overnight, and Dodek was fishing them out for breakfast. Dodek didn't use a plate, and the cabbage was still dripping with whatever liquid it was stewed in onto the floor. Milo knew he was here to clean, but watching a crime in action was something he couldn't stand by and do nothing about.

Dodek saw Milo, but didn't see any problem with what he was doing.

Milo realised he was staring, and Dodek realised Milo was staring.

Dodek worked out why Milo was staring, and had an idea.

The child put his hand in the now cold stock and lifted out a cupped hand of the liquid.

Milo shook his head to tell Dodek no.

Dodek nodded his head to tell Milo yes.

Milo tried to grab the child before he could ruin the floor even more, but Dodek saw the approach, and threw the cabbage water in Milo's face. Dodek laughed hard. Milo wiped his face of the stock and stared down the child, then without breaking eye contact, took another cabbage parcel from the pot, and held it over Dodek's head, letting it drip over him. Cold broth trickled down the child's back and made him wince. Once Dodek had regained control of himself, he used both hands to splash the stock over Milo, and without realising it, the two of them were splashing each other with cold cabbage water, and it quickly turned from a fight into a competition. Milo was smarter, and had the idea to separate some cabbage leaves as wet flannels, but

Dodek was more nimble, and took advantage of stealth tactics. Very quickly, the battle had both of them rubbing their soaked hands over each other's faces and laughing maniacally.

This didn't please Tola, who had watched it all happen.

Milo and Dodek both became incredibly embarrassed, and stopped the fight without a conclusive winner. Dodek stood up first and said something to his mother. Milo didn't say anything, unsure what the child just told his mother. That was stupid of me, thought Milo, but of the decisions he had made so far during this trip, this one only just broke his top three. Tola took both of them by the hand over to the sink, before taking a wet flannel and washing both of their faces. Milo wasn't used to the over-motherly treatment, and thought if this was how Tola treated everyone, he started to understand why she was single. Some time later, once everyone was cleaned and breakfast was eaten in the usual fashion, Tola left with Dodek, who was now wearing a dark green school uniform. Tola had left a list of things Milo needed to do, and he went on translating it. When Tola returned a while later, she went to her bedroom and, from the sounds of things, went straight to sleep. Milo realised it must be difficult to raise a child while working nights, especially Dodek, and tried to clean the flat as quietly as possible. Milo had worked as a housekeeper before moving to Pending, and he still remembered all the weird tricks his supervisors taught him, like using vinegar to get rid of lingering smells. Milo started wondering if Gunkar's Fafia would pay for this kind of treatment, before concluding that everything has their limits. At some point in the afternoon, Tola had woken up and went to retrieve Dodek from school, and when they returned, Dodek ran straight to Milo and tugged on his arm. Milo followed Dodek to the living room, where the kid proceeded to show Milo every single toy he owned. Milo had cleaned up all of them during the day, but the corpses of dishevelled teddy bears resurfaced quickly. Dodek talked his mouth off, but Milo still had no understanding of the language except a few words; it was like watching a lecture about cooking when all your meals come out of a bin. At some point in the evening, completely losing track of time, Dodek produced a poster for some kind of festival. There were words on the poster, but Milo didn't understand any of it; he had no idea if this was some kind of fairground or carnival, or if it was traditional, or just a fun day out, but Dodek was pulling at his shirt like he was trying to wake someone up from a coma, so seemed determined to have Milo join him. The festival was still weeks away, and Milo hoped he'd be gone by then, but Tola was in the room, and Milo was still quite dependent on his trachea. Whatever Milo was being asked, he agreed to it, and Dodek cheered. The rest of the day's events repeated like they had yesterday, and Milo went to sleep.

The next few days went by with little to no difficulty. Tola paid Milo daily, and was about half way to sending a letter back home. Milo really worried about what was happening back in Pending; he had interviews lined up, and a hospital appointment he'd missed, but thinking about it, he was fine with not going to a place populated by the sick, deranged, and mentally fatigued; he didn't mind missing the hospital appointment either. To be fair, being stranded in an unfamiliar country did have some benefits; the biggest one probably being he didn't have to listen to people's "nothing conversations," by which I mean discussions completely devoid of anything functional, funny or interesting; as much as Milo already didn't enjoy talking to people, conversations involving where the time had gone, how much something cost, or complaining about how many crisps were in a bag were some of a multitude of things Milo was pleased to not be a part of anymore. Dodek insisted on playing with and pranking Milo every day since the cabbage fight, and it seemed Milo's role had changed from a cleaner to a nanny. Tola still didn't speak/mime with Milo very much besides basic instructions, but it felt like things were as good as they were going to be. Tola left for work early one evening, and Dodek was still very much awake. Dodek played in the living room while Milo sat with him, making as much effort to seem excited as he could; Tola's fake interest seemed so effortless by comparison. Dodek was building some kind of wagon track using wood blocks in the shape of roads and bridges, taking immense enjoyment in crashing the wagon, and ruining the lives of the fictional occupants like some bored god. Milo tried to fix some of the out of place tracks, but ended up breaking it more by accident, which seemed to annoy Dodek.

"You're an idiot," said Dodek.

Milo looked at the child shocked. "What did you say?"

"You're an idiot."

Why did this kid suddenly know Milo's language? Milo hadn't spoken much, if at all, while staying with Tola, and it never even crossed his mind that the child might know his language. The validity of the insult could wait a minute; Milo took this chance and spoke as he normally would.

"Can you understand me?" asked Milo.

The child pulled a face that showed he didn't know those words.

"Where did you learn that?" asked Milo, becoming very desperate.

Dodek again didn't fully understand the question. Milo had to think for a minute; this was potentially a massive breakthrough for him. Milo hadn't let the dictionary out of his sight, so the kid didn't learn from there. Soon enough Milo had an idea.

"Hello," said Milo.

"Hello," replied Dodek.

Dodek wasn't just mimicking; he definitely knew something more than insults; Milo just had to find out from where he learnt it. Wait a second, the school! Where else could he have learnt it? Milo tried a couple of phrases and hoped Dodek would follow.

"School book?" asked Milo.

The child went away and came back with a homework book, and it was written in Milo's language. Milo hadn't been to school in years; he had completely forgotten that kids learn languages there, probably because too much of his long term memory was still being occupied by sine, cosine, and tangent (whatever they were; he couldn't remember exactly). Milo opened the book and looked inside; it was full of basic phrases that had been translated back and forth from both languages. Milo knew he had a valuable resource, and started reading. Dodek realised he was now being ignored, and retaliated by sitting next to Milo and going through the whole book with him. Dodek insisted on saying everything out loud, and going through the book in order, and wouldn't let Milo move on until he had finished, which was annoying considering some segments were quite pointless; Milo found the chapters on colours and animals particularly useless. Milo did know some foreign language when he was a young teenager, but it had completely left his brain now; he had known people who tried to speak a new language as an adult, but if we're being honest, all they did was learn the swear words. As arduous as the process was, Milo finally learned to properly say hello, goodbye, please, thank you, and a lot of other general terms everyone needs to know. Milo still didn't know where Dodek had learned the word idiot, but maybe he had a cool teacher. Before Milo had realised it, Tola had returned from work and was standing in the doorway; he looked out the window and saw it was well past dark. Tola shouted something a little too loud for the middle of the night, clearly telling off the boys for not going to sleep. Dodek showed the workbook to his mother and said Milo's name some way into the sentence. Tola and Dodek both stared at Milo.

"Un bruno," said Milo, having now learned to say I'm sorry properly.

Milo stood up and ushered Dodek to go to bed. Dodek sulked past his mother and Milo gave the school book to Tola, before going to his own room.

Milo woke up the next morning and walked into the kitchen, as was his pattern now, but Tola and Dodek were already there, which was out of the ordinary. Tola usually woke up only after Dodek made some horrible noise, but that hadn't happened today. The room was immediately uncomfortable for Milo; everyone's facial expressions were too clean, rehearsed even. What was about to happen? Milo prepared to dive away, just in case this was the time of his murder. Once Milo had inched himself far enough into the room, Tola looked his way.

"Kun Acar Onbyt?" said Tola.

This was the first time Tola had ever said a direct sentence to Milo without writing it down, but he knew what she said, and it was almost empowering now being able to understand basic sentences, spoiled only by the knowledge that this put him in similar standings as a four-year old. Milo answered "sa," meaning yes, knowing he had just been asked if he wanted breakfast. Tola then continued talking, going through a list of food stuffs, in fact, every food Tola mentioned was in the school book. Was Milo being tested? Milo answered the questions, and received his breakfast soon after; it was like training a dog, but it worked. Milo suddenly felt more confident about speaking, even if the only questions he really had committed to memory were "what's your name?" "where do you live?" and "how old are you?" which don't so easily slip into conversation when you've been living with someone for the best part of a week. The usual scene then followed: Dodek went to school as normal and Tola left Milo his pay, along with a new to-do list. Milo noticed the list had a few new tasks on it, and after translating it, he found out he had been asked to go shopping. Did Tola really trust Milo that much? Granted he could understand the list, but conversing with strangers was a different thing; they wouldn't understand his situation, especially considering Milo hadn't learned the swear words to accurately convey it. Milo summoned up the confidence to go out into the real world and test his new skill, and it could definitely be said that you need more than one day's teaching to properly learn a language. Milo found that merchants in Nunca love to haggle, and they aggressively lowered the price of their products whenever Milo said he didn't want them. None of the market stalls were in the same place as they were when Milo first arrived; it almost looked like some kind of first come, first served competition, as sellers were frequently moving their carts when better locations became available. The task took far longer than it would have back in Pending, and even knowing a few basic sentences didn't stop the trial by fire language barrier turning volcanic. Eventually, very eventually, Milo had completed his job and returned to Tola's home.

Day turned to night and morning again. After breakfast, Tola handed Milo his pay before going for her middle of the day sleep, but he noticed he'd received slightly more than the usual. Tola was already out cold by the time Milo realised her mistake, so he didn't wake her up. Milo noticed however that there was something written on the envelope; it was the word "caruto." After checking it through his dictionary, Milo realised caruto meant bonus. Tola really had paid Milo extra, and that made him so happy. Milo continued the day, and the following few days with a lot more enthusiasm. Tola was a lot more considerate of Milo, even if they never shared a real conversation, and once, he was sure she smiled at him. A little over a week in, and Milo finally had enough money for international postage. Milo didn't waste any time at all writing the letter and getting it to the post office, sending it to Hazel back in Pending, explaining everything that had happened and where he was (although he decided to omit the story regarding the brothel). Handing over the letter, Milo knew that it wouldn't be long until he was back home, and he almost jumped for joy.

All he had to do was wait for a reply.

Oh right, shipping was probably going to take a while, probably more than a week at least.

"Damn it!" shouted Milo.

Milo kept working for Tola and playing with Dodek for another week or so before the reply came; the morning it happened, Dodek was at school and Tola was asleep. Milo lunged for the envelope without even thinking; could it really be from

Hazel? Knowing his luck so far, Milo thought it could well have been an immigration agency. Milo tore open the letter and read it to himself.

"Dear Milo,

You twat!"

Yep, this was from Hazel.

"I'll save the aggressive language for when you return, but you have some nerve.

I've taken the courtesy to tell your work what's happened. I was kind enough to lie on your behalf, but if anyone asks, you had an aunty called Ruth who suddenly died, and you travelled back to your home town in a rush.

Heidi asks you to hurry up, as she doesn't exactly love having Rob be the replacement interviewer.

I've given you the money you asked for, but you better pay me back quick because business at the pub has gone down considerably since you've been missing for two weeks.

Regards, Hazel"

Milo was surprised with the speed of international post; back in Pending, you were lucky to get your letter delivered in the same year as sending it, but that wasn't worth thinking about now; Milo had his ticket home. This time tomorrow, he could be at home, drinking a... actually he thought he should lay off the drink considering how he got in this mess, but he would be home with all the comforts home brings.

Except could he go just yet?

He had promised to go to the festival with Dodek, and he didn't like the idea of breaking a promise to him, especially considering he was a fan of practical jokes, and forty miles of sea would not so easily stop the endless energy of a six-year-old. In fact, Milo realised he hadn't told anyone what his true objective was, and he started to feel guilty about doing it. Milo decided he would try and explain things to Tola and Dodek after the festival; that would probably make things easier. The festival was called Padmengent, but after checking his dictionary, Milo found it was a proper noun that had no equivalent translation.

Padmengent was only a few days away now, and what was a few more days on top of two weeks already. Milo kept quiet about the letter, and went about the rest of the day as he normally would.

When the day of the festival came around, Dodek didn't go to school, and Tola wasn't working. Milo had been given a very long to-do list, and Tola was busy cooking, ironing, and swearing.

Milo realised he had greatly underestimated the scale of this festival.

For just about all the daylight hours, Milo and Tola worked to prepare for whatever the heck Padmengent was, while Dodek was playing in the other room, completely oblivious to the stress that a fun festival can cause. As evening approached, Tola went away with Dodek, and threw some clothes Milo's way. The clothes in question were beige trousers, a belt that covered half his torso, and a black waistcoat with flowers embroidered on it. Whatever this costume was supposed to be, it was the tradition Milo was expected to follow. Like Milo's last clothing donation, these ones were far too large, and could have been used better to re-roof a church. Dodek and Tola were wearing similar outfits, although the latter wore a long flowing skirt with as many different coloured vertical stripes as would fit. Dodek seemed unhappy about the outfit, like he'd rather be wearing his usual clothes, but the mother wasn't having any of it. Tola fixed up Dodek and Milo's outfits; Milo had become weirdly used to Tola fixing his clothes that he just let it happen at this point. The three of them left the flat and went into the dark street, where many other people were strolling down, carrying lanterns. There were a lot more people on this island than Milo realised, and they all seemed to be congregating in the market plaza. Everyone in the street was dressed similarly; the colours and patterns were different, but the houses were painted in just the same fashion, so this wasn't surprising. When the three of them reached the plaza, it was not unlike the market, but a little more carefree. Despite the crowds being larger, no one was rushing around. The stalls were either games or selling street food, and

Dodek was adamant to get a pancake. Milo still didn't understand what this festival was about, if it was about anything, but you don't normally wear uncomfortable clothes unless it's important. The events went by fairly uneventfully, with people generally socialising and eating. One odd thing that Milo noticed were big hay wagons full of water dotted about the stalls, but no one paid them much attention. A few hours into the night, the stalls started disappearing, and people were beginning to look apprehensive. Milo could hear random people talking, and the time was mentioned over and over again, like something big had been scheduled, but what exactly? There was no evidence something was about to happen, so unless there was a call for a shirt that could be used as a parachute, Milo wasn't prepared. Eventually, everyone stopped, just to stare at the plaza's clock tower. What the heck was going to happen? While everyone was silent, Dodek made his way through the mob to the outskirts of the crowd, and Tola and Milo had to follow until their backs were on a building wall. Milo just stood there, waiting for whatever it was to happen, and looked around to try and get a grip on the situation. Milo thought he saw someone or something on the roof of a building, but he wasn't sure if that was just paranoia. After a little time passed, a bell sound rang throughout the plaza, and Milo heard the ocean.

No, wait, water was falling on him.

From the roof of the buildings, troughs and troughs of water pelted everyone below, soaking Milo head to toe in less than a second. Dodek laughed at Milo, who ran out of the way when the bell struck.

Milo was livid.

That little sod had completely duped him into standing in the perfect place for a soaking he wasn't expecting. Milo didn't care that he was wet, or even that the water was cold as a parent's guilt stare; what bothered Milo was that Dodek had pulled out of his pocket a cabbage leaf, and threw it at Milo's face. In the most calculated and roundabout way, Dodek had won the water fight they had in the kitchen two weeks ago. Milo looked around, and everyone in the plaza had suddenly found buckets and mugs that were being used to throw water over each other. It was clear that this was the celebration, but the reason why wasn't important to Milo; all he wanted to do was drench Dodek; there was no way Milo would give the kid the satisfaction of victory. Milo dived for the child, but his now soaked clothes added a lot of weight, making his movements sloppy. Dodek quickly became too hard to detect in the crowd, as everyone was splashing each other and getting spray in Milo's eyes, but the kid would show up again; he'd have to find his mother soon enough. Milo stole a bucket from the floor and wringed out his clothes into it, ready for attack. Now all he had to do was wait; if he could keep Tola in his line of sight, Milo would strike back soon enough.

Milo scanned the crowd.

Milo looked back at Tola.

Milo scanned the crowd.

Milo looked back at Tola.

Milo saw a sponge flying toward his face.

Dodek hit Milo square between the eyes and ran past him, smacking his bucket to the floor as he ran past. Milo wiped the water from his eyes and tried to regain focus. It was just when Milo regained his vision that Tola poured an entire bucket over his head, laughing hysterically.

Her too? Really?

The three of them and the rest of the town threw water on each other for what felt like hours, and the fight turned into play. At the end of it, every single person returned home with sodden clothes, high spirits, and, by next morning, probably the flu.

The next morning, Milo broke the news to Tola and Dodek that he had to leave. Tola understood, but Dodek didn't like it; he had no one oblivious enough to prank any more. Milo genuinely felt sorry for them, but he couldn't stay. Milo returned the pay he didn't need back to Tola, as a way to say "kozey kun" for the hospitality, as well as leaving his home address, in case they ever wanted to write. Milo hugged Dodek and gave Tola a kiss on the cheek before leaving for the port.

By the time evening came, Milo was home.

When Milo arrived in Dorcoast, he saw someone he recognised; it was the ship's captain that he had stowed away on originally, standing on the pier. Milo thought back to how he had tricked him into going to a brothel, not to mention the fact he showed up in Dorcoast before Milo when he said he couldn't sail him back here. Milo walked up quietly behind the captain, and tugged on his sleeve. The captain looked to his side, and saw no one, but felt Milo pushing into his back, and throwing the captain over the pier into the ocean.

If Dodek was good for one thing, it was in teaching how to get revenge.

***

Milo dipped into his home before quickly making his way to The Devil's Neckhole; as much as he wanted a drink, it was more important he paid Hazel back for his ferry ticket. As Milo was about to enter the building, the door rocketed open, and out flew two men wrestling with each other while a dolled up biddy screeched something unintelligible over the kerfuffle.

Good to be home, thought Milo.

Milo squeezed his way past the skirmish and met eyes with Hazel, who was stunned to find him still alive. Hazel broke off from the conversation she was having with the other patrons to address the man properly.

"You took your bloody time getting here," moaned Hazel.

"That's a fine 'How do you do?'" replied Milo. "What's going on out front?"

"Oh, the usual. Ethel's got a new boyfriend."

Milo peeked outside and saw both men on the ground, one of them using their legs to place the other in a choke hold. "Is she happy with him?"

"I imagine so," wondered Hazel. "Her new fella's got a lot

more money. Anyway, that's beside the point. How the heck did you end up in a different country?"

Milo explained the situation he had been though in greater detail now he wasn't restricted by pen and paper; everything from the brothel, to sleeping rough, to befriending a prostitute and her son; the whole ordeal was laid bare. Milo was relieved to finally have a proxy therapist to discuss the matter with, even if Hazel was holding back sniggers for some of the more ridiculous moments.

"Well, that's one heck of a chapter for your autobiography," offered Hazel. "At least now you know what to do if you ever go back there."

Milo looked distractedly through the window. "Yes, if I ever go back there."

CHAPTER NINE

Easier Said Than Done

You can generally tell how interesting a place is to live based on what people talk about. Chatting about recent events is no different anywhere in the world, but what those recent events are is the telltale sign. If you talk about your work, hobbies, or the news, you might be living in a place that is somewhat fascinating. If, however, you talk about mundane natural phenomena which you have no control over, you are very thin on the ground when it comes to interesting topics.

People in Pending talk about the weather a lot.

What the weather has been, will be, currently is, when it might improve, when it might turn crap; no subject concerning the climate is too tedious for the average Pending resident. Being in the colder south of Flatrock and located near the coast, Pending's weather is frequently awful, which some people might choose as a reason to focus on something more positive, like good transport links, or that their country isn't stricken with poverty, but no; the weather is people's favourite subject. This day in question was like most others; cold, cloudy, and complainable, with one major exception: It was snowing. You can tell you have become an adult when you worry about snow more than you appreciate it. A child who sees snow thinks of building snowmen and throwing snowballs, whereas an adult who sees the same thinks of difficult roads, and the potential misfire of kids throwing snowballs.

This is for everyone except Heidi, who was making snow

angels.

In the manner of fairness, it should be noted that Heidi had never seen snow before; having lived and travelled only north of Pending until now, she had never experienced a climate capable of snow. Heidi was enamoured with the sight before her; she had just finished work and hadn't realised what was happening outside. Snow was already thick on the ground, and Heidi jumped into it and shovelled it into her hands, surprised by how light it was, and how cold it could be (as stupid as that sounds). Heidi wasn't wearing gloves; she wasn't prepared for the sudden snowfall, and just wanted to feel the cold cotton balls slip between her fingers.

Milo looked on like Heidi was crazy.

Milo was seeing the exact same scene, but had a very different outlook. Milo was similarly ill-dressed for snow, and only thought about how his shoes were poorly suited for walking back home. Milo kept watch on Heidi, partly to make sure she didn't injure herself, but mostly because he was hoping the weather might clear up if he waited.

It didn't.

An hour passed with Heidi playing in the snow while Milo sheltered in the office, until he knew he had to make his excuses and leave.

"I'm going to try and head back home," started Milo. "You should probably leave before you catch a cold."

"No. I think I might sleep here," gushed Heidi.

Milo was fairly sure there was going to be no reasoning with Heidi right now, but he tried anyway.

"The snow will probably stick around for a few days, weeks even, and it's your day off tomorrow," stated Milo. "You'll have plenty of time to act like a child then."

"Actually, I can't. I got a part time job," announced Heidi.

"Really? Where?"

"Butcher's Bakery."

Working at The Bystander wasn't exactly the high paying job Heidi was hoping for to further her dream of having the money to travel, so she had found a placement at Butcher's Bakery. Basically, if she couldn't be a breadwinner, she could at least be a bread maker.

"Have you met the boss of that place?" asked Milo.

"You mean John? He seemed nice enough," replied Heidi.

"Most people call him Parmesan?"

"Why's that? He likes cheese?"

"No, skin condition," ended Milo.

Milo, shortly after that exchange, left Heidi to her business of rolling around in the snow, and trusted she would be fine, or as fine as a woman rolling in ice can be. It had somewhat surprised Milo that Heidi would find a part-time job considering she was the kind of person to use her spare time as fruitfully as possible, but then again, she had been in Pending for a while now, and there's very little a town with a cemetery next to the general practitioner can offer you.

Heidi arrived the next morning at Butcher's Bakery: Pending's most inspected food shop. Despite what you may think, the requirements to have a satisfactory hygiene score for an establishment is much easier than you think; this is partly because the standards of practice to create a hygienic working environment are easy, but it's mostly because your average food safety inspector is not the most thorough when it comes to their job. You might be expecting swabs and professional testing from these examinations, but generally it's nothing more than a quick look around with a few questions that won't be followed up on if you lie about the answers. Butcher's Bakery was good in comparison to Pending's competition, but that's like saying you kick the hardest out of all the paraplegics. The front of the shop looked fine; shelves stocked full as they could with appealing looking products, glazed and glistening golden in the daylight, and the scent of freshly baked bread filled Heidi with the kind of feeling one might get from intoxicating drugs. The back is where things started to become the usual Pending standard. Under the counters, just below where a customer could see was a layer of grime as thick as pâté; on top of that little problem, the dry stores were wet, the tables weren't stable, and the sink had sunk. Heidi had been instructed to meet Parmesan in the kitchen behind the counter early in the morning, and when she walked in, she saw the man looking dazed and confused.

"Who are you?" demanded Parmesan.

"Heidi Watson. I start working here today," answered Heidi.

"I know that!"

Heidi wondered why he had to ask at all, but didn't question anything.

"I'll be with you in a second," added Parmesan frustrated. "I lost the flour scoop."

"You mean this thing?" said Heidi, pointing to a scoop on the table directly in front of Parmesan.

"No, not that..." Parmesan's sentence trailed off as he looked at the table. A moment passed. "I found the flour scoop."

Parmesan had seemed a decent enough guy during the interview, but maybe this attitude had something to do with the fact he had clearly just dropped today's bread on the floor. Besides that, the baker had a shaved head, messy red apron, and hands that looked like they'd seen the bad side of a cheese grater. Parmesan (who very rarely had the respect to be known as John) was one of the few people in Pending who could perform magic; in times past, he wished to be a wizard, but after five years of trying, the only spell he seemed to perfect was "summon walnut," which while tricky to perform, its usage was limited to garnishing carrot cakes.

Heidi raised, "Would you like me to start immediately or-"

"There's no time. You'll have to start now," Parmesan interrupted.

Heidi was shoved an old apron and thrown out onto the shop floor to organise the day's stock. Heidi had four general responsibilities when it came to working at the bakery, first of which was packaging. When the bread and pastries were cooked, much of it was expected to be wrapped in wax paper to prevent it from going stale. This was in every regard the most tedious of all the tasks because every individual piece, every pie, every cake, every tiny cracker, had to be wrapped, as was Parmesan's instruction. It was also a process that was mostly useless as very few people leave a bakery without eating what they've bought within a few minutes. The most annoying of these items to wrap were the bread loaves, which could be shaped round, flat, twist, plait, cottage, knotted, baton, sat on, and every which way you can think of. Heidi determined that whoever was so picky about bread that they would only eat it if it was the shape of a crescent would need a serious talking to, not to mention the fact she had to wipe the dust away from when Parmesan had dropped the loaves on the floor. Heidi's second responsibility was shelf stacking, which demanded placing the produce out for display. It was here that Heidi realised why the shelves looked so full; they were all tiny. Each shelf could barely carry a few loaves, so as soon as one was sold, it looked empty again. It wasn't long before her job purely consisted of walking back and forth from the shelves with a couple of items at a time, making it the furthest she had ever walked without going anywhere. Heidi's third responsibility was cleaning, which while third on the list of priorities, should have been number one. Flour seemed to travel in the air like dandelion seeds, blooming into mite and weevil infestations. Heidi realised that many of these shelves had not been moved in some time, and lifting up one of them caused bugs to skitter on the underside, having used the shadow of the shelves to avoid light for who knows how long. The shelves themselves hadn't been well maintained either, with various jams and pickles marking their territory in the shop, which was odd, because the bakery didn't sell those products. The stains had clearly been there for some time, as they could not be shifted for all of Heidi's effort; the only thing more stubborn than the stains were the customers. Heidi's final responsibility was to serve customers and manage the till, and as nice and patient as Heidi can be when it comes to other people, customers do not count as people; they are parasites. The bakery had seemingly gotten into the habit of yielding to customers' requests, which while nice for the buyer, is absolutely awful for the seller. Heidi had to deal with every special customer request, and any time she didn't know or understand what the customer was asking, she was met with entitlement that even kings would call a bit much. More than once, Heidi would have loved to shout, "there are countries suffering from famine right now," but she refrained as she wanted to keep this job for more than six hours. The position was challenging on many fronts, primarily because she was the only one on the shop floor; Parmesan was there cooking, but it was clear Heidi was only employed so he could avoid serving customers. Heidi tried to chat with Parmesan whenever she popped into the kitchens, but he wasn't exactly the most receptive, unless you consider occasional darting glances proper communication. As the end of the day rolled around and all the customers had left, Heidi was left to sweep and mop the floors before she could leave.

"You're doing that wrong," said Parmesan offhandedly.

"What am I doing wrong?" asked Heidi.

"Mopping the floor."

Heidi was confused, as she was sure moping involved wiping a soapy wet mop across the floor, and to her knowledge, that was what she was doing.

"What's wrong about it?" asked Heidi.

"You're doing it side to side, you're supposed to do it up and down otherwise it smears," explained Parmesan.

Of all the requests people had made today, this one hit a nerve in Heidi's brain. She knew she wasn't doing anything wrong, in fact, she could see the floor she had already done, and it was fine. What the heck was he talking about, thought Heidi, but before she said anything she might regret, she repressed the anger and just did the floor as was requested. It had been a long day, and Heidi knew she was overreacting. Heidi finished the floor and went home, and it wasn't until she got into her flat that she realised how tired she was; it was like she had just finished a hike, but the destination was severe muscle tension. Heidi did not enjoy working in the bakery at all, but she had to do it; her dream was to visit every major city in the world and be a part of any culture that she could meet, and this was the best paying job she could get (legally). Heidi knew that the struggle wouldn't last long; just a few days a week for a few months and she'd be on the road again to who knows where. Heidi took a deep breath, and without even realising it, fell asleep from exhaustion.

The following days working in Butcher's Bakery were not the most pleasant; not that day one was very good, but days two, three, and four onwards were hardly an improvement. A routine quickly formed where Parmesan would cook and Heidi would package, which was a task that never seemed to end. The cleaning never seemed to be completed either, as every time one problem was solved, a new one would emerge from the deep recesses of the yeast cupboard. One day, Parmesan made it known that he would be in work late, and asked Heidi to set up shop before he got there; she wasn't trusted with making bread, but she was allowed to measure out the ingredients, which at this point, any little variety in tasks was a blessing. Heidi intended to start working as soon as she got in, but there was a slight problem in front of her.

It was a rabbit.

Normally, pests have to be small to creep in through the cracks of walls and doors to get inside a kitchen, so how a rabbit got in baffled Heidi. The rabbit was white all over bar a brown streak between its eyes, and it was poking its nose into the little corners of the room, as if it too had gained the feeling of an intoxicating drug. Heidi had to rack her brain for a full minute as to whether a rabbit actually is considered a pest, because it wasn't the kind of thing she'd ever had to think about before. What is the dividing line between a pet and a pest? Heidi soon determined she had to throw the rabbit out, as she remembered hearing once that rabbits eat their own droppings (not some fallen bread loaves, the other kind of droppings.) Heidi carried the rabbit out the back door, and then started on the day's work. Heidi did as she had been demanded, such as weighing the ingredients and heating water for yeast. Parmesan left many notes around the kitchen, and if you want a sample of how patronising they were, here is what was written on one in particular:

"To whom it may concern (Heidi) - Instructions for cooking sausage rolls

- Turn the oven on.
- Brush the sausage rolls with beaten egg.
- Once the oven has finished preheating, open the oven door.
- Place sausage rolls in the oven.
- Close the oven door.
- Set the timer for 30 minutes.
- Halfway through cooking (15 minutes), turn the trays around as the back of the oven is hotter than the front.
- After a further 15 minutes, remove the sausage rolls from the oven.
- If the sausage rolls are not to the desired colour (see attached chart), cook for a further 3-5 minutes.
- If you burn the sausage rolls, well, you're fucked."

Parmesan also reminded Heidi to put away any deliveries that came in, check the shelves, and make sure everything looked tidy, but that last task was a job that needed a master wizard, not one woman. Some time passed, and Parmesan arrived in the bakery carrying a large bag of something, which he placed on the floor.

"I'm here. You can go into the shop now," said Parmesan.

Heidi did as was asked, and as she walked away, made a quick glance into the bag. The bag looked like it was full of hay and grass, which Heidi was fairly sure didn't go into any of the cakes, unless they were planning on catering for a horse any time soon. Heidi went about her usual tasks for several hours, dealing with customers, the wrapping machine, and high blood pressure, until Parmesan went for his break. There was a lapse in customers at that time, and Heidi's curiosity around the bag of hay had been in the forefront of her mind since she saw it. Heidi walked into the kitchen and took a closer look inside the bag that Parmesan had tucked away into the back of the kitchen, and there were three things in there that raised Heidi's suspicions: a lettuce, some carrots, and a small dish that had the word "Snowy" professionally painted on it. Heidi realised this dish was a pet food bowl, and also came to the conclusion that the hay was probably bedding, and the other bits were most likely animal food.

Suddenly, Heidi remembered the white rabbit.

Oh, no, thought Heidi. Had she thrown Parmesan's new pet into the street? A name like Snowy would suit a white rabbit, and it did seem very tame when Heidi picked it up, not to mention if Parmesan brought the rabbit in, it would explain how the animal got into the bakery. Parmesan hadn't mentioned anything, but then again, he didn't mention anything ever, unless it wasn't a complaint. Heidi suddenly felt a wave of guilt wash over her, because the fact that Parmesan felt the need to go out early to get a bag full of pet supplies probably meant the animal was one of the few things he actually cared about. Heidi pulled herself together and tried to assess the situation: Parmesan hadn't noticed the rabbit was missing, and when things did go missing, he couldn't see them even when they were right in front of him. Heidi probably had some time before Parmesan would say anything, and a little more time before he could work out it was Heidi's fault. Heidi didn't want to leave the rabbit out in the cold, especially when it came to nighttime, and the foxes would be out looking for a good carcass to tear into. Heidi decided that when the workday was over, she would go out to look for Snowy; she also took a carrot from the bag to use as bait later. It was quite lucky that Parmesan rarely looked at Heidi, because she was not keeping totally calm. Every minute spent in the bakery was another minute the rabbit could run away, and after eight hours, who knows how far it might have gone. When the end of the day came, Heidi swept and mopped the floors very quickly, smears be damned, and left the bakery in a hurry. Heidi opened the door and went to search for the white rabbit before it could be mauled, except there was a slight problem: The snow.

Finding a white rabbit that has had eight hours to run away from you is one thing, searching for something white in a town covered six inches thick in snow is another. The one advantage Heidi had with snow was that she could follow the rabbit's tracks for at least some idea of the direction it had headed. Unfortunately, the tracks were quickly stamped out by other people's footsteps as soon as it passed through a slightly crowded area. All the while, Heidi was shouting, "Snowy, Snowy," in the hopes the rabbit understood its own name, but given the current weather, it made onlookers think of her to be quite simple minded. The best part of an hour passed before Heidi really started to feel the hopelessness of the situation; she didn't know where to look, and even if she did know, she was searching for something perfectly camouflage. Heidi had walked from the back of the bakery, to a stable, to a street, to a busy street, to a suspiciously quiet street, and ended up in a park. The rabbit tracks hadn't reemerged, and even then, what guarantee was there that it was the same rabbit? Heidi looked around the park briefly, but only saw a few children playing around; no sign of the rabbit at all. Heidi desperately wanted to rest, and couldn't help but collapse on a snowy bench, only in that moment discovering that her trousers were not as waterproof as she would have liked them to be. Heidi only had a few hours left, and no good ideas to hand; she didn't have the time to go out and find help; as soon as nightfall came, there was more chance of finding an honest politician than that rabbit. Heidi looked over to the children playing with snowballs and enjoying themselves, annoyed she wasn't in a better frame of mind to do the same.

Although, Heidi, at that moment, did think of something she could try.

Would it be worth asking the children to help search for the rabbit?

There were five children, somewhere in the region of four to eight years old, not perfect, but cognitive enough that they could help the investigation; even if they just acted as extra eyes and ears, it would be better than nothing. Heidi stood up and went over to the children, waving to get their attention.

"Hey, can you help me with something?" asked Heidi.

The children all looked on at the weird woman; she seemed to act like a rational adult (if only they knew), but she wasn't much taller than any of them. None of the children spoke.

"I need help finding a rabbit. It's white, and has big ears and a tiny button nose," explained Heidi.

"I know what a rabbit is, you knob," blurted out one of the older kids.

Heidi realised talking down to the children was a mistake; this was Pending after all, and people grow into pessimists fast.

"I need to find this rabbit before sunset. Can you help me?" asked Heidi, a little less calmly.

The kid who spoke out before was clearly the leader of the pack, as the others were waiting for him to talk.

"How much is it worth?" asked the boss.

"It's worth my job," answered Heidi, brutally honest.

"I don't want your job."

Was this a child or a dodgy salesman? No one this young should be so clued up on the world. Heidi wasn't expecting, nor was she exactly willing to bargain with the children, but she was too young and not scary enough to command the kids; she had all the authority of a wet floor sign. Heidi didn't have much money on her, and the whole reason she was in this mess in the first place was because she needed to save money for travelling. This was going nowhere fast; Heidi had to think of some way around this. The children wanted something, but she had nothing to give; if only there was a way to sell nothing to children. That was the moment that Heidi thought to say, "This is a competition. Whoever finds the white rabbit with a brown streak on its head wins."

The other four kids ran off in all directions to instantly search for the rabbit, leaving the oldest one dumbfounded;

Heidi hadn't even offered a prize, just the thinly veiled term of "winning." The older kid instantly lost all power and went off in a strop, as the other four scavenged the bushes for something that might not even be there. More ground was definitely being covered with the tactic, but Heidi had a hard time urging the children outside of the park; it was clear none of the kids expected the rabbit to be so far away. Heidi and the children circled around a school, the edge of the high street, and one of the kids was so desperate for victory, that they started going into people's gardens. Heidi thought about moving the child away from other people's property, but at the same time, there was every possibility the rabbit could have ended up there. After some time, maybe only half an hour before sunset, one of the kids shouted, "I found it." Heidi jumped towards the place where the child shouted, only to find the rabbit wasn't there.

Oh, of course, thought Heidi, the shouting scared it away.

Everything was fine though, because at least Heidi knew the rabbit must be around here somewhere. Heidi moved tentatively into the bushes, keeping her head above the shrubbery to see through the cracks in the leaves for where Snowy might be. The children meanwhile, still intent on "winning," crawled into the bushes when Heidi wasn't looking. The moment Heidi thought she caught a glimpse of the carrot munching prick, the same child again shouted, "It's there," and the rabbit hopped out of the shrubs in a hurry. Heidi tried to run out of the bush after it, but ended up falling face first into the branches. The rabbit scampered away as quickly as possible, the children unable to make up the ground between them, and Snowy burrowed itself into some kind of tunnel. It was a few minutes later that Heidi had managed to squirm her way out of the bush, picking off splinters as she walked towards the four children staring into a point on the ground.

"I found the rabbit," exclaimed one of the kids.

"No! I did!" shouted another.

The children bickered about who won the game, having not learned their lesson that shouting does not keep a rabbit calm, not that they needed to, because they had already won. Heidi had deceived them in a way, and the kids didn't know nor understand her real predicament.

"QUIET!" shouted Heidi sharply. The children suddenly paid attention; Heidi's authority had been promoted from wet floor sign to dinner lady. "Is the rabbit in there," asked Heidi, pointing to the burrow in the ground.

"Yes," replied one of the kids. "That means I win."

Heidi saw one of the children raise their hand in question of the previous statement, but Heidi grabbed the hand before the other child could speak. Heidi was already tired from work, add to that however many miles she had walked just for the rabbit, she was not in any mood or state to act with enthusiasm.

"Yes, congratulations. You won. All of you," said Heidi tiredly.

The children moaned, all feeling like they had been cheated with some half-arsed participation trophy. All of them left the burrow since there was nothing else to do, leaving Heidi alone with the rabbit.

Now came the new problem, how to get Snowy out of the hole.

Heidi still had the carrot, and left it at the edge of the burrow, but the rabbit wouldn't leave. It was obvious that Snowy had been spooked and was acting defensive, but Heidi couldn't give up here when the target was literally just out of arm's reach. Heidi was still waiting outside the burrow until dusk, when the temperature was even lower than usual, and most people with common sense were tucked up in bed, but she couldn't leave the rabbit in that burrow as she didn't know if it would even be there the following morning. Heidi was starting to shiver now, learning like every other adult in Pending to hate the snow; her bangles were especially good at conducting the cold temperature, frost biting her arms every time she shaked them even slightly. Waiting for the rabbit to come out was pointless; it might even be asleep by now, and if the rabbit wouldn't come out, Heidi needed to find a way in. Heidi did have a plan, not one she liked, but a plan; using her hands, she dug the burrow wider, gently as she possibly could until the hole was big enough to reach in and take Snowy out. Heidi had to watch out for any small landslides or avalanches, and took the process as slowly and carefully as possible. Unbenounced to Heidi, rabbit burrows can be quite deep, and she was digging for the best part of an hour until she felt the fiendish fuzzball on her fingertips. Heidi dived in, and gently picked up the creature, jittery and jumpy as it was, she had it in her hands, and checked that it had the same brown streak as the rabbit before.

"Victory!" whispered Heidi to herself.

Heidi was still shivering when she returned home with the rabbit; she couldn't give it to Parmesan now because the bakery was closed, and she didn't know where he lived; it would have to wait until morning. Parmesan would have undoubtedly noticed that Snowy was missing by now, and Heidi wasn't supposed to go to the bakery tomorrow, but she was sure she could explain the situation, right now, there was a bigger problem: Heidi didn't know how to take care of a rabbit. She thought back to a cat she had when she was younger, but being honest with herself, it was more her parents doing the work while she petted it every so often. Heidi's lifestyle demanded her to travel and live light, which is why she owned so little furniture, which meant that she didn't really have a bed for the creature. Heidi improvised some bedding out of her messier clothes, but the rabbit was more content to hop around the floor than stay in one place. Heidi understood now why most people prefer to keep animals in either cages or pies, because they were quite a hassle. Every other minute, Heidi had to pick up the rabbit to make sure it didn't jump onto the stove or chew up the stuff Heidi left on the floor. At the very least, the rabbit had food; Heidi had already fed Snowy the carrot she took, and she had some other vegetables in the flat, but besides giving it food and water, Heidi had no idea how to properly look after an animal. Heidi was struggling to stay awake, from both exhaustion, and because it was past her usual bedtime. It was only once Snowy fell asleep, that Heidi felt she could do the same.

Heidi woke up later than usual the next morning with a sniffly nose; as most could guess, she had caught a cold from staying in the snow for too long. Snowy woke up earlier, and had crapped on the floor next to Heidi's bed, only finding out for herself when she stepped in it. Realising now that rabbits don't eat *all* their droppings, Heidi did the bare minimum to make herself presentable, and walked down to Butcher's Bakery with the rabbit in hand. Heidi should have been going to The Bystander, but there was a rule about staying home if you're sick, and she needed at least a day to physically and mentally recover. Heidi knocked on the back door to the bakery and waited for someone to answer.

"It's open," shouted Parmesan from inside.

Heidi walked through and saw Parmesan, while another man, similarly dressed, was talking to him, which Heidi assumed was one of the permanent employees she covered for on her days working.

"Hello, I know I'm not supposed to be working today but I wanted to bring you your rabbit back," said Heidi through deep sniffles.

"What do you mean?" asked Parmesan.

"Are you using live animals?" asked the other man to Parmesan.

Everyone seemed somewhat confused.

"This is Snowy, isn't it?" asked Heidi. "Your pet?"

"No," said Parmesan bluntly.

Heidi, even with her stuffed up head and tired body, knew she was about to hear everything she didn't want to hear.

"Do you not have a pet rabbit called Snowy?" asked Heidi.

"No, my daughter has a pet Gerbil called Snowy," answered Parmesan.

"Does she work for you?" asked the other man to Parmesan, pointing at Heidi.

The other man seemed like he wasn't following a lot of this, which was fair. When face to face with a visibly ill person holding what was now understood to be a wild animal, you would have a few questions.

"Sorry. I'm Heidi," said Heidi. "Who are you?"

"I'm the food safety inspector," answered the man.

Heidi, upon returning home, thought about what she had done: She had caused Parmesan a lot of trouble with the food safety inspector for bringing pests into the kitchen, she showed up to a workplace visibly cadaverous, she had taken a wild animal from its home, and to top it all off, she didn't even find out how it got into the kitchen. Heidi, if it wasn't for the fact she was fired, would have left the job, deciding the stress it caused was not worth the paycheck. Heidi lay in bed for the rest of the day, trying to recover from her cold, and could hear children outside playing in the snow; she was in no right mood to listen to the screams of joy. Heidi still needed to get some more money before she could leave Pending, and thought about the other potential jobs she could go for, but decided that as long as none of them were for a pet shop, she would be fine.

**

A couple weeks passed, and Heidi was in The Devil's Neckhole; she had only been passing by to see if there were any job adverts in the window, but there were none at the time. Since she was there, Heidi decided to pop in quickly to say hello to Milo and Hazel, wondering if they knew anything on the job front.

"Hey, Hazel," called Heidi.

"Oh dear," muttered Hazel. "You're looking a bit down. Something the matter?"

"I'm looking for part time work. I need some more money if I want to start travelling again."

"Oh right. Milo mentioned something along those lines. Sorry, but I can't help."

Heidi felt a tad downtrodden, but wasn't surprised; she had

pushed her luck too far and it was now careening off the cliff side.

"Why don't you do portraits for commission?" suggested Hazel. "Didn't you say you've done that before."

"I did, but..." Heidi's sentence trailed off while she tried to think of the right words. "Some customers can be quite demanding, and Pending is..."

"You don't need to say anymore," insisted Hazel. "If you change your mind, you can put an advert in the window."

"Thanks."

Heidi sat at the bar for a minute to rest her legs, looking around, and eventually noticing something was off.

"Where's Milo?" asked Heidi.

"Couldn't tell you," answered Hazel. "He hasn't shown up today."

Heidi checked the clock, and it was showing any time of the day, so Milo should have been there.

"Is he sick?" asked Heidi.

"That wouldn't stop him," said Hazel. "Though he was unusually happy last time I saw him."

Heidi was becoming morbidly curious. "What do you think he's up to?"

"In my mind, he's paid for a fancy woman, but I know he wouldn't really do that. Don't worry. I'll get the information out of him next time he's here."

Heidi thanked Hazel then excused herself; there were still a few places where job adverts could be found. Heidi ruminated on other ways she could make money, but she was rather attached to her internal organs, so dismissed most of her own suggestions. There was no point selling any of her possessions either, as they only had sentimental value, which has a very poor exchange rate. Heidi racked her brain for a while, but nothing clean and easy was presenting itself. By the end of the day, Heidi fell asleep having not progressed an inch; all she could do was sigh and hope tomorrow would be better.

CHAPTER TEN

War Of The Window

Bureaucracy is the worst thing in the world, period. Some people might argue that genocide is worse, but those people have never had to move house in an upward chain. Primitive cultures don't care for paperwork; if you want something built, you build it, but in the more "modern and civilised societies" that exists now, bureaucracy now entails transforming yourself into a circus animal just to gain easier access to hoops for you to jump through. In bygone days, if someone argued about your construction work, you could kill them, but unfortunately, prisons have been invented since then. If this universe has an afterlife, and a punishment for your misdeeds, I believe it involves reading a housing agreement until you understand it, at which point an even more complicated agreement will be drafted to amend the original, continuing for eternity. Milo was about to experience something akin to hell soon, as upon returning home from work, he found one of his windows had just been smashed.

If you are not experienced with life as an adult, then it might surprise you why a simple window replacement would create so much red tape; in all honesty, recounting the tale I am about to, I don't understand it either, but that is bureaucracy in a nutshell. Milo's last major dealing with administration was when he tried to join a pension scheme. Milo, in theory, only had to send one letter to the pension office in order to have the matter sorted;

in practice however, it involved four letters. The first letter was rejected because Milo failed to get his birth certificate double validated by a person in a professional occupation, the second letter was rejected because he failed to get that birth certificate double validated by a person in a professional occupation who also wasn't a family member, and the third letter was rejected because he wrote in a handwriting that made the "i" in his name look slightly like a "j." It's worth noting here that the rules concerning Milo's pension and birth certificate were not explained to him beforehand; this is just one of many examples in how bureaucracy fails in the "modern and civilised society." While there are more talked about problems such as corruption in powerful positions, it's generally the people further down the corporate food chain, the tired and underappreciated, that cause issues for the average consumer, and one inadequate explanation of the terms and conditions can snowball into an avalanche. The only reason the fourth letter wasn't rejected was because it never arrived at the pension office; it got lost in transit, birth certificate included. It took a month to get a response from the pension office each time, and it was only after a far longer than average waiting time that Milo snapped, and travelled to the office in person to have the matter sorted. The stagecoach ride to the pension office was two days long, and it's amazing how steadfast Milo could hold a grudge for.

Milo has not since applied for a replacement birth certificate, for obvious reasons.

Milo examined his living room, which had the newly broken window in it; it seemed at some point in the day, some unruly children (actually, unruly is a redundant word there) had thrown a ball through the window, and then thrown their friend through in order to retrieve it, as a child was still passed out on the floor. The child was uninjured, which Milo considered a shame, because at least the kid would have received due punishment for their stupidity. Milo removed the child as one does with pests, cleaned up the mess, and boarded up the window with cardboard to stop the draft. Milo sighed as he realised now the worst was to come: He would need to hire someone to fix it. Milo's obsession with being tidy racked his brain; he couldn't stand having a broken window in his home ruining the safe atmosphere he spent the past few years harbouring, but he also hated having people over, especially ones he didn't know. Milo convinced himself that it would be a relatively painless experience, as he could request quotes from a few companies, choose one, and have the matter sorted within a few days.

But of course, this is a bureaucratic process, and nothing ever lasts a few days.

Milo sent out the letters, and by the end of the week, the first window company showed up, however, they couldn't simply measure the window frame, do some basic maths, and then calculate the cost; he was forced to listen to a woman drone on for two hours, reciting a presentation about the quality of the windows they sold. The woman wore a lot of shiny jewellery, probably to compensate for how dull she actually was. Milo didn't personally care about the millimetre depths of the locks or the heat retention index; all he wanted to know was "do they open, and can I see through them?" When the lecture was over, a price was finally uttered, and Milo's eyes bulged wide open, in what is known by body language experts as the "fuck off, you're lying" face. Unfortunately, the woman was not lying, and the windows were as expensive as she said; a figure halfway between "way too much," and "how much do kidneys sell for?"

The next day, the second company showed up, but an entire hour earlier than planned. Milo was at The Bystander that day, meaning the tradesman had been waiting outside for Milo to answer the door he wasn't behind. With the tradesman in a huff, and probably late/not as early as he wanted for his next appointment, measured the windows and gave the numbers. While the windows were being measured however, the tradesperson decided to chat, and Milo didn't like chatting. First the tradesman asked why Milo wanted the windows changed, as if the child shaped hole wasn't a big enough clue, then he asked about which other companies Milo had shown interest in. Milo told the tradesperson about the last quote, to which the tradesperson responded with how crap that business was. The basic gist was that the first company Milo spoke to were liars, which was hard to believe considering the two-hour presentation; tedious as it was, there were a lot of facts. Normally a good salesperson will try to upsell their own products, but this man was very much going for the opposite approach, which basically gave Milo the feeling of someone saying "in a world where you can trust no one, trust me." The quote was cheaper, and the tradesman even offered a discounted rate if Milo had the window fitted on a specific day, but if this guy couldn't get the time of day right, what were the chances he'd be able to get the days of the year correct?

The third company just didn't show up; a time and day was organised, and Milo being one of those people who can't help but listen for the slightest noise coming from the door, was on edge the whole time. Milo even checked the confirming letter again to make sure he had read it correctly, imagining a world where he forgot what the number four looked like, but no, he was in the right.

Milo decided to cast his net wider, wasting a few more days before settling for a company that seemed the least worst. A longer time than was intended had passed, but Milo had his windows sorted, and they would be fitted in a few days' time; everything was fine.

At least, that's what Milo thought.

Two days after sorting the window, shortly after Milo woke up, there was a knock at the door; answering it, he saw an old man in a clean and pressed suit, holding a clipboard with the same care and attention one might give to their own child.

"Are you Mr. Milo Point?" said the old man with the annoyed infliction one might give to someone else's child.

"Yes," replied Milo.

"Hello. I'm Ernest, and I'm from the Home & Land Registry. I am to understand you are having a new window fitted."

"That's right."

Milo was nervous, and rightly so. Home & Land Registry wasn't simply a faction of the local council; this was the council that other councils had to answer to, and how they found out Milo was getting a new window was anyone's guess.

"I'm afraid you don't have permission to have a new window fitted," remarked Ernest.

"Why not?" asked Milo.

"This house is a leasehold property, and unless you get leaseholder permission, you can't have any new features fitted."

Milo was perplexed; he did know his home was leasehold, but he had bought it on mortgage, and had full ownership of the house, which Milo questioned.

"When the leasehold period ends, the property will be repossessed by the housing agency we represent," answered Ernest, "and as such, you can't make changes without their consent."

Milo had to ask, "Do you know how long the remaining leasehold period is?"

"One hundred and ninety-seven years," answered the old man.

Milo thought about that for a moment. "We're both going to be dead before that time comes. Does it really matter?"

"Yes, it does."

"But it's one window!"

"But it needs permission, or you'll go to court."

Milo could see this man came with a loaded gun, and there wasn't a lot that could be done, not without filing the administration.

"Here is the appropriate paperwork," declared Ernest, handing over an encyclopaedia of tedium. "Please fill it out and send it to the address listed. If you have any further questions, fill out the questions and answer form, and we will be in touch within seven working days of receiving the form."

"Wow, thank you," Milo ended sarcastically.

Milo studied through the papers, and winced the more he read. Besides the usual name, address, date of birth, etc. there were some quite patronising questions like "When do you expect the work to start?" to which the answer is impossible to tell; Milo had planned the work to start in four days' time, but thanks to the bureaucratic process forced upon him like a punch to the face, it would be at least seven working days before it would be approved, and that was assuming the request was accepted, which it probably wouldn't be for some inane reason like not being able to remember the name of his first pet. Milo also knew he couldn't simply write "as soon as possible," even if it was the honest answer, because anything less than an exact date would make the paperwork void. Milo was also expected to read the terms and conditions, which was the most pointless exercise in the world. Terms and conditions were a thing created by bureaucrats in order to get away with murder, should they want to. By making the terms and conditions incredibly long winded and confusing so no one would read them, let alone understand them, officials could hide little clauses in there that, for all you know, could ruin your lives. Who knows for sure if terms and conditions have their own terms and conditions to follow, all Milo could work out was that his personal information would be held onto, and what happened with that information was simply the whim of fate. No one at the home and land registry genuinely cared at what age Milo last pissed the bed, or whatever question he was being asked, it was just a thing that they needed to ask because someone, somewhere, a hundred years ago in some high up building away from functional society, thought it might be important. As soon as Milo had finished writing his autobiography, he sent it out to the home and land registry in Dorcoast.

Now, he could only wait.

As much as I could say Milo waited patiently, he didn't.

Waiting for the letter was awful, and Milo didn't take well to looking at the cardboard over his window; Heidi had offered to draw a landscape over it, but Milo didn't want to be complacent with the construction work. Close to ten days later, Milo finally got a response back from the home registry. Milo opened up the letter, and to the surprise of pretty much no one, his request was rejected. Milo was annoyed, at first because of the obvious: Milo wasn't getting his window fixed, but then he was confused by a box on the form titled "Reason for rejected request."

The text box was blank.

Milo had not been given a reason as to why he couldn't have the window fixed, and yet it had been rejected. Milo needed to find out what happened; surely the bureaucrats hadn't become so absurd as to write with invisible ink, had they? Milo went for his pencil and paper, suddenly remembering what happened when he tried to get a pension; he wasn't going to sit down, and seeing how it was still morning, and Dorcoast was marginally less than two days' travel away, Milo decided to walk to the home and land registry office and sort it out right now.

Two hours later, Milo was standing at the foot of the Home & Land Registry office in Dorcoast. Milo didn't see the bureaucracy office as a collection of people, it was more like a slimy hive mind of insects, one big conglomerate of crap, a place where creatures do meaningless busy work while nothing gets accomplished, like a monkey pissing into its own face and wondering how it got wet; an office populated with people who use the word "technically" when they "technically" don't need to, and can explain in detail the legal difference between littering and fly-tipping, and why that means they can't sort out your problem; a place where discrepancy is created but can never exist.

Did I mention that I hate bureaucracy?

In the real world, the building was a three-story block, as plain and grey as could be, with uninteresting square windows, laid with colourless curtains, and lifeless people sitting on bland furniture drinking humdrum tea from their insipid mugs; it was a prison fitted with nicer doors. Milo walked into the building and met eyes with the receptionist.

"Can I help you?" asked the receptionist.

"Yes, I was rejected getting new windows, but no reason was given," explained Milo. "Can I find out why?"

"I'm afraid I can't answer that. If you fill out a question-and-answer form, you'll have a response within seven working days."

Milo looked to the side of the desk and found a stack of forms with fillable spaces printed on.

"Can I not speak to Ernest?" asked Milo, pointing to the signature at the bottom of his rejection notice.

"I'm afraid everyone here is busy," replied the receptionist bluntly. "If you fill out a question-and-answer form, you'll have a response within seven working days."

"It will only take a minute," begged Milo.

"I'm afraid everyone here is busy. If you fill out a question-and-answer form, you'll have a response within seven working days."

Milo knew he wasn't going to get through to this woman, who was repeating like a bad curry. While the receptionist wasn't looking, Milo milled about the ground floor of the building and tried to spy through the windows of the doors to find out if he could see the offices, but he couldn't, and the doors were locked anyway. Milo saw no other option than to fill out the question-and-answer form. Milo scribbled down his question, as well as tried to write his name in a box that was far too small for anyone to write their name in; Milo, having been blessed with a surname only five letters long, just about managed it, before folding the paper and placing it in a post box device.

Now came the long wait for yet another letter.

Another needlessly long wait later, Milo found the answer to his question form; as it had turned out, Milo had not filled out *all* the paperwork, as there was a page that had to be completed concerning the window company he was using. I say there was a page Milo hadn't filled out, but in reality, the page had not been given to Milo when he was handed the documents all that time ago. Milo despised how the registry made him pay for their mistake, but there was no use shouting about it now, as the end was seemingly in sight.

Note how I said *seemingly* in sight, because the truth is, in bureaucracy, the end is always seemingly in sight, but very rarely is it actually there. One big reason why paperwork is so annoying is the feeling that you are near the end while making no progress at all. There's no rush of happiness gained from the feeling of progress if progress never happens, and when the red tape finally is cut, you become too numb to feel the pleasure.

Milo filled in the missing form that was now provided to him, as well as all the previous forms again because they were now officially out of date, before sealing the envelope and posting the letter.

Ten days later, the request was rejected again.

As it turned out, the window company Milo wanted to go with, which was the cheapest and most no-nonsense of the ones he got quotes from, wasn't a registered company. Due to the fact that someone else never filled in the admin, Milo now had even more to do. Milo had to go through all his old window quotes, which he had to recite from memory because he threw out all but the one he wanted a long time ago, and once he had decided on a new company, filled out all the forms *again*, and sent them off *again* to be reviewed. Milo had completed all the forms three times now, no doubt destroying a forest in the process of their printing. Milo knew he had all relevant papers, and he knew the new company he had chosen was definitely registered; things were finally going to be sorted.

Things were not sorted, as the window request was rejected again.

Milo was apoplectic with rage as he read the phrase "We apologise, but we do not have your identification on record."

Never mind the fact that Milo's papers were missing, it was hardly surprising at this point that no one knew how to use a filing cabinet; Milo was enraged that these creatures were pretending to be apologetic. They weren't apologetic, they weren't sorry, there's probably a guy at the top of that office wanking himself witless thinking of all the misery their causing, thought Milo. They probably have portraits of all the disgruntled faces they cause; they're probably spying on people through the office window at the reception desks, and laughing as they watch people get rejected for their new conservatory; they probably wouldn't give someone with arthritis their medicine without making them do ten push-ups first. Milo was irate, and once again snapped like he had with the pension office. Milo didn't just walk to Dorcoast, he ran with all the rage of a bull, using athleticism he didn't know he had, fuelled high on adrenaline. By the time he reached the housing office and stopped running, he was exhausted, which may have been for the best, because he probably would have straggled someone if he had the remaining strength.

"Can I help you?" asked the receptionist slightly nervous as she saw Milo breathing heavily.

"Probably not, but let's try it," growled Milo. "I've just been told you don't have my records in your office," he explained while showing the now crumpled rejection letter. "Can you explain how this has happened?"

"... If you fill out a question-and-answer for-"

"NO!" shouted Milo. "Don't make me fill in another bloody form! All I want is a new window. For the love of all that is good, find Ernest so he can sort this out now."

The receptionist, showing the first bit of emotion she had ever done at work in years, went into one of the locked offices. The other people in the reception area had watched Milo's outburst, and were keeping their distance from the lunatic. After a few minutes, the receptionist returned with a man who worked there, but definitely wasn't Ernest.

"How can I help?" asked the man.

"Where's Ernest?" replied Milo quickly.

"Don't worry. I'll be able to sort out your problem."

"I want to see Ernest," demanded Milo.

The man tried to calm Milo, but to no avail, before addressing matters again.

"I'm afraid Ernest has retired," answered the man.

Milo's eyebrows raised, and his nostrils flared, in what is known by body language experts as the "I could kill you and feel nothing" face. In the who-knows-how-long time it had taken to get the problem up to this moment, the man who first raised the supposed issue with Milo didn't even work there anymore, and probably failed to file Milo's papers to whoever he was supposed to pass them on to, so not only would Milo have to make *another* window request, but he also had to have his home registered before he could even make said window request.

"Sir," said the man, trying to regain Milo's attention, "I don't want to beat around the bush but-"

"What do you mean beat around the bush? It's all bush! This entire process has been nothing but bush!" screamed Milo.

"Sir, we can have everything sorted for you. I understand we don't have your records, but if you can provide us a copy of your birth certificate, we can-"

Milo didn't remember what happened after that, but the police explained that he was fined for criminal damage. Oddly enough, the administrative process for Milo handing over a chunk of his money wasn't nearly as difficult as getting a window fixed. By the end of the day, Milo was home, his house still slightly chilly from where the cardboard didn't perfectly fit the window frame. Milo sat down with a full bottle of whiskey, wrestling with the indignation of the whole process, and was emotionally exhausted. Milo could see the critical path in front of him: Get a new birth certificate, register at the housing office, then apply for a new window again, but how long would that take? A month? Ha! Closer to a year, thought Milo. If Milo knew how to forge documents, or even knew someone who could, he would do it in a heartbeat, money no object. Milo had next to nothing in the way of personal documents.

Although, thought Milo, that could be used to my advantage.

A few weeks had passed since Milo was arrested, and he sat calmly in his living room, reading a history book and excluding himself from the world, until there was a knock at the door. The person knocking was from the home and land registry; not Ernest, who was retired, nor the other man Milo talked to in the reception, who had since also made a career change, but a completely new face.

"Are you Mr. Milo Point?" asked the housing official.

"Yes," replied Milo.

"Hello. I understand you were interested in having a new window fitted."

"I was, but it's already been done."

Milo pointed to the brand-new window in the front of his house, that both opened, and could be seen through.

The housing official looked slightly bewildered. "Did you get permission for that?"

"No," replied Milo bluntly.

"You performed illegal construction on your house?"

"I did."

The housing official was caught off guard by the readiness that Milo was willing to admit his crime. Milo stood in the doorway, seemingly without a care in the world as one might when idly chatting to a work colleague.

"Do you realise the implications of that?" questioned the official. "The leaseholder has every right to take you to court."

"You can try it," smirked Milo, "but unfortunately, you don't have my identification on your records."

Milo knew the home and land registry might come back for a routine check, but they would only find his address from his recently filed documents, and not his personal records. While Milo was smiling like a clown, the housing official was not best pleased.

"I can find out which contractor you used and report you through them," argued the official.

"I'm sure you could," admitted Milo, "but unfortunately

again, I used an unregistered company."

Milo, through a collection of other people's mistakes and a little underhand deception, had created a paperless trial to get his new window, and without paperwork, he was uncatchable to a bureaucrat, because without solid proof, there is no proof at all; Milo wasn't even "technically" a homeowner. Milo was about to slam the door in the officials' face and go back to his quiet, happy, paperwork free life, but before doing so, wanted to make one thing abundantly clear.

"Let it be known," said Milo, leaning towards the official, "I'll be happy to meet you in court, but you have a lot of paperwork to fill out first."

***

Milo showed up at The Devil's Neckhole around mid-afternoon, no specific agenda in mind besides inebriation. Milo was about to go through the door when he noticed an advert in the window accompanying a portrait. The advert was written by Heidi, and promoted her service as an artist for hire. Heidi had made it clear she was looking for additional work, even asking The Big Cheese at The Bystander for any extra jobs, but she'd been so far unlucky. Milo had no idea that the advert had been posted, but come to think of it, Milo realised he hadn't had a proper walk around Pending for a while. Milo thought about questioning Heidi next time he saw her, but that could wait until tomorrow. Milo wandered into the bar, and was greeted by his usual favourite barmaid.

"Hello stranger," announced Hazel. "Where have you been?"

"What do you mean?"

"I don't think I've seen much of you recently. Don't tell me you've turned sober."

"No. I've just been busy."

Milo purchased a couple of his usual brews as Hazel made idle chit-chat. It became apparent to Hazel that Milo wasn't aware of a lot of current happenings around town; he only knew a few headlines from his work at the newspaper. Hazel's curiosity had been sparked, but it was truly ignited when she noticed a change in Milo's attire.

"That's a nice shirt," commented Hazel.

"Thanks" responded Milo. Hazel noticed Milo smiling after that compliment, a much wider grin than he normally would.

"Was it a gift?" asked Hazel.

"Yes it…" Milo's sentence trailed off for seemingly no reason.

"Is something the matter?"

"No. Not at all."

"I see," muttered Hazel. "Who's the present from?"

Milo dithered. "It's from no one."

"What? You bought a gift for yourself. Milo, are you hiding something."

Milo remained silent; he was going on the defensive in this interrogation, and Hazel realised she needed to change her tact.

"When you said you were busy," started Hazel, "why were you so busy?"

Milo remained silent still.

"Where were you that stopped you visiting?"

Milo kept his mouth shut.

"Who were you busy with?"

Milo's eyes widened slightly, a twitch you'd never notice if you weren't looking, but Hazel was.

"You were with someone! Out of town."

"I was not."

"You definitely were," beamed Hazel, having cracked the nut. "Come on. No secrets between friends. Tell me everything."

Milo gave in to peer pressure; it would only be a matter of time anyway, and he confessed where he had been, what he'd been doing, and most pressingly, why he was suddenly happy all the time. The answer was surprising to Hazel considering the nature of the man, but it was nothing worth hiding. When the situation was properly explained, Hazel was happy to let Milo drink in peace, and left him in his daydreaming state.

I never had him down as a romantic, thought Hazel.

CHAPTER ELEVEN

Orchestrated Madness

It was an unremarkable day in (what is fair to say) the most unremarkable town in Flatrock, and Hazel was enjoying the peace and quiet that life in an unremarkable town grants a person. Hazel was at home, making the most out of a game of solitaire early in the day, and there was not a modicum of reason in the woman's mind to believe why the peace should be disturbed. The weather was not cold enough to cause discomfort, nor hot enough to attract day drinkers; only the most determined of spiders might poke its head from its hovel to test the purity of the day. The noise outside was not loud, nor quiet enough to assume the apocalypse. Everything was mediocre, which for Hazel, was perfect.

That previous statement was true until a knock came at the door.

Hazel was startled and perturbed, as she was not expecting company. Unexpected guests usually bring with them inconvenience, and with inconvenience comes annoyance, and with annoyance comes violence, so Hazel ignored the sound.

There was a second knock at the door.

Hazel remained still, for she knew if she made a sound, whoever was at the door would know there was someone in, and keep trying.

There was a third knock on the door.

This was almost certain to be the final attempt. One time may be misheard. Twice might be a mistake. Thrice indicates there is no one home. Hazel held her breath for a moment longer and listened carefully for footsteps slowly becoming distant.

There was a fourth knock at the door.

This was beginning to take the mick. Even a genuinely important messenger would have left a note through the letterbox to give details of their impending return. Hazel was becoming quite aggravated.

A fifth knock.

A sixth knock.

It was after the eleventh attempt that Hazel got up and stormed to the door, opening it with the force of a typhoon. Hazel looked at the unfamiliar man standing in front of her, and spoke firmly.

"What do you want?" demanded Hazel.

"Hello, would you mind if I talked to you for a second," asked the man.

This was bad. Only two kinds of people want to talk to you on your doorstep: Police officers to tell you a loved one has died, or political campaigners. Unfortunately for Hazel, no one was dead.

It has possibly become apparent in my recounting of these stories of Flatrock that I hold some kind of grudge against politicians and political figures, but that's what they get for being such self-satisfying swine suckers. In the early days of established democratic politics, many politicians could be held in disdain for wrong doings by the general population. Going to war with other countries for underhanded reasons, not following the laws they establish, or simply calling people pricks to their faces were just some of the things politicians would often do. To avoid vicious scrutiny, politicians devised a way to make politics insufferable to talk about, taking some inspiration from competitive sports. Politicians divided into two "parties" (ironic considering a party is supposed to imply fun) of slightly different beliefs, meaning there also became a divide in populations. With clearly established "teams" in the election, there would now be winners and losers, creating a delusion of competition, and people who supported one party instinctively hated the opposition, but the plan was much more devious than simple titles. The most ingenious part of the plan went as follows: Newspapers were founded by friends and colleagues of the then leading politicians, which pedalled specially curated stories to affirm peoples' empty beliefs, which worked to tremendous effect. It is a commonly observed fact that the more frequently someone tells you a lie, even if you know the truth, you slowly start to believe the lie (or so I've been told a few times). Just like competitive sports, this led to arguments, but unlike competitive sports, politics actually mattered. People who grew tired of the quarrels stopped following politics for their own sanity, and now with half the world not wanting to read the news, and the other half arguing blindly, there were less people to scrutinise politics, and politicians got away with a lot more because of it. It wasn't long before the multi-party system came to be used worldwide, and the entire planet was bent over to be given a damn good rogering.

Traditionally speaking, politicians are supposed to serve for the benefit of the population in their designated area using laws governing health, welfare, immigration, economy, crime, military, education, and many other departments, while accepting a portion of state tax funds for the work provided, but it was argued (by politicians) that the people doing these important jobs deserved a high salary for their work. This is where the party system started to fall apart. While intending to give the illusion of competition, there was still a prize for the winner, and the fake divide became very real. Politics no longer became a public service; it was a game; a game that you won by manipulating the minds of the public. Influencing local prejudices, acting charismatic, and even flat out lying became common practice in the mad race for power. People were competing for the opportunity to screw over the public, and charge them tax for the privilege. This is why you will not find it hard to believe that Hazel was wishing for death.

The creature standing in Hazel's doorway was a politician named Lawrence Braker, made evident by the name badge he was wearing. He was a person of average height with brown hair and a face you could trust (hanging over his mantelpiece). He held in his left hand a thick paper folder loaded with statistics, surveys and a dead baby sandwich. With a sterile jet black blazer, chalk white shirt, and brown leather shoes, it's fair to say he was dressed to kill (the mood). Hazel stood at the door for a split second before Lawrence raised the question again.

"I said can we speak for a second?" asked Lawrence.

"No," asserted Hazel, quickly while slamming the door, only to find it blocked by a foot.

"Are you aware of the upcoming election?"

"No, and I don't care," replied Hazel, rhythmically continuing to slam the door on Lawrence's foot, but he seemed to not feel the pain, which isn't too surprising considering insects are known for their hard skins.

"Are you also aware," started Lawrence, watching the timing between each slam, and slipping through the second the doorway was wide enough to crawl through, "that the current government has failed to deliver on its promises."

"I wasn't keeping track but to be honest, I'm not surprised. Would you leave?"

"You see," started Lawrence, turning away from Hazel and walking around her small flat, speaking out loud and obviously ignoring the previous comment, "I represent the Central Unions National Trust Society (a bit of a mouthful but for some reason, they don't like acronyms) and I work for the benefit of businesses in the area."

Hazel rolled her eyes. "Do you really?"

"Indeed I am. Tell me, are you employed?"

Hazel thought about her response carefully, knowing that whatever she said would have a prepared response, unless she said, "I have a corpse in the floorboards."

"Ah, you work as a gravedigger," returned Lawrence.

"I killed them myself and ate their face."

"Ah, I am unfamiliar with the current practices. Getting back on point."

Hazel threw her hands to the side in disbelief; she knew her ploy was absurd, but anything was better than entertaining this cockroach, who was clearly following a script, and would stick to it as much as possible.

"I am working hard to ensure the job security of all people, from the freelance and self-employed, to the unionised and non-unionised workers. Small businesses are the cornerstone of the blah blah blah boo boo whatsamajiger foodlefudge," is what Hazel heard the wasp saying. Lawrence was probably saying intelligible words, but Hazel had pulled out two pieces of cotton from a drawer and stuffed them in her ear; she stared at Lawrence, so enraptured by the sound of his own voice that he hadn't even noticed. Hazel stood in front of him for quite some time, but Lawrence never twigged to what was happening. Hazel edged closer to the politician in the hopes he might notice, but to no avail. A not insubstantial amount of time passed before Lawrence's jaw stopped biting at the air, and he looked once again at Hazel, who quickly removed the cotton from her ears.

"Yes, yes, very interesting," said Hazel.

"I don't believe you were listening to what I was saying," noted Lawrence.

"You're right, I wasn't. If we're being honest, I don't really care for you, or whatever you represent."

Most people would take that open letter as an invitation to go away, but some termites are not so easily stamped out. As a political campaigner, it was Lawrence's job to change people's way of thinking, and simply saw Hazel as another challenge to overcome.

"Why is it that you don't care about the central unions?" asked Lawrence.

"I don't even know what the central unions are," moaned Hazel.

This was a bad choice of words considering the creature in

front of her was holding a folder the size of a small dog. What led was what felt like revenge for all the schoolwork that was never completed or taken seriously. Hazel was reaching her breaking point and wandered through her home to find peace, which didn't last long as only a minute later, Mr. Braker was following. After a time, Hazel entered the kitchen looking for the hardest work surface in the home to smash her face against, until a sudden idea popped into her head; she reached into a drawer and pulled out the biggest knife she owned, before prodding the tip into the blazer of the still rambling mosquito. Lawrence saw the blade, but it only distracted him for half a second as he continued his lecture. Hazel pressed the knife slightly deeper into the fabric, but there was no further reaction. Harder still, this time there was no way Lawrence couldn't feel the point digging into his chest. Lawrence was worried about his suit becoming torn, so stepped back from the blade. Hazel noticed the slight movement and walked forward. Before long, Hazel was the new lead dancer in this tango of twats; all the while, Lawrence was still talking. Hazel edged the intruder towards the exit, and influenced him out into the door. When Lawrence was outside, making extra care to poke a hole in his shoe which was trying to block the doorway, Hazel slammed the door in his face. A detailed discussion on the central unions was still in progress, but it slowly diminished. When the subtle hint had finally sunk through Lawrence's thick skull, he walked away.

It would be worth noting at this point that Hazel would not have stabbed Lawrence, but this was only because she fell out of the habit of sharpening her knives, and even her best weapon struggled to slice an onion. Hazel relaxed her muscles again, returned her knife to the drawer, and sat back down in front of her game. It was here that Hazel became incredibly irate.

"That knobhead finished my solitaire game!"

A few hours later in the day, Milo was sitting in his study, copying research material into a blank book while he ate lunch. Milo often ate in his study, and could be described as a workaholic, but that was only the second worst kind of "holic" he could be called. When it came to eating in the study, Milo had a strict set of rules: One, the food must be placed a suitable distance away from any research material. Two, the food must not contain any sauce or liquid content that could splash or stain. Three, any food eaten with bare hands requires the use of white linen gloves, which will be removed when returning to writing, and washed after every meal (if it wasn't already clear, Milo lived alone.) Milo was lost in thought when there came a knock at the door. This knock didn't come as much of a surprise to Milo like it had done Hazel. Milo, if only by proxy of working for a newspaper, knew full well this could have happened, and who might be at the door. It was for this reason he had double checked the locks on the windows, and blocked every possible entry point. Milo peeked through the curtains to ascertain who exactly it was, and how troublesome they might be. Ignoring the problem rarely worked, and affirmative action would have to be taken to remove the pest.

"Hello," shouted Milo from the safe side of a window.

Milo had no recognition exactly who the politician was from appearance alone, or their political party, but that wasn't too surprising considering many insects look identical to each other.

"Hello," said Lawrence. "Pleasure to meet you."

"No, it isn't," replied Milo.

"Would you mind if I talked to you for a second?"

"We can, but we'll have to do it here. My door won't open."

"Why's that?"

"I refuse to open it."

"Oh, that shouldn't be a problem. Let me just-"

Lawrence left Milo's line of vision as the politician stepped away from the window. Milo tried to listen carefully, and rearranged himself at the glass frame to get a better view of the thing in the street, but with no luck. As Milo was transfixed on the outside...

"Are you aware of the upcoming election?" asked Lawrence,

who was standing behind Milo as if he had crawled through a crack in the floorboards.

Milo jumped, and if it wasn't for the window, he would have fallen into the street.

"How did you get in here?" asked Milo slightly panicked.

"I represent the Central Unions National Trust Society," started Lawrence, avoiding the question like a seasoned politician would, "and I work for the benefit of businesses in the area. Tell me, are you employed?"

Milo was a newspaper interviewer, and had talked to a fair few politicians in his work. He was familiar with the language, the tricks, the facades and masquerade balls these cretins would prance through. Once they start talking, they won't stop until their statement is completed, regardless of how loud someone shouts over them, or who might be wielding a knife. Lawrence continued to discuss his plans for a strong economic foundation, a higher standard of living for working families, and other buzzwords that could have been taken from a moron's guide to popular political lies. Milo was at no point interested, but listened regardless. When the annoying white noise emanating from Lawrence's mouth ceased, Milo spoke up.

"This is all very interesting," lied Milo, "but before I cast my vote, I want one question answered first."

"Absolutely. Ask away," invited Lawrence.

"Why should I trust you?"

Lawrence dithered. "Excuse me."

"How do I know you can be trusted to keep your promises? I'll take anything. Anything at all. A personal anecdote. A friend of yours I could meet who would vouch for you. Do you have any means by which I can use to believe you?"

Lawrence swallowed. "I care deeply about business owners and their employees."

"No, you care about them paying tax," countered Milo. "How can I know that you'll follow through with your plans."

Lawrence wasn't sure what to say to this, as he didn't have a prepared response; he looked through his folder for a chart or diagram that could prove his humanity, but to no avail. It was while searching through the folder that Lawrence committed the ultimate faux pas.

A sandwich dropped on the floor.

Milo's eyes widened, analysing just how many rules were being broken and their possible severity (again, lives alone).

"That's my lunch," said Lawrence unapologetically.

As Lawrence picked up his meal, Milo examined with newly sharpened eyes the contents of the bread. It was red, wet, chunky, the kind of thing that would attract ants if it was not handled carefully. Milo scrambled in his head as to whether he had some kind of container to conceal the problem, but the internal skirmish was cut short, as Lawrence helped himself to a piece of paper, the one Milo was copying, from the nearby desk, which he used to wipe his hands. Milo became irate. The feeling boiled away inside him, and he was more than prepared to get rid of this louse.

"Leave now," demanded Milo.

"I haven't answered your question," argued Lawrence.

"Your silence told me everything I needed to know. Goodbye."

Milo had grabbed hold of Lawrence and was using his limited strength to push the politician to the door. Lawrence continued to speak, but Milo wasn't listening anymore, and shoved the termite outside. Milo made sure to check every lock again, paranoid of the security breach, and used the rest of his day trying to decipher the words below the sandwich spread. Lawrence had caused a great inconvenience to Milo that day, not that Lawrence would ever know that, as he was too busy eating his lunch.

It was becoming late in the day, but there were still plenty more stops left in the campaign trail for Lawrence. For the final stretch, Lawrence walked through the district where it seemed the lower classes could be found, which caused him to shudder at the thought, who could possibly help these poor people, he didn't think to himself. After several visits, Lawrence walked to the first floor of a building and knocked on the door, which was quickly answered.

"Hello," said Heidi.

"Hello, would you mind if I talked to you for a second," said Lawrence.

"Absolutely, come in."

Heidi welcomed the guest into her apartment and invited him to sit down. She didn't have chairs, but she did have a pile of crap with a blanket over it that wouldn't break under a person's weight. Heidi let Lawrence sit down on the crap while she made a seat of the floor.

"Are you aware of the upcoming election?" asked Lawrence.

The election seemed to ring a bell with Heidi, considering she worked at the same place as Milo, but unlike her colleague, she only paid half as much attention.

"No, I hadn't," confessed Heidi.

"Are you also aware that the current government has failed to deliver on its promises," asked Lawrence.

"No, I haven't lived in the area for very long."

Lawrence smiled, knowing he had found an easy target for influence. "You see, I represent the Central Unions National Trust Society and I work for the benefit of businesses in the area. Tell me, are you employed?"

Heidi listened intently to what Lawrence had to say. Lawrence seemed to speak with passion about the necessity of business to the grand scheme of society, and other local social issues Heidi didn't fully understand. Being someone who doesn't understand politics is not uncommon; someone who doesn't understand politics, and *knows* they don't understand politics is very rare indeed. When Lawrence reached the end of his speech, Heidi did indeed have something to ask.

"Oh, sorry, I should have said when you came in. Would you like a cup of tea?"

Heidi didn't wait for an answer before preparing the kettle, and urged Lawrence to talk on. She pressed more questions about other opposing parties and their policies, the history of the current government, and even an in depth discussion on the central unions. As someone who was relatively new to the area, many things were a mystery to Heidi, and she listened studiously, which Lawrence noticed. This was one of those rare occasions when someone seemed to genuinely care about politics without being toxic; it came from a place of interest, and the want to understand and educate, which Lawrence was happy to oblige, as an idiot was much easier to influence than someone who knew half what they were talking about. However, with a clueless individual comes clueless questions.

"There's one thing I'm still wondering," asked Heidi. "If all the political parties want the best for the public, why don't they work together?"

Of course, you know the answer to this question as I stated it at the beginning of this story, but I have the benefit of knowing Flatrock's complete history and can tell you it. In this age of Flatrock, that fact was never made public, and happened many, many centuries ago, so the original answer is no longer correct.

"The parties wouldn't work together. Their beliefs are too radically different," answered Lawrence.

"But I thought it was the beliefs of the people that mattered," questioned Heidi.

What Heidi just said is the most common lie politicians tell people to make them feel like they mattered. Ages ago, in the founding of democracy, such a statement might be true, but not anymore. Fortunately for Lawrence, a question like this was easily answered.

"That's why the public vote for the party they believe represents them, and the new leader passes laws on behalf of the majority voters," explained Lawrence.

"So, people don't get to directly vote on new laws?" asked Heidi.

Most politicians actually hate the idea of people voting, as it gives the public an opportunity to do something in their own interest.

"That's correct," answered Lawrence.

"Hm, so there's clearly a lot of trust put in politicians around here," said Heidi.

Lawrence had to stop himself from chuckling. "Correct again."

Lawrence talked further to assure Heidi the political system was foolproof, and she believed him. In the end, a significant amount of time had passed, and Lawrence was feeling confident he had recruited someone into his way of thinking. Once the conversation had reached its natural conclusion, Lawrence rose from his seat.

"Thank you for listening," said Lawrence. "I assume I can count on your vote in the election."

"Oh, no. I don't vote," replied Heidi.

Lawrence froze. "What!"

"I don't stay in one place for very long, and I don't think it would be right to vote on laws that won't affect me."

After Lawrence stormed out of Heidi's apartment, he realised he had lost the remainder of his day, and he would have to return to the rock he crawled out of before it became too dark. The day had proved quite pointless for Lawrence, considering his greatest achievement during the whole endeavour was a free cup of tea. It seemed he had no support in the upcoming election, the Central Unions National Trust Society would fail, and he would never be in a position of power.

Serves the bastard right.

***

Heidi showed up at The Devil's Neckhole immediately after finishing work at The Bystander, looking for Hazel and hoping that her advert had successfully drawn in a few clients, or at least some curiosity. Unfortunately, no such luck. Heidi knew it was possible a pub was not the best place for an advert, but it was the only place that offered advertising for free, and that was only because she was friends with Hazel. Heidi was starting to get the itch of impatience; she wanted desperately to start travelling again, but nothing was working in her favour.

"Chin up," said Hazel, trying to comfort Heidi.

Heidi forced a smile, and knew things weren't all that bad; at least her itch was caused by impatience and not a horrible infection. Hazel still knew that the smile was fake to an extent, and she knew she didn't have an answer for the predicament, but she was sure she could take Heidi's mind off the subject.

"Want to know a secret?" asked Hazel.

"What is it?" answered Heidi, never able to resist opening a closed box.

"Milo has a girlfriend."

Heidi was flabbergasted. "No! You're joking."

"It's true. Her name's Tola. She's lives in Nunca and works as a prostitute."

Heidi thought for a moment. "I'm not sure if that's a girlfriend."

"Apparently he gets the service for free, so technically, it is."

Heidi was at a loss for words for a moment. "Wow. Good on him. I thought he hated travelling."

"He had a change of heart, I guess."

Heidi was happy for Milo; though it was hard to believe considering his outward disdain for most things, but she supposed he wasn't totally closed minded. Milo had become pretty firm friends with Heidi, and Heidi friends with Milo; she was pleased that he was pleased, but the curiosity didn't stop there.

"Tell me everything you know about her," demanded Heidi.

Hazel was more than happy to assist, glad she had distracted Heidi from her worries, if just for a few minutes. There was nothing wrong with a little friendly gossip, and it's not like Milo could hide it forever; his girlfriend lived in another country, and there's only so many times you can claim you're going on a trip before people start asking where and why. Hazel and Heidi would have rambled aimlessly for hours, if it wasn't for the fact that the man of the moment had shown up.

"You have a girlfriend!" shouted Heidi, as Milo walked through the door to The Devil's Neckhole.

"Yes, I do," thought Milo out loud, unsure whether the comment was one to take with pride or offence.

"That's so good for you. How did it all happen? Why have you been keeping it a secret?"

Milo reiterated the story of his chance encounter with Tola to Heidi, explained what it was like in Nunca, and even discussed Dodek with a sense of admiration.

"You're a stepdad now!" congratulated Heidi.

"Calm down," demanded Milo. "I haven't known her that long. We're not married yet."

"You said yet! You're planning it, aren't you?"

Milo acted defensive around the whole situation, trying to make out that his and Tola's relationship was not the world changing event Heidi was making it out to be. There was only so much of the arguing Hazel could take before she blurted out, "Oh, stop being so embarrassed, you knob! You've fallen in love, not shat yourself. Something good has finally happened in your life, so stop acting like it's nothing."

Hazel's words silenced Milo immediately, and for a while. Heidi teased for a confession like a child, and didn't give in until the words were out of Milo's mouth.

"Fine. I admit it," started Milo. "I'm in love, and I want to spend my life with her and her son."

Heidi and Hazel simultaneously said, "Awww," unintentionally embarrassing Milo; the words had been forced out of him, but he meant them, he just wasn't used to vocalising it so bluntly. Milo quickly took a prolonged sip of his beverage to hide his face, but the secret was out, and there was nothing more to hide.

CHAPTER TWELVE

Relics Of A Bygone Word

Milo, Heidi, and Hazel stayed in The Devil's Neckhole for no small amount of time, losing themselves in conversation, but besides the revelation that Milo had somehow managed to get his leg over, the evening was like any other; Milo was drinking, Hazel was serving, and Heidi was on damage control. Time passed as it normally did within those oft-examined walls until Heidi had a sudden sense of realisation.

"What's the date today?" asked Heidi.

"Tenth day, tenth month," answered Hazel.

"Hey! That means it's Mask's Day," declared Heidi.

"Who's day?" queried Milo with liquor dribbling down his chin.

"In my home country we celebrate Mask's Day, where children wear masks and prank each other. The mask is so no one knows that it's you."

"And the point is?"

"I don't think there is a point. It's just one of those fun things you do every year."

"It doesn't sound like fun."

"That's only because you know you'd be the victim," remarked Hazel. "Is Mask's Day based on anything?"

"Well, according to legend," started Heidi, "there was a man with a suit and walking stick who wandered around town. No one saw his face because he always wore a mask. Some people say he was really a monster. When you weren't looking, he would prank you. He only moved when you couldn't see him, and he travelled lightning fast. I don't know the exact origin, but it became a tradition to mess with people, and you're only supposed to do it when their back is turned."

"I think I've heard about this," added Milo. "Didn't it have something to do with a masked man who went around killing a bunch of farmers."

There was a pause, then Hazel broke the silence. "I suppose that would be quite the prank."

"You've heard about that too, right?" asked Milo to Hazel.

"I have, but I wasn't going to ruin Heidi's fun, on Mask's Day of all days." Hazel turned to face Heidi. "You'll have to ignore Milo; he gets unsettled by monster stories."

"I'm not scared of monsters," snapped Milo. "They don't exist."

"You say that, but if there's such a thing as God, why can't there be monsters?" countered Hazel.

"They're always some kind of misunderstanding. It's either magic, or magic items, or drunk people trying to rationalise events in the way a drunk person would."

"But monsters do exist," said Heidi, jumping in on the argument. "There's so many folk tales in the world that not all of them can be mistakes."

"I assure you they are," stated Milo.

"You're wasting your time," said Hazel. "He won't admit he's wrong."

"Let's try it," suggested Heidi. "I bet you I can find some kind of monster story that you can't explain."

"Try it," challenged Milo. "You have until I go home."

"Take your time Heidi. You've got all night," mumbled Hazel.

When God created life, he instilled in them the emotion of fear, so whenever a dangerous situation presented itself, a person may run or fight in order to survive, but I can't help in thinking that if God didn't spend so much time on fear, and instead spent all that spare time on better refining common sense, you wouldn't need fear at all. When you think about it, several emotions are somewhat useless. Anger is there to help mentally prepare you for a fight, a fight that, by law of averages, was started because someone got angry. Jealousy exists in order to motivate us to compete against each other and better ourselves, but again, it causes more conflict than it resolves. The only reason we experience sadness is because of all the trouble caused by anger and jealousy.

But I'm getting sidetracked.

Fear, generally speaking, is used as a way to avoid unpleasant situations via subconscious control of the body through the mind. It is unfortunate however that fear's potency has been somewhat watered down by the existence of folk stories. As if the threat of an actual sabre-toothed tiger wasn't enough, people also invented myths and monsters that would use the controlling power of fear to manipulate people's whim, even though these rumours never really existed. Of course, in the post-religious world of Flatrock, folk stories are usually reserved for children who haven't eaten all their vegetables, but they do still exist, and Heidi was just about to recite one.

It didn't take Heidi long to recount her first story; she had travelled a decent portion of the world, so had a good repertoire to pull from. "Out in the oceans far north, there's a group of islands called the Lichians, one of the hottest inhabited countries in the world. Growing farm animals there is difficult, so they import meat from the mainland continent. Every week, a boat load of ready butchered farm animals arrives at port, except one day, none appeared."

"Wow, I didn't see that coming," groaned Milo.

"Shut up!" barked Hazel. "Continue, please."

"After the shipment didn't show up," resumed Heidi, "the Lichian locals sent out a boat to see what happened, except they never returned. Weeks went by without a shipment of meat, and the reason was still unknown. It wasn't until the locals started to starve that someone from the mainland washed up on shore.

When they were asked what happened to them, the survivor had no idea; the only thing they remembered was sailing towards the island, then a big cloud of fog covered the deck of the ship. The boat started breaking to pieces, and the crew fell into the water, surviving only by luck. Since that day, you still hear stories of disappearances from around those seas. Accounts differ depending on who you ask, but the result is always the same: Boats that sail around the sea of the Lichians frequently go missing."

When it appeared that Heidi's story had ended, Milo piped up and said, "It's simply not true. While boats have disappeared there, the water around the Lichian Sea is no more deadly than any other part of the ocean. The legend was most likely started as a tourism stunt based on a one-time occurrence."

Heidi didn't have any way to disprove the argument, so had to give up almost instantly.

"If that's the best you have, this isn't going to take very long," chirped Milo.

"Might I add a story to the mix," asked Hazel.

"Go ahead," said Milo, welcoming his new opponent to the ring.

"Have you heard of a prizore?" asked Hazel, adopting a tone of voice to better portray a sense of menacing. "They're creatures that hide behind the moon and prowl around the cities looking for people to execute. When they move, they leave trails of ash because their skin is so hot, it burns their clothes as they run. If you feel a sudden wave of heat, or a gust of wind when you're walking alone at night, it's because a prizore crossed your path, but you were lucky enough not to be noticed. Their skin is yellow, like rotten bones, their eyes are green as ivy, and their breath reeks from the rotten flesh caught between their piercingly sharp teeth-"

"And they're not real," interrupted Milo bluntly. "Prizores are from a satirical book about King Basco of Doninger. He never went out during the day for fear of assassination, his skin was hot and yellow because of a disease, and his breath stinking was an allegory for the fact that his preferred method of execution was feeding people poison until they died of diarrhea induced dehydration."

There was a pause, then Heidi broke the silence. "I never did *that* kind of prank for Mask's Day."

There was a lapse in the chosen conversation while Heidi thought of her next story; she knew that simply rattling off all the folk stories she knew wouldn't work, nor would recounting some of her favourites. Heidi's challenge was to come up with a story that had no explanation, and she was going to do that. Soon enough, Heidi settled on a story that she thought might work, as the details of it led her to believe it was based on a real-world event.

"You must have heard of the legendary explorer Bradstein, right?" asked Heidi.

"I know vaguely of him," stated Milo.

"Well, have you heard the legend of the crocodile with diamond teeth? Out in the swamps somewhere west of the world, Bradstein found the territory of a huge crocodile, its mouth as big as the tallest man you've ever seen. The other creatures in the wilderness feared it, and wouldn't so much as look at it. When Bradstein's crew went to investigate the creature, they saw all its teeth were diamonds, the largest gemstones you would ever find. A member of the crew couldn't help themselves, and reached into the crocodile's mouth to pull at its teeth. They pulled and pulled so hard until the tooth was yanked from the animal's jaw, but unfortunately-"

"Its jaw snapped down and ate the person's arm," said Milo and Heidi in unison.

"How did you know?" asked Heidi.

"Because I have the mental capacity of someone older than two, and before you get too carried away, I'll tell you now that your whole story is just a cautionary tale about not letting greed distract you from danger. I'll admit that this was your best one so far; it at least had a person I know was real, but besides that, it was cack."

"Let me have another try," suggested Hazel. "I want to know your explanation for all the local disappearances in Dorcoast at the hands of the dockland devil."

"Oo, I want to hear about this," burst Heidi.

"I don't," added Milo.

"You already know that Dorcoast is a big port town with lots of tradespeople coming and going, but did you know that many of them go missing?" explained Hazel.

"Interesting how a lot of these stories involve sailors: the kind of people who are stereotypically the biggest drinkers."

Hazel ignored the heckle and continued on. "Sometimes, in the dark nights of Dorcoast, when the streets are quiet and the merchants rely on the street lamps for direction, they often lose their way. Sometimes, they fall. Sometimes, they fall unconscious. When they wake up, they've found their body covered in scars, but they're the lucky ones."

Milo was rolling his eyes at this point in the story, but Hazel continued for Heidi's benefit.

"Out from the sea, there's a creature that crawls up the pier and onto land; a hulking beast with muscles like rocks, deep blue scales, and blade-like spines running the whole way down its arm. This is the dockland devil, and it searches for those sailors who lose themselves in Dorcoast's maze-like buildings. When the monster finds a particularly meaty victim, it will drag them back to the docks, and take them into the water, drowning them to never be seen again."

Heidi was in awe of the storyteller. "Wow, that's really creepy."

"Now that you're finished, do I have permission to ruin your fun?" interjected Milo. "It's just a story of drunk people getting mugged. Anyone who disappeared fell into the ocean on the way back to their ships," said Milo, unwilling to wait for his previous question to be answered.

Hazel was starting to get annoyed by Milo's self-satisfied attitude.

"Alright then, how about this," started Hazel, dropping the intimidating voice and instead speaking as bluntly as possible. "There once was a creature who stalked women. When that creature saw a woman that they like, it'd often follow them, but was always too shy to get their attention. There was one time when this creature walked six miles before eventually being stopped by the police, who asked why the creature was stalking an innocent young girl. When the creature couldn't give a good enough answer, the monster spent three days in a prison cell until they were bailed out."

Milo was silent.

"Can't you explain that story?" asked Hazel.

"I can," countered Milo.

"Why don't you want to?"

"You know why."

"Oh, that's right. That wasn't a monster at all. That was you."

Heidi burst out laughing as Milo's face failed to hide the sheer embarrassment that had washed over him.

"I want to clarify that I don't stalk women. I was drunk, and this only happened once," argued Milo.

"Of course it only happened once. You were too scared to try it again," objected Hazel.

Heidi almost toppled over her barstool laughing as Milo ducked to cover his face.

When the argument had calmed down, and the clientele of the bar who were listening in had decided to reserve their judgement of Milo to private conversations, Heidi and Hazel were still thinking between them of a story that Milo couldn't explain; now he had been outed as a pervert, he seemed a little more susceptible to open mindedness.

"I got it," exclaimed Heidi. "I have one folk story that you won't be able to disprove. I heard it from some people who served the patron of honesty, so it can't be fake."

Milo waved his hand as if to say "I'm all ears," as he was currently feeling too sheepish to speak out loud.

"There's a temple up in the mountains north of here," started Heidi. "The temple was decorated with bright blues and golds, and the ceiling was as high as a hundred of me."

"You mean it was the size of a normal house," said Milo to the incredibly short woman.

Hazel turned to look at Milo, which silenced him in an instant, before Heidi continued.

"One day, the chief of the temple died, and in accordance with tradition, they were cremated, and sealed their ashes in an urn. The urn was completely unassuming according to the followers. It wasn't until after the cremation that things got hairy. The urn suddenly came to life and jumped about the place. It moved like a trapped bird, and crashed into everything. The followers instantly knew it must be the spirit of their old chief possessing the urn and trying to tell them something. It was a while before someone managed to grab the urn mid-flight and remove the lid, but when they opened it to pour the ashes out, there was barely anything left. The chief used all the spirit power they had and wore out all that remained of themself. The worst part was that they never discovered what the chief was trying to say."

"Come on then," jeered Hazel. "Tell us what's wrong with that story. No one could lie, so there can't be anything fake."

"You're right that there isn't anything fake," replied Milo, "but that doesn't mean they didn't make an honest mistake. This urn," said Milo looking at Heidi, "was it by any chance a rusty brown colour and had two small handles on either side?"

"It was, yes," answered Heidi.

"That urn was a magic item," stated Milo. "I've heard of a jar that has the ability to move on its own, but it requires some kind of fuel to be placed inside."

Heidi had to think about that statement for a moment, "You mean..."

"That old chief's ashes were eaten up by the urn," confirmed Milo.

"Oh dear," muttered Heidi.

"I hate to be the bearer of bad news, but you still haven't told me a story I couldn't explain."

Heidi had to hang her head; she had no good ammunition left in the chamber. Hazel was also out of ideas as her knowledge was limited on the subject, however, she was not the kind of person to let a convicted stalker have a moment of victory when they had such a swollen sense of pride. While Milo was taking a swig of his drink, Hazel walked over and talked to another customer of the pub. Milo tried to look at what Hazel was doing, but didn't have a good angle to see. Heidi, who was sitting in a different position, realised what Hazel was doing, and decided to shuffle her barstool a few feet away. A moment later, Hazel walked up to Milo, careful to cover his vision of the thing that was behind her.

"I think I've got another story for you," said Hazel.

"Go ahead," invited Milo.

"Oh, no, I won't be telling it. Rob will," announced Hazel, moving to the side and revealing the most boring man in the world.

Rob instantly started droning, "Have you heard the story of the pigs who suddenly started suffering from optometry disorders?" is how it started, but any further detailed recollection will be cut for the benefit of you reading this. It goes without saying that Rob, not having work to distract him, was happy to recount tales of the odd migratory patterns of buffalo, and the suspiciously accelerated coastal erosion of the eastern territories. It was just after Rob started that Hazel walked to Milo's other side, and whispered in his ear, "Happy Mask's Day."

**

The following day, Milo and Heidi had just finished work at The Bystander offices. Milo noticed Heidi had been somewhat antsy all day, constantly looking in her bag and checking the time. Milo asked if Heidi was feeling agitated, but she claimed to be fine. When the end of the workday was upon them, Heidi asked Milo, "Do you mind waiting for me? I want to talk to you on the way home."

Milo accepted the request as Heidi took herself into The Big Cheese's office. Milo waited in the hallway by the front door, idly observing the patterns in the wallpaper and the tops of his shoes. After a few minutes had passed, Heidi rejoined Milo, but the man was interested to know something.

"What did you need from The Big Cheese?" asked Milo.

"I've handed in my notice," confessed Heidi. "I'm leaving Pending in two weeks."

CHAPTER THIRTEEN

Last Call

Milo and Heidi left The Bystander offices, soaking in the revelation that the woman would be leaving very soon. Heidi walked through the streets she had spent the last few months becoming accustomed to with a renewed sense of appreciation, knowing now it would be one of only a few more times. Milo was somewhat astonished by the news; Heidi made plenty of allusions to the fact she would leave in due course, but he wasn't expecting the announcement to be made quite so abruptly.

"Are you sure you want to leave so soon?" asked Milo.

"I'm leaving the morning after my last workday," affirmed Heidi. "My mind is made up."

Milo admired the determination, but he had to question something. "I thought you didn't have the money to start travelling again."

"I don't, but I can't wait any longer. I've spent way more time in Pending than I have anywhere else."

"Where are you going to go?"

"I thought I should continue south while I'm close to the bottom of the continent, but it might be easier to go to Dorcoast and board the cheapest ship I can. I haven't decided yet, but I've got two weeks to think about it."

Milo was concerned. "Are you sure you're going to be fine?"

"Not at all, but you went travelling without any money and ended up with a girlfriend, so I'm not totally scared."

Heidi may have been joking a tad, but she couldn't stop

herself from revealing flecks of the truth; Milo noticed she wasn't speaking with her usual upbeat enthusiasm, as if hiding how fearful she really was to stop anyone worrying about her.

"Do you want some money?" offered Milo.

"No," insisted Heidi. "I made my decision. It's my fault if it goes bad."

Milo couldn't help but feel slightly perturbed, but Heidi was making out like she was ready to deal with the consequences, so he decided to let the matter fall to the side.

"What was the reason you wanted to talk to me on the way home?" asked Milo.

Heidi jumped to life. "Oh, right. I completely forgot. Do you mind joining me on market day? I need your help choosing something."

"What exactly?"

"Well," Heidi tried to dance around the point, but caved fairly quickly. "Don't laugh; it's really cheesy. You know how I always wear these bangles?" It was hard for Milo to forget; working with Heidi was like working with a xylophone. "Because I travel around so much, I meet a lot of people I don't want to forget, so every one of these bangles represents someone I've met. I want you to pick the bangle that reminds me of Pending."

Milo felt warmed by the offer, as saccharine as it was.

"I can do that for you," confirmed Milo.

"Great. I'll see you there," beamed Heidi.

Milo and Heidi's path home soon diverged after that request, and the two made their own ways home. Milo decided to take a diversion into The Devil's Neckhole, walking into those ever familiar walls and seeing his ever familiar favourite barmaid.

"Evening, Hazel," said Milo.

Hazel returned the greeting and poured Milo his usual. It didn't take long for the conversation to draw onto its newest story.

"Heidi's leaving in two weeks," revealed Milo. "She just told me."

"She's finally getting out. Good for her," declared Hazel.

"Yes," mumbled Milo.

Hazel saw Milo was looking a tad despondent. "I haven't seen you like this since we stopped selling triple strength wine. Are you getting sentimental for Heidi?"

"I might be. I think I'm going to miss having her around."

"And so you should. It probably isn't said enough, but you're a sweet guy. It just took a little culture shock to get it out of you."

It was hard to deny that Milo's life had changed in subtle ways since Heidi had arrived; he still regularly reminisced about a handful of their excursions, and she had become a firm friend of his, despite her childish demeanour.

"It feels like ages since I left home," reflected Milo. "I haven't had to say goodbye to someone in a long time."

"That's because you moved to Pending: Flatrock's biggest dungeon," declared Hazel.

Milo politely nodded and kept drinking; he was lost heavily in thought and didn't converse much while Hazel chatted with other clientele. There was an unsettling feeling within Milo he couldn't define, like an unopened box, or a suspiciously shaking bush. The man found it difficult to simply brush the feeling aside; this feeling needed a proper scrub and polish before it could dirty anything else. In the end, Milo was half drunk and no more clear minded than he was when he had started, and simply walked back to his house.

Milo returned home and decided to lie on his sofa for the night; he felt he needed a moment to mentally process some things, which was rare for him. The man wasn't sad that Heidi was leaving, he'd come to terms with it a while ago, but there was some other feeling Milo was struggling to digest; his mind meandered down the river of thought, wondering where Heidi was going to end up next, which led to him thinking about the world around him. There were a lot of countries close by, and Heidi had no end of options. Milo was broken from his mental diving experience when he noticed there was a letter by the door that he missed when walking in, and it was from Tola. Feverishly ripping the letter from its envelope, Milo read its contents, heart sinking a little bit at the sentiment. Milo missed Tola when he returned to Pending, but he wasn't exactly in the best position to move away; he wished he was brave enough to take the plunge like Heidi was, but Milo was the kind of man who spent five hours deciding if he was going to be spontaneous. Inviting Tola to live in Pending was just as fraught with issues considering the nature of her work, not to mention her son. Milo realised he was trapped in a rut, and this must be the reason for his feelings. Milo wanted to leave Pending like Heidi was, and it wasn't until she announced her plans that he realised he was jealous of her. Heidi was achieving things Milo wouldn't dare try. When did this start? I used to be motivated, thought Milo. I left my home town to be a journalist, and I don't even like working there anymore. Why don't I just leave!

Milo struck a chord in his head with his last thought.

Why *don't* I just leave?

Everything I want is out there, across the ocean. If I board a boat now, I can do it, and I'll never look back. No, this is stupid, interrupted a thought. I have to think this through. Oh, for cack's sake! Why do I have to think everything through!

Milo was stuck in the prison that was being himself. He hated himself, but he couldn't stop himself from being himself. In a fit of rage, Milo threw a book on the table next to him at the window, before shitting himself at the possibility of it breaking again, but he was lucky this time. Milo knew he needed to calm down; he wasn't achieving anything, just have a drink and go to bed, thought Milo. I'll feel better in the morning.

I hope.

The day after was market day, and fake smiles were in full bloom as Milo and Heidi wandered the pinstripe stalls looking for some jewellery. Milo was partially hungover, but that wasn't the reason he was feeling so despondent; he was still living the nightmare that was being Milo, and had no clear vision of what he should do. Moving to Nunca wasn't something Milo could do in an instant; he had to find work, move his possessions overseas, find enough time to cry about the house sales process, and what if he changed his mind in that time? What would happen then? The only saving grace Milo had was Heidi, because for just shy of the next two weeks, she was the only person who had experience with this kind of torment, and he could ask questions.

"Heidi," started Milo, "have you ever thought twice about leaving somewhere?"

"If I only think twice, then it's an easy decision," affirmed Heidi.

"Do you ever worry you've made the wrong decision?"

"All the time, but things usually work out well in the end."

Milo couldn't help but hang up on a particular word. "Usually?"

"I try not to think about the past. I prefer to look to the future."

"Aren't all those bangles to remind you of the past."

"Remind me, but I don't reminisce. I get lonely if I think about it too much, and that doesn't help anyone. I don't think about what I had, I think about what I will have."

Milo tried this, and thought about living with Tola and Dodek, but he couldn't help focusing on the empty space around that; he couldn't justify with himself that a family was enough. Milo didn't tell Heidi about his internal struggle; he was a naturally private person, and he convinced himself it wasn't anyone else's problem but his own. It was while Milo was dissociating that Heidi had come across a decent jewellery shop.

"Here," announced Heidi. "Choose one for me."

Heidi turned to face away from the shop.

"Which one do you want?" asked Milo.

"I want whichever one you choose," answered Heidi.

Milo didn't know anything about fashion, or really what Heidi preferred; she had deliberately faced away from the shop front to not give any clues about what she might want. There was no pattern to any of Heidi's other bangles besides the fact they were metal; some were multicoloured, some had stones and etchings; there was no way to tell her favourites. If Milo wanted a piece of jewellery that truly reflected Pending, he would choose the worst one of the lot, but that would be a cruel joke. Milo scanned the shop's wares again and again, but every bangle was different, it was potluck what he could see. Eventually, after digging through the scrapyard, Milo fished out a piece he thought was fitting.

"I've got one," announced Milo.

Heidi turned around and was met with a shining rose-gold bangle with a small flower set on top.

"It's beautiful," cheered Heidi. "What made you pick that one?"

"It reminded me of the river blossom festival," answered Milo.

Milo and Heidi walked around town for a while; neither had anything else planned for the day. Being so secretive was proving difficult for Milo, who wanted desperately to ask more questions without directly addressing the problem, but failing any decent avenues, he tried small talk instead.

"What are your final thoughts on Pending?" asked Milo.

"I liked it," answered Heidi. "The old buildings, how green everything is, the snow; I haven't seen another place like it."

"How does it rank to other places?"

"I told you I don't like to think about the past."

That was enough of an answer for Milo.

"Any more ideas about what you're going to do next?" questioned Milo.

"Still nothing. Maybe I should visit your girlfriend," teased Heidi. "That reminds me, are you still learning the language?"

"I am, one children's book at a time."

"Do you know how to say, 'I would like a cup of tea, please'?"

Milo needed a second to translate the sentence in his head. "Un acar punchar erbata, zozey."

"Impressive. You could live there if you wanted to."

"I do want to, but I can't," muttered Milo.

"What was that?"

Milo froze; he didn't realise he was speaking out loud. "Nothing."

"I thought you said you wanted to live in Nunca but you can't."

Milo stopped for a moment to think, but gave up and dismissively said, "Don't worry about it."

Heidi could see the man was distressed. "Milo, are you alright? You look like you're about to cry."

Milo had started tearing up, and his fingers began to jitter; he stopped in the street as he fought against his urge to break down and cry, but the fuse had been lit, and the bomb exploded.

"I'm no longer happy here," confessed Milo. "I've lived in Pending for nearly half my life, and I found someone I love just across the ocean. I let my life stagnate by refusing to move from one place. I can see why you travel; there's so much in the world, and staying in one place is just a waste of time, but I've got a job, and a house, and so many other things to worry about, and I don't even know if everything will work out between me and Tola. It's just," Milo caught his tongue, and slowed himself down. "I just don't know what to do."

Heidi had to wait for a moment; she had never seen Milo lay himself bare like that; she didn't know what to do except give him a hug, which Milo returned.

"Those things are nuisances, but they're not really stopping you," comforted Heidi. "If things don't work with Tola, you'll have to move out, but it doesn't mean you'll be homeless. Nothing ever goes as bad as you think it might as long as you try something." Milo sobbed between sentences. "I once met someone who used to say things like 'A broken wheel can be fixed, but someone needs to hold the hammer.' I'm not really good with metaphors, but I think it means any problem can be fixed as long as someone makes an effort. That's why I'm not scared about leaving Pending with no money. If I keep trying, or I can find someone to help me, I'll always be fine in the end."

Milo continued to quiver for some time, but it slowed down eventually. Once she was certain he had calmed down, Heidi let go of Milo.

"Thanks," said Milo. "Or *kozey*, as they say in Nunca."

Heidi smiled, and the duo walked for a while longer. There was silence between the pair, but it seemed an unspoken agreement was made, and neither felt awkward. Milo was suffering from mild embarrassment, but the relief of having his problem vocalised to the world outweighed any shame. Heidi didn't feel like a natural advice giver, but there was some evidence that she had helped; she just hoped Milo would be able to solve this conundrum in a way that made him happy. After some time, the two of them passed the church of Roland, and the portrayal of Heidi's patron namesake that she made months ago: Patron Heidi of Gratitude. It looked like the painting had been maintained well; there were no graffiti marks to be seen, and the colour was barely faded. As they passed, Milo stared at the artwork for a while, focusing more than he had done before; he had only seen the painting once or twice, since he didn't normally walk down these roads, but now he was noticing details he hadn't before.

"Did you put me in that painting?" asked Milo.

"Oh, yes. I did," admitted Heidi. "I can't come up with faces out of thin air, so I modelled everyone out of people around me."

Milo could see now that Hazel, Rob, and a handful of people from The Bystander offices also made cameo appearances among the crowd; he couldn't recognise everyone, but there was undoubtedly some of Heidi's family there too.

"That makes sense," started Milo, "but why did you make me the bread giver?"

"Well, the story in the painting shows a man helping a girl when she's in a difficult part of her life. That's a little bit like what it was like when we first met. I was new to this country, and you agreed to meet with me," answered Heidi.

Milo could see where Heidi was coming from, but it felt overly generous. When Heidi painted that scene, she and Milo were not close friends like they were now.

"Are you being honest?" asked Milo.

"When have I ever lied to you?" challenged Heidi.

Milo didn't realise how rude he was being; there was absolutely no reason to doubt Heidi. It was while he stood in front of that illustration a moment longer that Milo had an idea.

"Are you still taking portrait commissions?" asked Milo.

"I could do," answered Heidi.

"I'd like you to paint something before you go."

"Alright. What did you have in mind?"

"Tola and Dodek are visiting soon. Could you do a group portrait?"

Heidi burst out with excitement. "Yes, absolutely."

A small handful of days later, Milo walked into The Devil's Neckhole, nicest shirt and shoes on, and waved over to the barmaid.

"You're looking a bit posh today," inquired Hazel. "Is today the day I'm finally going to meet your fancy woman?"

"What are you talking about? She's right..." Milo turned around and noticed someone was missing. "Tola?"

After a few seconds, Milo found Tola trying to calm Dodek down from a minor tantrum; the child hated to wear anything vaguely nice looking because it made him itch, and anything itchy needed throwing on the floor. Milo had yet to learn the Nunca equivalent of "for cack's sake," so had to leave this problem with Tola. When Hazel realised what was happening, she retrieved a jar of sweets from under the bar, and threw one towards Milo. The Devil's Neckhole always kept sweets to hand whenever someone brought their child in so they would associate the pub with happy times, rather than the cesspool it really was. Milo used the sweet as a bargaining tool, and Dodek went silent very quickly.

"Aren't you going to introduce us?" asked Hazel.

"Hazel, this is Tola and Dodek. Tola, sun alm Hazel."

Hazel and Tola shook hands; Tola's grasp was incredibly firm, almost hurting Hazel.

"Bloody heck," muttered Hazel. "You're a prostitute with grip like that?"

Milo motioned Hazel to shut up and took everyone inside while they waited for Heidi, late as expected. There was some time before the artist's arrival, and Milo spent most of that wait chatting with Tola; Hazel couldn't work out what the two were saying, but body language was enough. Milo was smiling, fingers entwined with Tola, who was smiling back, enthusiastically explaining something Hazel couldn't even begin to guess at, but the joy was radiating outwards, and Hazel smiled too. Hazel's cheerfulness dropped down a few notches when she noticed Dodek worming through behind the bar.

"Hey, hey, hey," snapped Hazel, picking the child off the floor and sitting him on the bar. "No."

"Yes," replied Dodek.

"No," repeated Hazel.

"Idiot," laughed Dodek, as he pulled a handful of sweets from his pockets, then scrambled out of Hazel's arms.

As Dodek returned to his mother's side, Heidi walked into the room, and waved towards the group. Milo quickly got out of his seat and brought everyone in for introductions.

"Heidi, this is Tola and Dodek," said Milo pleasingly.

"Buna," started Heidi. "Uni alm Heidi. No kun?"

"Un bom, kozey kun," replied Tola. "Un wizdec kun switini artya."

Heidi stopped in her tracks; two sentences in and she'd already spent all she knew of the language. As translator, Milo explained Tola was simply asking if Heidi was the artist, and after a few pleasantries, the family left with Heidi to her apartment.

Milo hadn't actually visited Heidi's home since the first time he was invited, although little had changed; she still had close to no furniture or decorations, although the charcoal faces of the people she knew still remained, redrawn and repositioned.

The only thing that Milo noticed that was different was Heidi's futon had been transformed into a seating area for her portrait models. Tola made sure Milo and Dodek's clothes were properly pristine before taking their seats and allowing Heidi to work. Milo and Tola sat with hands held on the sofa, while Dodek tried to sit anywhere except next to them; the kid already had his own supply of sweets, so negotiations were difficult from this stage onwards. Fortunately, a little bit of create licence can be taken with a painting, and Heidi simply pretended Dodek was sitting on Tola's lap. At some point in the process, Dodek seemed to have found one of Heidi's charcoal pencils, and added to the collage of faces on the wall by drawing a cow eating a farmer.

He was a strange kid.

There was relative silence in the room besides occasional pencil scratches as Heidi glanced back and forth at the happy couple on the sofa. Heidi remembered the first time she drew Milo; he was stilted and nervous before, but he was clearly more comfortable in Tola's presence. The couple were smiling pleasantly, clearly happy simply to be in each other's company. As gleeful as they both obviously were, Milo was clearly more love struck than the other, barely stopping himself from glancing Tola's way every other minute. Heidi was proud of Milo; when they first met, he was delighted to declare himself king of the knobheads, but now he was holding down a relationship, and if he was commissioning a portrait, making a conscious effort to keep hold of it. No one was very certain just how much time had passed when it finally came for Heidi to declare she had finished her work. Everyone stood up as Heidi flipped the canvas over, showing exactly what you would expect: a truly happy couple, with a six-year-old imposed to their side. Tola gave Heidi a thumbs up, realising she didn't speak as much of the language as she had let on, before Dodek started hounding his mother to leave because he was bored. The family knew they had to depart and take Dodek to a park, otherwise he may become so bored as to erupt snot for his own amusement, so everyone said their goodbyes and left. As they walked out, Milo waved back to Heidi and shouted, "Thank you."

"My pleasure," replied Heidi.

The following day, Tola had to return home, so she would have to wait for the final portrait to come her way. The following morning was Heidi's last day in The Bystander office, and one more sleep after that was the fateful final hour. Milo, Heidi, and Hazel agreed to meet up one last time in The Devil's Neckhole before saying farewell, and it allowed Heidi to give Milo the final painting. Heidi was eager to shoot off, and arrived early carrying a large duffle bag, ready to fly the first moment it was polite to leave; she wasn't waiting long before Milo and Hazel showed up.

"How are you feeling?" started Hazel to Heidi. "Nervous?"

"Obviously," answered Heidi. "But never mind me. Here's the finished painting."

Heidi had the portrait wrapped in parcel paper for safe transportation, then passed it to Milo; he didn't need to open it to know it was quality work.

"Thank you," said Milo, before pulling an envelope from his pocket. "Here's the money."

"Oh no, I wasn't expecting payment," blurted Heidi. "You're a friend."

"Alright, then. Here's a present from me and Hazel," said Milo, presenting the same envelope.

Heidi tentatively took the envelope and opened it, realising there was far more money in it than her usual portrait price.

"I can't accept this," argued Heidi.

"Yes, you can," countered Milo.

"It's too much."

"It's worth every bit of it."

"But you should keep it."

"Oh for cack's sake! Just take the money," interrupted Hazel. "Do you really think we're going to leave you out in the wild without any money and have a good conscience about it?"

"But it was my decision to leave."

"And it's our decision to give you the money, so stop

arguing."

Heidi held the weighty envelope in her hands and started reflecting.

"If someone offers you something, it's rude not to take it," added Hazel. "As long as I don't have to feed it, fetch it, or fondle it, you shouldn't have an issue."

Hazel stopped joking when she saw Heidi's head curl down; with Heidi being so short, it was hard to tell what emotion was on her face. It sounded like Heidi was choking slightly.

"Heidi, are you al-"

"Thank you. Thank you, thank you, thank you, thank you, thank you!" Heidi leaped on Milo and held him tight as a vice, before jumping over the bar and doing the same to Hazel. "Thank you so much!"

Heidi went manic, practically jumping off the walls and swinging on the ceiling; there was so much she could do with that money, and she didn't know how to express it. Milo and Hazel just had to wait until Heidi expended her excess energy.

"I take it you're not so nervous anymore?" asked Hazel.

Heidi couldn't manage words, but shook her hand to let Hazel know she was correct. Heidi hugged everyone again, wiped her eyes, took a deep breath, and eventually calmed down to a manageable level.

"Well," muttered Heidi, arms still shaking with adrenaline. "This is goodbye."

"Yes, it is," confirmed Milo.

Everyone stood still for a moment.

"Is it wise to drag this out for so long?" asked Milo.

"No," said Heidi through tearful eyes.

No one wanted to end things, but Milo was the first to say the words to move Heidi along. "Don't think about what you had. Think about what you will have."

"Right," replied Heidi, before nodding deeply and facing away, running as fast as she could.

"Goodbye!" shouted Heidi.

"Goodbye," returned Milo and Hazel. "And good luck."

EPILOGUE

Destination Unknown

Life in Pending moved as it always did; fires burned, buildings burned, everything burned, the usual. Hazel remained a trusty barmaid of The Devil's Neckhole; she practically lived there, but she didn't mind so much, although she couldn't help but wonder what might happen if she tried something new. Reflecting on their lives, maybe Hazel had been a bad influence on Milo; maybe she should have listened to Heidi. Hazel was the older of the two women, but had half the life experience; she rested her arm on the bar and pondered some things, reflexively tapping at her forehead before muttering to herself, "I suppose it couldn't hurt to try."

A boat left Dorcoast's port, carrying on it a short woman with long hair and a bag prepared for the worst that travelling has to offer. Heidi had picked out the first country she didn't recognise and set sail; she had no idea what was waiting for her on the other side of that ocean, but that was how she liked it. Strong wind streamed through Heidi's hair as the weather slowly became warmer; she'd forgotten just how cold Pending was. Heidi kept checking her pocket to make sure the envelope she was gifted hadn't fallen out, but after a few investigations, she realised there was a piece of paper among the banknotes. Opening the paper, Heidi read what it said, and it took her a second to recognise the handwriting, and to work out the reason why she'd been given an address for somewhere in Nunca.

"Oops," said Milo.

These words were uttered just after dropping Heidi's portrait on the floor. Maybe it was middle age getting to him, but Milo was struggling to see without glasses. Thankfully the portrait was still wrapped; he wasn't finding another artist like Heidi for a long time. Milo may have met someone new through work, but chances were slim considering he had already handed in his notice. It was hard for Milo to go back to his "normal" life after everything had been shaken up so violently, and it was impossible to deny anymore that he had fallen in love. Once all the god-forsaken admin was sorted/ignored, Milo would be living with Tola and Dodek for the foreseeable future.

This was the life Milo wanted: One of complete tranquility, with the changes that he made happen, and would continue to make happen until the day he died.

Milo was content.

LUKE HARROWER

A Final Message From The Author:

Hello again. First of all, thanks for picking up this book and reading to the end (I'm assuming you're not one of those people who reads the last page first). I wrote this book primarily because I felt like no one was making the type of novels I wanted to read: A light-hearted comedy story where each chapter reads like an episode to a sitcom. The world isn't going to end, there's no greater force threatening the main character's life; it's just interesting and funny characters existing in an interesting and funny world. If you try to look up cosy books online, half of them are murder mysteries; when did people get so desensitised to murder?

This is all beside the point. What I want to draw attention to is the fact that there's a lot more magic in the world than we think, and even in a world of literal magic like Flatrock, the most beautiful things are the people and places within it.

It's worth tilting your head up slightly and watching the clouds, or to lie on your back and count the stars. The world is, without exaggeration, fucking huge, so go explore it. If you can't afford travel, learn about it. Travel broadens the mind, and with that wealth of wisdom, share it. There have probably been friends who've recommended music to you that you still listen to. Heck, you might have introduced someone to their future husband or wife. We, as people, have a super power, and it shouldn't be wasted. Show kindness, and make a difference.

Special thanks to my parents, and best
friend, Michael, who were my three
unwitting proofreaders.

Printed in Poland
by Amazon Fulfillment
Poland Sp. z o.o., Wrocław

16640838R00146